E.R. PUNSHON
SO MANY DOORS

Ernest Robertson Punshon was born in London in 1872.

At the age of fourteen he started life in an office. His employers soon informed him that he would never make a really satisfactory clerk, and he, agreeing, spent the next few years wandering about Canada and the United States, endeavouring without great success to earn a living in any occupation that offered. Returning home by way of working a passage on a cattle boat, he began to write. He contributed to many magazines and periodicals, wrote plays, and published nearly fifty novels, among which his detective stories proved the most popular and enduring.

He died in 1956.

The Bobby Owen Mysteries

E.R. PUNSHON

SO MANY DOORS

With an introduction
by Curtis Evans

DEAN STREET PRESS

'Death hath so many doors whereby to let out life.'

BEAUMONT AND FLETCHER.

The Custom of the Country.

Detective Stories, the Detection Club and Death: The Final Years of E. R. Punshon

> . . . but, they dead,
> Death has so many doors to let out life,
> I will not long survive them.
>
> *The Custom of the Country* (c. 1619-23; 1647)
> JOHN FLETCHER AND PHILLIP MASSINGER

WHEN IN 1949 E.R. Punshon published *So Many Doors*, his twenty-sixth Bobby Owen detective novel, the Englishman was seventy-seven years old, with nearly a half-century of published novels behind him and a comparatively scant seven years of life and letters remaining before him. 1901, the year of the appearance of Punshon's first novel, *Earth's Great Lord*, saw the death of Queen Victoria, the long reigning granddaughter of King George III for whom a regal age of European global dominion has been named; while 1949, a year during which a convalescent Europe was still bleakly recovering from a world war that had reduced much of its civilization to ashes and rubble, saw the testing by the USSR of its first atomic bomb and the proclamation of the formation of the People's Republic of China. The world was changing with a fearsome fleetness that not merely old men who had first glimpsed light in the Victorian era were finding hard to follow.

Rapidly changing too was the craft of crime and mystery fiction that E.R. Punshon had long practiced (this admittedly a minor thing compared to unsettling phenomena like armed revolution and atom splitting). Like the once seemingly imperishable British Empire, the hegemony of the between-the-wars "Golden Age" clue-puzzle detective novel was breaking asunder, under pressure from increasingly popular rival forms of mystery fiction, such as hard-boiled, noir, psychological suspense and espionage. Already stalked by Raymond Chandler's famous gumshoe, Philip Marlowe, as well as ill-humored and hard-drinking would-be Marlowe doppelgangers like Mickey Spillane's brutish Mike Hammer, Punshon's well-born English policeman Bobby Owen, along with other of his surviving gentlemanly detective colleagues from the era of classic crime fiction, soon found himself in the sights of no less deadly a professional killer than James Bond. Agent 007's creator, Ian Fleming, who cited as his literary influences Raymond Chandler, Dashiell Hammett, Eric Ambler and Graham Greene, published his first Bond spy novel, *Casino Royale*, in the United Kingdom in 1953, where it enjoyed immediate popular and critical success. In the United States, where the novel appeared in 1954, the same year as Raymond Chandler's much-lauded *The Long Goodbye*, *Time* magazine wryly declared that "Bond . . . might well be [Philip] Marlowe's younger brother, except that he never takes coffee for a bracer, just one large martini laced with vodka."

Upon the publication of *So Many Doors* in the UK and the US (in the latter country it would prove the last Punshon mystery published during the author's lifetime), crime fiction reviewers deemed the novel and its author representatives of a vanished era. "The twenties were the plotter's heyday (consider Freeman Wills Crofts, J.J. Connington, Dorothy L. Sayers)," observed the Democratic-Socialist *London Tribune* in its review of the "well-plotted" and "studiously told" *So Many Doors*, "and to the twenties, in spirit at least, belongs Mr. Punshon." In the United States, Anthony Boucher, dean of American mystery critics, allowed in the *New York Times Book Review* that the narration of *So Many Doors* was "leisurely"; yet, after noting the seventeenth-century English stage derivation of the novel's title, he approvingly added that there "is something Elizabethan, even Jacobean, about the obscure destinies that drive [Punshon's] obsessed and tormented characters, and about the frightful violence that concludes the story." Punshon, it seemed, still had something to say in the harried and hectic atomic age, when crime fiction reviewers and readers alike seemed increasingly to believe that brevity was the soul of death.

* * * * *

To his death in 1956 E.R. Punshon maintained a loyal following in the United Kingdom among readers who staunchly adhered to the strict standard of fair play puzzle plotting associated with Golden Age detective fiction. During the Fifties the aging but seemingly indefatigable author, who still lived quietly with his wife Sarah at their house at 23 Nimrod Road, Streatham, produced, through the medium of his prestigious longtime publisher Victor Gollancz, nine new mystery titles-- *Everybody Always Tells* (1950), *The Secret Search* (1951), The Golden Dagger (1951), *The Attending Truth* (1952), *Strange Ending* (1953), *Brought to Light* (1954), *Dark Is the Clue* (1955), *Triple Quest* (1955) and *Six Were Present* (1956)— that detailed the final criminal investigations of his longtime series police detective, Bobby Owen, now risen to the august rank of Commander (unattached), Metropolitan Police. Additionally Punshon continued to remain active in his cherished Detection Club, a London-based social organization of distinguished detective novelists, in which the author had been inducted, along with Anthony Gilbert and Gladys Mitchell, in 1933, three years after the Club's founding, joining such luminaries from the crime writing world as G.K. Chesterton, Dorothy L. Sayers, Agatha Christie, E.C. Bentley, Anthony Berkeley, R. Austin Freeman and Freeman Wills Crofts.

Like other British institutions the Detection Club from 1939 to 1945 bore the bitter burdens of war, including the devastating Nazi air raids known collectively as "the Blitz." When the Club revived its meetings and annual dinners in 1946, it became immediately apparent that time had wrought cruel changes with its membership. On seeing his brother and sister detective novelists again at the Club premises after the long interval of war years, John Dickson Carr, a comparative stripling at the age of forty, recalled that he had been "shocked" by their appearance, which he had found decidedly "greyer and more worn."

By 1946 eight of the original twenty-eight Detection Club members, including G.K. Chesterton, R. Austin Freeman and Helen Simpson, had passed away and many other members were now elderly and inactive. Several more members would expire over the next few years. Even the formerly quite engaged Freeman Wills Crofts and John Rhode (Cecil John Charles Street), now in their sixties and living in the country, became markedly less involved with Club affairs, as did an increasingly infirm Henry Wade (the landed baronet Henry Lancelot Aubrey-Fletcher). For his part, John Dickson Carr, deeming British life under postwar conditions and the governance of the Labour party intolerable, would in 1948 depart for his native United States. Besides Punshon, only Christie, John Rhode and Henry Wade, among original members, and Anthony Gilbert, Gladys Mitchell, Margery Allingham, John Dickson Carr, Nicholas Blake, Christopher Bush and E.C.R. Lorac, among the smaller number of Thirties inductees, remained substantially active as crime writers into the 1950s. Of these Lorac and Wade, like Punshon, would not survive the decade, and another, John Rhode, would barely outlast it.

Clearly some new blood was badly needed. During Punshon's remaining span of life the aged and ailing Detection Club received transfusions, so to speak, from seventeen new members. Although with the deaths of Baroness Emma Orczy and A.E.W. Mason (in 1947 and 1948 respectively), Punshon became the oldest surviving member of the Detection Club, the author, who served as Club treasurer between 1946 and 1949, during the postwar years remained extensively involved in Club affairs, actively participating in hearty debates concerning prospective new members, like Christianna Brand, Michael Innes, Michael Gilbert, Elizabeth Ferrars and Julian Symons, as to whether or not they practiced fair play and sufficiently respected the King's (later Queen's) English, the Club's chief requirements for induction. (These debates are chronicled in detail in my CADS booklet *Was Corinne's Murder Clued? The Detection Club and Fair Play, 1930-1953.*)

In 1949 Punshon found himself at odds over the matter of new enrollments with the man who unquestionably was the Club's crankiest and most cantankerous member: Anthony Berkeley, famed author of *The Poisoned Chocolates Case* (1928) and, under the pseudonym Francis Iles, of *Malice Aforethought* (1931) and *Before the Fact* (1932), three of the best regarded British crime novels from the Golden Age. In April Berkeley wrote a provocative letter to Punshon in which he claimed that as the Club's "First Freeman" he possessed blanket veto power over prospective members, despite the fact that he no longer served on the membership committee. During the early days of the Detection Club, Berkeley had observed at a meeting that the Club had two "Freemans" as members (R. Austin Freeman and Freeman Wills Crofts), and he pronounced that as the person who had originally suggested forming the Club he would be its "First Freeman." To this suggestion everyone else had laughingly assented, taking the office as a joke; yet now, nearly two decades later, it seemed that Berkeley had not been joking.

Incensed by Berkeley's gambit and the rude language in which he had couched it, Punshon wrote Sayers, enclosing his antagonist's "offensive" letter (which evidently has not survived) and warning that "[Berkeley] intends to make some sort of fuss." Punshon speculated that "possibly it is better to take no notice [of the letter], except perhaps as regards the absurd claim of his to hold some special position as what he calls 'First Freeman.' I have a vague idea that once before he put forward a claim to be a permanent member of the [membership] committee on the same ground." He noted dryly that while he had forborne responding to the specifics of Berkeley's letter, he had sent the notoriously tightfisted "First Freeman" a reminder that his annual membership fee was due, to which he had received no reply.

"Bother AB!" responded Sayers in a letter to Punshon that she composed the day after receiving his missive. "I do wish he was not so rude and silly." She entirely concurred with Punshon's recollection of the once comical but now rather annoying office of First Freeman and added resignedly: "If he tries to make a fuss at the meeting, the committee will have to cope; but I hope he will have more sense. I am sorry he should have written to you so impertinently."

By the summer of 1949 the First Freeman's irksome machinations had been checked--but only, Punshon feared, for the moment. With considerable skepticism Punshon wrote Sayers, "I gather the reconciliation with Anthony Berkeley is now complete and the hatchet well and truly buried. Until dug up again." Sayers, who soon would succeed E.C. Bentley as President of the Detection Club, advised members to tread carefully around Berkeley's tender sensibilities. "Let a (more or less) sleeping Berkeley lie," she urged. Nevertheless Sayers agreed with Punshon that the Club members would have to keep Berkeley off the membership committee, because were he to be on it the Club would "never get any new member . . . he turns them all down on sight." She lamented that "Berkeley is a difficult man to work with."

Sayers found working with Punshon, whose detective fiction she had enthusiastically promoted as a book reviewer for the *Sunday Times* between 1933 and 1935, to be an altogether more pleasant experience. Surviving correspondence between the two authors suggests that Punshon was, along with Anthony Gilbert (Lucy Beatrice Malleson), the Detection Club member with whom Sayers got along most amicably at this time. The two communicated fairly frequently during the postwar years, chatting not only about Detection Club matters, but more personal affairs as well.

As treasurer of the Detection Club, Punshon gave his attention to matters large--such as any taxes the Club might have to pay to a revenue-hungry British government ("we have to remember that we may be dropped on by the Income tax people")—and matters small. As an example of the latter, Punshon advised Sayers in December 1948 that the Club should give a "small Christmas present" to Mrs. Buchanan, caretaker of the Club premises at 12 Kingly Street, Soho. ("A room and loo in a clergy house," Christianna Brand bluntly recalled of the locale.) Although payment for services was included with the rent, Punshon pointed out that "services included are very often badly neglected and so far as I have noticed in this case they have been quite well carried out and the room always seemed neat and tidy." "[E]ven in this sordid age," he reflected with characteristic gentle irony, "a few thanks and expressions of satisfaction . . . often please as much as gifts—at any rate if accompanied by a gift." A few days later Sayers gave Mrs. Buchanan a £1 Christmas tip (about £32 today).

Sadly, Punshon suffered a serious setback to his health in August 1949, not long after a busy summer that saw the English publication of *So Many Doors*, his nettlesome skirmish with Anthony Berkeley and the annual Detection Club dinner at the

Hotel Café Royal, Piccadilly. (Recorded treasurer Punshon of the latter event: "L87/9/9—Miss Gilbert paid L6/9/4 for after dinner drinks. I gave the head waiter L1. Total 95/9/1. Great success.") After writing Freeman Wills Crofts and John Rhode to inform them about the Berkeley brouhaha, Punshon went into hospital for an operation. In September Sayers wrote Punshon that she was pleased to hear from his wife that he was "making a really good convalescence," adding: "We will miss you greatly at the October meeting, but of course you must have a good long holiday and get quite fit."

By early November Punshon, recuperating at Christopher Bush's house, Little Horsepen, near Rye in East Sussex, was able to report that he was "very much better," though the same month he resigned as Detection Club treasurer. (Christopher Bush succeeded him to the office.) Later that month Punshon wrote Sayers from Bournemouth, where he was taking a "long rest." He wished her good fortune with the recently published Penguin paperback edition of her translation of Dante's *Inferno*, remarking, "I don't know any translation of Dante except the old one [1805] by [Henry Francis] Cary, and that was a fairly pedestrian performance." He also heaped praise on Penguin's ambitious paperback publishing scheme, deeming it a "very praiseworthy attempt to turn us into a nation of book buyers instead of borrowers. A Real Revolution—if they can bring it off." Punshon had particular reason to applaud Penguin's effort, as the previous year the company had issued a pair of 1930s Bobby Owen mystery titles as paperbacks. (Three more titles would follow in the next half-dozen years.)

Punshon remained active in Detection Club affairs in 1950, though he urged that Michael Gilbert be tapped to replace him on the membership committee. "Would [Anthony Berkeley] take the suggestion as an insult," he sarcastically queried Sayers, obviously still smarting over the events of the previous year. Punshon also participated in evaluations of the work of proposed new member Julian Symons (1912-1994), one of Britain's new wave of consciously self-styled "crime writers." Of Symons's recent *Bland Beginning* (1949), a novel based, as was Punshon's own *Comes a Stranger* (1938), on the Thomas J. Wise literary forgery scandal, Punshon wrote Sayers, "On the whole I should be inclined to say 'yes,' even though I think the character drawing deplorable and the construction and final explanation a bit shaky. But he does manage to produce a readable story and it is certainly an intelligent and clever book."

By 1952, Punshon's health had declined to the point where he felt unable to attend the Detection Club's annual dinner. "[A]s they used to say in the war, the situation on the (health) front has deteriorated," he mordantly wrote Sayers, adding ominously that he had scheduled an "appointment with a specialist." The next year, however, both he and his wife, now octogenarians, managed to make it to the dinner, much to the pleasure of Sayers, who promised, "you shan't be bothered with the [initiation] ceremony at all—there will be plenty of people to carry candles." Sayers promised the Punshons good seats at the High Table to hear philosopher Bertrand Russell speak, and in a contemporary letter Christianna Brand somewhat cattily reported observing Mrs. Punshon sitting "terribly close to the speakers so as not to miss a word, and sound asleep."

Sometime in the 1950s an increasingly fragile Punshon took a dreadful tumble down the landing steps at the Detection Club premises at Kingly Street, an event Christianna Brand vividly recollected many years later in 1979, with what seems rather callous amusement on her part:

> My last memory, or the most abiding one, of the club room in the clergy house, was of an evening when two members were initiated there instead of at the annual dinner [possibly Glyn Carr and Roy Vickers, 1955 initiates]. As they left, they stepped over the body of an elderly gentleman lying with his head in a pool of blood, just outside the door.... dear old Mr. Punshon, E.R. Punshon, tottering up the stone stair steps upon his private business, had fallen all the way down again and severely lacerated his scalp. My [physician] husband, groaning, dealt with all but the gore, which remained in a slowly congealing pool upon the clergy house floor.... However, Miss Sayers had, predictably, just the right guest for such an event, a small, brisk lady, delighted to cope. She came out on the landing and stood for a moment peering

down at the unlovely mess. Not myself one to delight in hospital matters, I hovered ineffectively as much as possible in the rear. She made up her mind. "Well, I think we can manage *that* all right. Can you find me a tablespoon?"

The club room was unaccountably lacking in tablespoons. I went out and diffidently offered a large fork. "A fork? Oh, well . . ." She bent again and studied the pool of gore. "I think we can manage," she said again, cheerfully. "It's splendidly clotted."

I returned once more to the club room and closed the door; and I can only report that when it opened again, not a sign remained of any blood, anywhere. "I thought," said my husband as we took our departure before even worse might befall, "that in your oath you foreswore vampires." "She was only a *guest*," I said apologetically.

"Dear old Mr. Punshon," no vampire he, passed through a door to death in his 84th year on 23 October 1956, four years after his elder brother, Robert Halket Punshon. On 25 January 1957 the widowed Sarah Punshon presented Dorothy L. Sayers with a copy of her husband's thirty-fifth and final Bobby Owen mystery, the charmingly retrospective *Six Were Present*. "He would like to think that you had one," wrote Sarah, warmly thanking Sayers "for your appreciation of my husband's work during his writing life" and wistfully adding that she would miss her "occasional visits to the club evenings." Sayers obligingly invited Sarah to the next Detection Club dinner as her guest, but Sarah died in May, having survived her longtime spouse by merely seven months. Sayers herself would not outlast the year. As Christianna Brand rather flippantly reports, Sayers was discovered, just a week before Christmas, collapsed dead "at the foot of the stairs in her house surrounded by bereaved cats." Having ascended and descended the stairs after a busy day of shopping, Sayers had discovered her own door to death.

* * * * *

Dorothy L. Sayers's literary reputation has risen ever higher in the years since her demise, with modern authorities like the esteemed late crime writer P.D. James particularly lauding

Sayers's ambitious penultimate Peter Wimsey mystery, *Gaudy Night*--a novel E.R. Punshon himself had lavishly praised in his review column in the *Manchester Guardian*--as not only a great detective novel but a great novel, with no delimiting qualification. Although he was one of Sayers's favorite crime writers, Punshon was not so fortunate with his own reputation, with his work falling into unmerited neglect for more than a half-century after his death. With the reprinting by Dean Street Press of Punshon's complete set of Bobby Owen mystery investigations—chronicled in 35 novels, five short stories and a radio play—this long period of neglect now happily has ended, however, allowing a major writer from the Golden Age of detective fiction a golden opportunity to receive, six decades after his death, his full and lasting due.

Crime Fiction Reviews by E.R. Punshon

E.R. PUNSHON reviewed crime fiction for the *Manchester Guardian*, a newspaper congenial to his own Liberal Party sympathies, in 70 insightful and witty columns published between 13 November 1935 and 27 May 1942. A total of 369 books were included in Punshon's near-monthly column, making his reviews one of the larger bodies of crime fiction criticism by a Golden Age detective novelist. (In Punshon's company we also find, among others, Dashiell Hammett, Anthony Boucher, Todd Downing and Punshon's Detection Club colleagues Dorothy L. Sayers, John Dickson Carr, Anthony Berkeley, Milward Kennedy, Julian Symons and Edmund Crispin.)

Punshon's crime fiction reviews, selections from which are included in Dean Street Press's new editions of the novels *So Many Doors, Everybody Always Tells, The Secret Search* and *The Golden Dagger*, indicate a partiality on the author and critic's part toward classical detective fiction, especially works by present and future Detection Club members, including, for example, both richly literary whodunits by Dorothy L. Sayers, E.C. Bentley and Michael Innes and ingenious yet austere efforts by John Rhode, J.J. Connington and Freeman Wills

Crofts. Yet though Punshon figuratively threw bouquets at the feet of Dorothy L. Sayers, whose own rave review of Punshon's first Bobby Owen detective novel, *Information Received* (1933), was a great boon to Punshon's career as a mystery writer, in his columns he forbore neither from occasionally criticizing works by other Detection Club members nor from tendering advice on improvement. He also demonstrated interest in American crime fiction, reviewing not just detective novels by classicists like S.S. Van Dine and Ellery Queen, but suspense novels by Mignon Eberhart and tougher fare like Raymond Chandler's *Farewell, My Lovely*. Altogether Punshon's crime fiction reviews offer both the mystery scholar a valuable research tool and the mystery fan wise pointers for further reading.

Curtis Evans

CHAPTER I
"FULL MOON TO-NIGHT"

Bobby Owen, lately honoured, slightly to his embarrassment, by the somewhat ambiguous title of 'Commander (unattached), Metropolitan Police', raised his eyebrows.

This was a trick he had learned since his return to Scotland Yard. He had found it useful both to indicate disagreement with his superiors and disapproval of too zealous subordinates. His wife did not even notice it. But she was waiting for a reply. He said:

"My dear child, I can't do anything. No one can. Even if a silly girl runs off with some undesirable or another, it's not a police matter. We can't interfere."

"Yes, but they're so terribly upset," pleaded Olive. "Mr Winlock was almost crying himself. Isobel's their only child, and they say they believe Mr Mark Monk is married already."

"Enough to upset any one," Bobby agreed. "It's always pretty bad when your children make fools of themselves. It's not the one who goes to gaol who suffers most, it's wife or husband, the parents or the children. But there it is, and elopement's no crime—or, if it is, it's one that carries its own punishment with it."

"Mrs Winlock says some of her jewellery is missing, too," Olive said.

"Of course, that's different," Bobby admitted gravely. "If jewellery is missing and there are reasonable grounds for thinking that Miss Winlock has taken it, and if it is reported to the police, action will be taken at once. But do the Winlocks really want this Isobel girl prosecuted for theft?"

"Oh, no," exclaimed Olive, shocked. "Only Mrs Winlock thought if you could find out where Isobel is before it's too late and you went to see her—and—" Olive subsided, for Bobby was looking at her very sternly indeed. "Well, you've often said yourself," she protested defensively, "that more things are done by pulling strings than this world ever knows."

"That," Bobby explained, "only applies to politicians and the topmost social peaks. But I'm neither an M.P. nor a duke, I'm only a humble cop, and I'm not going to risk my job tripping up over any string-pulling. If the loss of jewellery is reported, action will be taken as usual, and if Miss Isobel is caught she'll go into the dock like any one else. Of course," Bobby added thoughtfully, "a clever counsel might pull off the kleptomania stunt. If he did, nothing to prevent the girl going back at once to what's-his name—Mark Monk, did you say? I suppose she's of age?"

"A month ago," Olive said.

"Well, then," Bobby said with finality. "We don't know them, do we?" he asked. "What brought them here? Cheeky, wasn't it?"

"Mrs Winlock is a sister of Mrs Barrett in the flat opposite," Olive explained. "Isobel was her favourite niece, and she's almost as much upset as Mrs Winlock. Oh, Bobby, can't you do anything to help?"

"No, I can't," Bobby told her crossly. "You ought to have told them so. I know it's a tragedy, but it's a private tragedy. I can't do anything, any more than I could if the girl got pneumonia and died. Hang it all, don't you see enough trouble and tragedy in the Force without having this sort of thing pushed on you as well?"

"It's the man, too," Olive said. "He frightens them—the Winlocks, I mean. Mr Winlock tried to forbid him the house, but he went on coming all the same."

"He doesn't seem to have frightened the girl," Bobby remarked.

"Mrs Barrett says she's sure he did," Olive told him. "Isobel is such a quiet little thing, awfully timid and shy. Mrs Barrett says the man must have terrorized her. Very likely pushed her into a car and drove off with her."

"Oh, well, if there's any reason to suppose that, that's different again," Bobby agreed once more. "But it must be reported in the ordinary way."

"They do so want to avoid any scandal," Olive said pleadingly. "It might ruin her whole life, and she did seem such a nice, sweet little thing. She was at that party the Barretts gave that we went to, sitting in a corner all by herself and hardly speaking to any one. Different from most girls to-day. Don't you remember her?"

Bobby searched his memory. He was growing rather tired of this tale of the escapades of Miss Isobel, who, having made her bed, must lie on it. Olive had evidently been a good deal upset by the sight of the very natural distress of the parents, and that did not make Bobby any more sympathetic towards the young woman who was the cause of so much trouble. He did not in the least see why Olive should be asked to share a grief that neither he nor she could do anything to help. Gradually into his mind came a faint recollection of a small, nondescript young woman, sitting alone and taking very little part in the proceedings. He thought he remembered offering to get her a cocktail and of the offer being flutteringly refused in a rather shocked and frightened tone. But the image was so faint that it faded away almost at once. Bobby shook a disapproving, slightly uneasy head.

"Just the sort of innocent little fool," he pronounced, "likely to let herself be bullied into doing anything any one wanted who got hold of her. That's no help, though. Not unless some definite charge is laid. And that wouldn't help the girl much—or the father and mother's happiness either, if it's her they're thinking of and her future."

"Oh, it is," Olive declared. "I wish you had been here when they called."

Bobby was devoutly thankful that hadn't been the case. The police have quite sufficient experience of listening to sad and tragic tales where they can do nothing to help, without seeking more.

"All they can do," he said briskly, hoping the subject was now disposed of, "is to wait till they hear from the girl. It may not turn out so badly. She may be married by now, or if there's already a wife in the background Mr Mark Monk may get a divorce and Miss Isobel settle down as a respectable married woman."

"I suppose it might happen," Olive agreed, though doubtfully. "Mrs Barrett saw him once, and she says, too, that there's something about him that's positively frightening, the way he looks at you. It makes you chilly all up and down your back. Even when he's being most awfully formal and polite. I told you Mr Winlock tried to forbid him the house and he just listened and said of course, of course, but he went on coming all the same. And then it's so funny about the money."

"What money?" Bobby asked.

"Isobel had a small allowance as well as all her salary, and she's a little extravagant, so generally there wasn't any left at the end of the month," Olive explained. "Sometimes she tried to coax a little more from her father. But just lately she never did, and instead she's been paying quite large sums into the Post Office. Mr. Winlock found the old book, and it had all been drawn out the day before Isobel went away. Five hundred pounds."

"That's a bit unusual," Bobby agreed. "Sounds as if this Mr Mark Monk had plenty of money and had been handing it out. Funny, though. Generally, it's rings and bracelets and wrist-watches you make the running with—not crude cash. What's the value of the missing jewellery?"

"Mrs Winlock didn't say exactly, but I don't think it was anything very great," Olive answered. "Mrs Winlock did say something about it's being some Isobel had been promised when she got married."

"That means she may have thought she had a right to take it," Bobby remarked. "I suppose they've no idea where the runaways are likely to have gone?"

"Mr Winlock talked about Thameside Village," Olive answered. "Isobel was rung up sometimes from there by an old schoolfellow she met recently—a Miss Bella Brown. She's a journalist, and Isobel thought she would like to be one, too, and Miss Brown promised to help. The Winlocks met her once. They say she tried to be very nice to them, but they didn't care for her—thought her common. She let Isobel come with her sometimes on some of her assignments, and once or twice Isobel stayed the night with her. But there's no Bella Brown in the 'phone book living anywhere near Thameside. You know, Bobby, there's something very queer about it all. I don't believe it's just an ordinary elopement."

"Well, what else can it be?" Bobby asked. Olive shook her head and said she didn't know. Bobby said he didn't either. Then he said: "It's a bit queer, too, about Thameside. I don't suppose there's any connection, but we think there's gambling going on there in one of the big houses along the river-bank, and we think we know the house. And the chap handling the case thinks it may be a black-market centre as well—the gambling possibly a cover for the black marketing."

"Mrs Barrett has a photograph of Mr Monk," Olive said. "She showed it me. He did look horrid. The Winlocks found it in Isobel's room after she had gone. It was pushed away at the back of a drawer. I'll slip across and ask Mrs Barrett to let me have it to show you. You might recognize it."

"Wouldn't help if I did," Bobby told her. "Not unless it's some one wanted, and that's not likely."

But Olive had gone already, and soon was back with a small photograph she handed to Bobby. She said:

"Mrs Barrett says it doesn't show the look in his eyes she thought so horrid. Bobby, why do you look like that?"

"I know him all right," Bobby answered slowly. "I've seen him once. He was Matt Myers then, and he was in the dock, charged with the murder of his wife—if she was his wife, which seemed doubtful. Some one had put a knife into her, but he had a good alibi, and he was brilliantly defended. He was acquitted— after the jury had been out nearly six hours. I had nothing to do with the case, but I was in court part of the time, and had a good look at him. An ugly customer, but women were said to fall for him in the way women do sometimes for ugly men. They like the contrast, probably. After that we didn't hear of him again till he was questioned three or four years ago about a girl he had been friendly with and who had disappeared. She has never been heard of since. There were no grounds on which proceedings could be taken. The Public Prosecutor's office made that clear. Part of my job at the Yard just now is to help in the periodic revision of uncleared cases, and I've been reading the papers in this one. I quite agree with the Public Prosecutor people. Nothing was dug up to take to a jury. Strong suspicion only. Very possibly the girl is living quite happily somewhere or another—or, again, quite possibly she isn't. I don't suppose any one will ever know." He paused and added slowly: "I expect it's only a coincidence, and I would never dare shove it into an official report, but the first murder was on the night of a full moon. And it was full moon again when the other girl disappeared."

"It's full moon to-night," Olive said.

CHAPTER II
"NOT A POLICE MATTER"

THEY WERE both silent. Olive was remembering uncomfortably the quiet, demure, gentle-looking young girl she had seen sitting in a corner at the Barretts' party, content, as it seemed, to be alone with her thoughts, and yet brightening with shy gratitude if any one spoke to her. Bobby was asking himself what he ought to do and finding it difficult to decide. No grounds for official interference. It is an inalienable right of all young women to run away from their homes if they wish to. A man formerly acquitted on a murder charge retains his full rights as a citizen and can resent, like any one else, any attempt at police interference that has not full legal justification. Mere suspicion gives no ground for action. And yet . . . and yet . . .

Nor was Bobby altogether unaware of another consideration. People, both in and out of the police force, are very fond of being wise after the event. Suppose, in fact, these faint hints, premonitions—what you will—of impending tragedy that were troubling him did become concrete fact, almost certainly he would be asked why he had done nothing, knowing and suspecting what he did? It would be a question not too easy to answer, and one that would certainly be pressed by those, not a few in number or uninfluential in position, who had watched his rapid rise in the Service with a certain envy. Nothing fails like success, some one has said, and very certainly nothing else breeds such an envious and often malicious jealousy.

Besides, there was the girl herself. Not very pleasant, if any thing did happen to her, to have to reflect that she might have been saved but for cautious official scruples. Playing safe for himself, Bobby knew, might well mean, would mean, leaving this unknown Isobel he had only seen once and hardly remembered, to run into dreadful danger. But then, again, that danger might well be entirely imaginary. Had Olive not been watching him he would, in his perplexity, probably have fallen back on that old trick of his of which she had tried to break him—that of rubbing the end of his nose so hard that she had professed alarm lest he should rub it all away, or at least flatten it for good.

Instead he thrust his hands deep into his pockets, to keep them safe, and went across to the window.

The flat was on the fifth floor, and from the window there was a wide and extensive view. He stared out moodily, watching the many twinkling London lights. On the distant horizon a silver rim appeared and grew, and under its quiet, shining radiance the twinkling London lights grew less brilliant. It was the full moon, and as it rose in all its loveliness Bobby made up his mind. For soon that increasing radiance would illumine the whole land, as it had done, he knew, that other night when a wife had met a sudden and dreadful death, and again as it had done when a girl had vanished for ever from all human ken.

Not that he supposed for even a passing moment that even in a world so strange, so little understood, as this, either the moon or any other heavenly body could in itself affect human minds or wills. But he knew well—too well—the power of suggestion, and the compelling effect it can at times exercise on both mind and will.

He turned and said:

"I think I'll go and prowl round Thameside Village for an hour or two."

Olive said nothing. She had been looking forward to a quiet evening with Bobby at home for once—not too common an occurrence for any wife with a husband in a Force in which at any moment the telephone may ring with urgent clamour.

Bobby began to make his preparations in a slow, reluctant, worried manner. He had a strong impression that he was going to a great deal of unnecessary and thankless trouble. In fact, he felt he was being the complete busybody, meddling in things that did not in the least concern him. He went along a corridor and knocked at the door of the Barretts' flat. Mrs Barrett appeared; for gone are those days when a knock at the door produced inevitably a correct and uniformed maid. Bobby asked if he might keep for the present the photograph Olive had just borrowed. He asked also if Mrs Barrett had ever seen Mr Mark Monk, and if so what impression he had made on her.

Mrs Barrett hesitated and looked uncomfortable.

"I've only seen him once," she said. "At my sister's. He's—well, he's rather plain himself, but he has a most fascinating voice. I can't describe it: it's almost like soft, far-away music."

Bobby nodded. The odd, almost hypnotic effect of Mr Matt Myers's voice had been mentioned more than once during that murder trial of past years. He asked:

"What sort of an impression would you say he made on people in general?"

Mrs Barrett hesitated again, and then laughed uneasily.

"I suppose most people were fascinated in a way, and yet in a way I think he made them rather afraid. I think it was rather like a rabbit must feel when it's dropped into a boa-constrictor's cage. Not every one, of course. My husband disliked him intensely on sight. He said he looked and talked like a crook. He called his voice soapy when I said how nice it was." She hesitated again, and then went on: "One man who was there said something to him. I don't know what, but it must have made Mr Monk very angry, because I saw him give the other man such a look—it made me feel all funny and creepy up and down my back. Afterwards, I didn't think his voice so nice, after all. And there was the oddest sort of glassy look in his eyes sometimes. I can't describe it exactly, and it wasn't always there. It came and went. I remember thinking that if he was only talking to you, and you couldn't see him, he could most likely make you do anything. But if you saw him looking like that, then you would be far too frightened to do it, or listen any longer. My husband said it was all nonsense; but, then, men always tell you that till," said Mrs Barrett comfortably, "they find out different."

"Yes, I know," said Bobby, and he remembered also that this strange 'glassy' look had been mentioned in the trial that had ended in a verdict of 'Not guilty'.

"I expect it's what you think, too," Mrs Barrett said abruptly. "Just an old woman's chatter. But I can't help feeling so very uneasy about dear little Isobel."

"Not the least reason to suppose anything's happened to her," Bobby declared cheerfully. "Nothing much to be done, anyhow. It's not a police matter. All I can do is to make a few discreet inquiries. If we do happen to get to know where the young lady is, we can tell her parents. Sometimes young ladies who run away from home get disillusioned very quickly. I may take it, may I, that her parents would be willing to have her back home?"

"Oh, yes, yes," Mrs Barrett exclaimed fervently. "It's all they're living for. She is such a dear child. She could come here, for that matter, if she feels nervous about going straight home. She came to me when she ran away from school and was afraid to face her father."

"Why was that?" Bobby asked, with his insatiable curiosity for every detail throwing any light on the character or personality of those with whom his duty brought him in contact. "Wasn't she happy there?"

"I never knew exactly," Mrs Barrett told him. "Something to do with one of the mistresses. What school-girls call a 'crush'. I think Isobel got the idea that the mistress was laughing at her behind her back. There was a terrible scene, and Isobel ran away."

"Did she go back?"

"Oh, no. She didn't want to, and the school didn't either. They had been really frightened, apparently. Isobel is very emotional, poor child, though she always seems so quiet."

"Quiet people sometimes are," Bobby remarked. "Emotional, I mean. Quiet because they feel so strongly they feel they mustn't let themselves go."

"Oh, yes," said Mrs Barrett, but doubtfully, for to her this was a new idea, and she wasn't much inclined to accept it.

Bobby took his leave then. He got his car from the near-by garage where he kept it and drove to Thameside Village, now a little less fashionable but a good deal more populous than in former days. Along the bank of the river stood a number of large houses with gardens leading down to the water. Some were now hotels or boarding-houses or were occupied by societies of one sort or another or as business offices. One or two were still in private hands. Others were unoccupied, waiting the inevitable day of doom when they would be converted into uncomfortable, inconvenient, and extremely expensive flats.

Bobby went first to the Thameside Village police station. Without explaining exactly his reasons, he showed the photograph of the one-time Matt Myers. He hoped it might be recognized as that of a Thameside resident. But the station sergeant shook his head. No one he had ever seen. If Mr Owen cared to leave the photograph with him, though, he would show it his men, and perhaps one of them might recognize it. He made much the same suggestion about Miss Bella Brown when Bobby mentioned her name. He had never heard of her, but some of the men might know something. The local knowledge of the men on the beat was extensive. They kept their eyes and ears open. Bobby said the local knowledge of the ordinary uniform man was the foundation stone of all sound police work. The station sergeant purred a little, and suggested that the staff of the local paper, 'The Thameside Awakener', might know her. The office would be closed now, but he could ring up the editor at his private address, if Mr Owen wished.

Bobby said that was a splendid idea. Unfortunately, the editor's reply was to the effect that he knew nothing of any Miss Bella Brown. Some people called themselves journalists on the strength of having once had a letter published in a national newspaper. But he would ask at the office next morning. Some of the staff might know her. So the station sergeant thanked him and hung up, and Bobby thanked the station sergeant for the trouble he had taken and prepared to go. Then he asked casually if anything was being done about the suspected gambling going on locally.

"Wasn't there a raid being planned?" he asked.

"Been put off," the station sergeant explained. "There's some information just come in that makes Mr Ferris"—this was the name of the D.D.I. (the Divisional Detective Inspector)—"think there's more to it than gambling: that the gambling is only a sort of cover, and that the place is also a depot for getting rid of stolen goods. There was a whacking big haul of cigarettes last week, you remember, sir, and one of our contacts has tipped us off that the whole lot is being brought here one night. Nice night for it, too—almost like day, with this moon. We've got a man on the look-out."

"Well, I don't see how that can have anything to do with what I've been asking," Bobby remarked. "Who is it you've got on watch? It may be a big thing if you can bring it off."

"Sergeant Long," answered the other. "Tommy Long—got his stripes only the other day."

"Oh, yes, I know," Bobby agreed. "Good man. Had a commendation or two, I believe. I'll go round and have a word with him, shall I? Tell him to keep up the good work."

The station sergeant looked pleased, and said young fellows appreciated it when they got a word or two of encouragement from their seniors. The personal touch went a long way.

So Bobby, having received directions, went off to find Bexley House, the name of the house Sergeant Long was watching. As the station sergeant had remarked, it was almost as clear as day, with the full moon riding majestically in the heavens above. But to Bobby to-night this pale moonlight had a slightly sinister effect. He did not know why. It made him think of a lovely woman offering a poisoned cup to her lover, or of her who brought forth butter in a lordly dish. He found himself murmuring a line he had once heard or read somewhere—Shakespeare, probably. 'The pale-faced moon looks bloody on the earth.' Stupid! Why on earth should this lovely night remind him of those only half-acknowledged fears he had been doing his best to forget?

Anyhow, no reason to suppose there could be any connecting thread between this story of a suspected private gambling saloon that might also be a depot for storing stolen goods before distribution, and the tale of the girl who had run away in the company of a man who once had stood his trial for murder?

CHAPTER III
"NOT ALIVE, THAT IS"

Bexley House, the scene of so many suspected activities, was only some three or four hundred yards from the police station. Thither Bobby now made his way through that contrasted pattern of deep shadow and thin, pale pools of light which marks the night when the full moon shines from a cloudless sky.

As he walked on, following the directions given him by the station sergeant, he noticed on hoardings some bills advertising a dramatic performance given at Bexley House by a local amateur company in aid of some charity or another. Another bill advertised a political meeting. So some innocent activities at least were carried on there. But, then, innocent activities can at times provide a very useful cover for activities very far from innocent.

By this time Bobby was nearing his destination, and he began to keep a sharp look-out for Sergeant Tommy Long, whose presence he supposed, however, would not be unduly obvious. Presently he came to Bexley House itself, a huge, square old building of the days when domestic help was cheap and plentiful and no one dreamed that it would one day be very much the reverse. It stood back from the road in a large garden that at the rear reached down to the river's bank. Here in former days there had been a small private landing-stage, now much decayed. In front it was approached by a wide, circular drive, overgrown by weeds and grass, and here again was repeated that alternate pattern of shadow and light, for the drive was bathed in the clear moonlight, and on each side the shadows lay dark and impenetrable under tall trees and thick, close-growing bushes.

No sign anywhere, that Bobby could see, of Sergeant Long. Not, of course, Sergeant Long's business to advertise his presence. Natural, though, when Bobby had walked a few yards past the open iron gates at the entrance to the drive and saw a darker shadow apparently trying to make itself inconspicuous against a tree on the other side of the road, that he should assume it was probably the sergeant. But when he crossed towards it he saw that it was a smaller, slighter man, and saw, too, that this stranger was trying to tie a handkerchief round his right hand, which was apparently bleeding rather freely. A trifling incident, but just a little unusual to find a man trying to tie up a wounded hand late in the evening in a deserted suburban street. More especially outside a house under police observation. And anything unusual always interested Bobby, lest it should be a sign or a suggestion of something more unusual still.

"Hurt yourself?" Bobby asked amiably. "Can I help?"

There was a distinct pause before the other replied, and Bobby was aware of an impression that his offer had not been welcome, and that a first and strong impulse had been to reject it with vigour. But apparently second thoughts had been different, for the reply, when it came, was friendly enough.

"Oh, thanks: it's nothing much," the stranger said. "I've managed to give myself a nasty cut, that's all. On a razorblade in my pocket. Silly trick. It must have worked loose. If you could just fasten my handkerchief for me. It's bleeding a bit."

"Let me look," Bobby said. A deep cut, evidently, and bleeding a good deal more than a bit. Bobby produced the first-aid pack he always carried with him. He soon had the wound bandaged. "That'll be all right," he said when he had finished. "At least, it will be till you get home. Live near?"

The other did not answer this inquiry, but he thanked Bobby for his help. He had a deep, distinctive voice, harsh and penetrating. He remarked that Bobby seemed well prepared for emergencies, and asked if he were a doctor. Bobby laughed and said no, but he had passed his first-aid examinations and always carried a first-aid pack ready for accidents. The stranger thanked him again, and they said good night. Bobby walked on; but presently glanced back. In the moonlight he saw the stranger cross the road and stand for a moment, looking through the open iron gates of the Bexley House drive. Bobby thought at first he was going to enter, but, after two or three minutes of apparent hesitation, the stranger walked briskly away.

A little curious, the whole incident. And was it, Bobby asked himself, only the influence of the pale and ghostly moonlight that filled his mind with such vague but troubling fears? Was this blood that he had seen upon the right hand of a wandering stranger a kind of warning or suggestion of ill things to come? His mind went back to those other nights of the full moon when the then Matt Myers's wife had met a strange, a violent, a still unavenged death; and when another woman had stepped from the warm safety of her home and family into the moonlight of just such another night and been heard of no more.

He had still seen nothing of Sergeant Long, and he wondered if the sergeant had taken up his post within the Bexley House garden itself. Not permissible, of course, since the police do not trespass on private property without clear and sufficient reason; but, then, the impermissible does sometimes occur. Bobby told himself that perhaps he had better go home. Indeed, he was not very clear what he was doing here. Moonshine in his mind, perhaps, he thought, as well as on the earth. He turned back; and now when he came to the Bexley House gates he heard a murmur of voices, carrying far in the calm of that quiet evening. He walked up the drive. He had decided suddenly that he would knock and ask if Miss Isobel Winlock were there, and, if so, could he see her, as he had a message for her from her aunt, Mrs Barrett. She might be more willing to listen if he said he came from her aunt rather than from her parents.

Besides, he was curious to know who was talking at this late hour in the shadows by the side of the moonlit drive. Possibly Sergeant Long might be one of the invisible speakers. The voices ceased as he drew near, and from the shelter of one of the trees a man stepped out. In a surprised tone, he said:

"Oh, it's Mr Owen."

"Evening, sergeant," Bobby said, in his turn recognizing Long.

Another man came lumbering out of the shadows where he and Sergeant Long had been talking. He was a short, heavily built, fat man, with a large, flat, white face and short arms and legs, hopelessly out of proportion with his big and heavy body. His voice was high and squeaky, again out of harmony with his massive torso, and his eyes were pale and small and hidden. He said resentfully:

"Mr Owen now? Commander Owen, isn't it? There you are," he complained. "All Scotland Yard nosing round, and all for nothing."

"You know me, then?" Bobby remarked. "Have we met? I don't think I remember you, do I?"

"It's Mr Jerry George," Sergeant Long said. "A very enterprising gentleman."

"Oh, yes," Bobby said. "I remember the name. Not a case I had anything to do with. Something about a whisky deal, wasn't it?"

"How was I to know there was anything wrong?" Mr Jerry George demanded. "All I did was put up the money. Discharged I was, without a stain on my character."

"That wasn't quite what the judge said," Long remarked.

"Prejudiced old blighter," commented Jerry. "All very well for him sitting up there in his wig, telling other people off, and him just like the rest of us, most likely."

"Didn't one of the documents you produced turn out to be a forgery?" Bobby asked.

"That was Mark," Jerry said, and now his shrill, thin voice took on a whining note. "Mark," he repeated. "It's him as put you on to this, isn't it? A pack of lies. Spite. That's all it is. Spite and malice."

"Mark?" Bobby said questioningly.

"A man named Mark Monk," Sergeant Long explained. "Mr George told us at the time it was all Mark Monk's doing about that whisky business."

"So it was," Jerry said. "Done me down proper, he did. Cost me over a thousand before I was clear. I knew all right, but nothing to show. No proof."

"No proof against any one," Long agreed, "but plenty of suspicion. You and Mark Monk, you passed the ball to each other a fair treat. Good as anything any football team ever put up."

"You've no call to say that," protested Jerry angrily. "It was all Mark Monk trying to wriggle out himself and put me in—a dirty trick, but that's him every time. I told him straight out if he tried that again he had better look after himself. So now he's trying this game on, trying to do me down for keeps."

"Jerry," explained the sergeant, "thinks Mark Monk tipped us off about this place."

"And well you know it," declared Jerry. "Or what's brought you here—you and a big noise like Mr Owen? Black-market centre he told you, most likely. Eh? Well, didn't he? Get that about and have it known there's police watching, and no more lets. The moment Vea Burden told me there was a busy snooping round here I knew it was Mark's doing—and Mark's going to know I know it before long."

"Who is Vea Burden?" Bobby asked.

"It was her spotted me," Long admitted with some reluctance. "It was the moonlight. Shows you up."

"More likely," Bobby remarked, "they were watching. Probably had some one on the look out."

"Not us," Jerry protested. "Why should we? Nothing to hide."

"Are you the occupier here, Mr George?" Bobby asked.

"Well, in a manner of speaking," Jerry admitted. "Mrs Burden is the resident housekeeper, but the lease is in my name. We're not doing so badly. Entertainments. Parties. Dances. That's our line. Pays well enough—not a gold-mine, but pays. Not one public hall left in the whole district. They were short of 'em before the blitz, and now every single one has been bombed or requisitioned or put out of action for one reason or another. Dances. Fine ballroom here. Receptions. Public meetings. Theatrical shows. We do 'em all—all except dinners. Can't manage dinners—no facilities. Besides, there are hotels people can go to."

"Catering licence?" Bobby asked.

"Don't do any," Jerry answered. "If refreshments required, that's up to them to see to. We provide accessories—a band, a magnificent ballroom and the best dance-floor ever, bar none. Them who lived here once had a craze for dancing and spent thousands on it—millionaires they were, but went smash in the 1930 slump."

"I see," said Bobby. "Interesting. Is Mr Mark Monk here now?"

"Him? Not likely!" Jerry exclaimed. "He knows better: he'll take care to keep out of my way all right," and this time the note of threat in his voice was evident, or at least so Bobby thought.

"Mind if I ask?" Bobby said.

"You're police," Jerry answered. "Go ahead. Anything you want is O.K. by me. Very decent lot, the police, in my opinion. Fair-minded and reasonable and all that, I always say. Treat 'em right, and they'll treat you right."

"Very kind of you to say so, I'm sure," Bobby observed amiably, accepting this tribute for what it was worth, and deciding in his own mind that Mr Jerry George was a formidable and probably quite unscrupulous personality.

"Miss Burden's there," Jerry said. "You ask her. Ask her to let you see round the place, if you want. Tell her it's what I said. I must be off. Dance on to-morrow night. Quite a swell affair. I've just been seeing everything's ready on our side."

He said good night and bustled away down the drive, his short fat legs covering the ground with unexpected rapidity. Sergeant Long began to make excuses for having been seen. Bobby said that was all right. The fact that he had been so quickly noticed, and his errand immediately guessed, was fairly good proof that a sharp look-out was kept, and that would certainly not be the case had not good reason existed. Useful confirmation of their suspicions. They were close to the house now—a ponderous, square mass of a place that must have needed a small army of servants to keep in good order. On one side had been added to the original building the ballroom spoken of by Jerry George. In the prosperous and feverish early twenties after the First World War it had been the scene of some remarkable and extremely extravagant festivities.

"Big place," Bobby remarked. "Why hasn't it been requisitioned? Looks as if it would house a dozen families if it were turned into flats."

"Bomb damage," Long explained. "Not much roof left, and whole of upper part more than shaky. Now they've found bad dry rot. Scheduled to be pulled down and a block of modern flats put up as soon as possible."

"How much of that fellow's story can we accept?" Bobby asked.

"Well, sir, it's all true as far as it goes, and I should say all of it cover," Long answered. "Gambling we are sure of. Most likely that'll be going on to-morrow night, though the people at the dance won't know a thing about it. Black market, probably. Stolen goods, too. Easy enough, when a contractor sends in stuff for some do or another, to send in as well a consignment of stolen whisky or cigarettes or what not."

"Quite clever," Bobby agreed. "We can watch garages and warehouses and so on, but a place used as a kind of public hall might seem all right. Do you think there is really bad feeling between Mr Jerry George and the Mark Monk he talked about? Or are they just playing ball together?"

"Both, sir, if you ask me," Long answered. "They play together against us, but either would shop the other any day if he saw a way to do it safely. They are two dangerous men. Jerry would cut his mother's throat for half a crown if he thought he could get away with it; Mark Monk was tried for murder once, though he got off, thanks to a smart counsel. One of my contacts says they've been using threats to each other recently over some deal or another they've quarrelled about. He said most likely one of 'em would do the other in one day, and he thought it was anybody's bet which way it would be."

"Nice couple," Bobby remarked. "It's Monk I want to see. It seems he's got hold of some wretched fool of a girl who hasn't any idea what the fellow's really like."

The sergeant whistled softly.

"Then the sooner she's got away again the better," he said. "Or else she'll be in it up to the neck before she knows where she is, and then she's done for. They would never let her go again—not alive, that is."

CHAPTER IV
"I HEARD A CRY"

BOBBY WAS more than a little startled by this remark. Nor did he much like it. It fitted in too well with his own thoughts and with the obscure unease he had felt all through this eerie, moonlit night. He did not answer, but went on to the house and banged on the knocker as if making more noise than necessary would be a relief. The door opened instantly and a flood of light streamed out. Two women were standing immediately within, so that only a hand had had to be put out to throw back the door.

The nearer woman was tall, dark, and thin; her complexion deathly pale, her face thin and ravaged, though there was about it a certain quality of intensity and purpose, even of defiance, that was in its way impressive. She was innocent of make-up, her most striking feature dark, deep-set and angry eyes beneath thin, black brows that met in a pencilled line above the well-shaped nose. She had on a close-fitting black frock with what looked like good pearl beads—cultured pearls, perhaps—and long pearl earrings that swung to and fro with every movement of her head. Even as she stood there without moving she gave an idea of being poised for instant action, as though the eager vitality within her had to be held carefully in check. The other woman was of a different type, tall and fair and much younger, heavier in expression, and a little clumsy both in build and movement. Again in contrast to her companion, she was heavily and not very skilfully made up. Her hair, however, had certainly been subjected to the attention of a skilled hairdresser. It was once more a contrast to that of the other, who wore hers brushed back from her forehead into a plain knot behind, almost as though she disdained fashion and trusted solely to the impact of her personality. Bobby noticed, too, this younger woman's hands—large and capable, the hands of a man, indeed, but for the smoothness of the skin and a certain feminine shapeliness; hands that looked capable of giving any service required. She was wearing an overall, one not too clean, and if she had little of the other's oddly impressive personality, her heavy eyes, her large mouth and prominent chin gave an idea of a kind of dull obstinacy of disposition that might quite easily, under provocation, kindle into flame.

Two interesting and oddly contrasting characters, Bobby thought, both unusual in their own different ways, and neither negligible. He noticed something else, too, though noticed is hardly the word, since the thing was so plain. They had evidently been quarrelling violently. Their attitudes as they stood there proved that. In spite of her heavy make-up, the second woman's face showed flushed and angry, the pallor of the other's skin had become even more accentuated, and the anger in their eyes was still visible as they turned towards the two newcomers. It was the lady of the swinging earrings who spoke first, as, in a surprised tone, she said:

"Oh!" Then she said "Oh!" again, and added: "It's that snooper fellow back again."

"Two snooper fellows," Bobby said in his most dulcet tones. "Have I the pleasure of speaking to Miss Vea Burden?"

"Suppose you have, what about it?" the lady snapped.

Before Bobby could answer, the other woman intervened.

"There is blood on his hand," she said, pointing, and in fact, when Bobby looked, he saw what before he had not been aware of—that his right hand was stained and red. "I told you," she muttered half to herself; "I told you."

Miss Burden stared, and then drew back a step or two, as if in defence or alarm. Bobby said:

"I'm so sorry." He took out his handkerchief and tried to rub the blood away, but without much success. "It was some one in the road outside," he explained. "He had managed to cut his hand. It was bleeding quite a lot, and I helped him to tie it up."

"Well, what is it? What do you want?" Vea Burden asked.

"We are police officers, and we are here on duty," Bobby said; and then, to the other woman he said: "What was it you told?"

"I heard a cry," she answered. "It was some one crying out. I think it was a woman. I told Vea. She said I was a liar."

"Shut up, Grace, you fool!" Vea said, and her voice was furious, her face all one pallid mask of rage.

The woman called Grace stared back, less fiercely, more sullenly. Speaking to Vea, still watching her, she said:

"I heard it all right, and so did you, though you said you didn't." To Bobby, but her eyes still on Vea, she said: "What was he like? Was he as quick as a cat and as false, and had he a voice like a saw?"

"You . . . you . . ." Vea muttered, and choked on whatever else she had tried to say. Bobby thought that only his presence and that of Sergeant Long prevented actual blows. She said: "You wait, Gracie, my girl, till Jerry knows." Turning suddenly her rage on Bobby, she shouted: "You get out, both of you! Quick!"

She would have banged the door on them, but Bobby was too quick for her, and held it back.

"One moment," he said. "If the Jerry you spoke of is Mr Jerry George, we've just been talking to him, and he told us to ask for Miss Vea Burden and to tell her we had his permission to see over the house."

"Good thing, too," Grace said loudly, plainly intending her words for her companion as much as for Bobby. "People don't cry out like that for nothing."

"Aren't you saying just a little too much, my dear?" Vea asked, speaking very quietly now, smiling a little—an uncomfortable, a daunting smile. "If you ask me," she said. Grace did not answer—to Bobby's disappointment, for he had been hoping to hear more. But plainly Vea's new mood was proving much more effective than had done her previous fierce intensity of rage. To that Grace had responded with sullen defiance, but now she was beginning to have an uneasy air. Vea began to walk away, as if leaving the others to it. Then she turned back and said: "If Jerry said so, I suppose it's all right. Grace can take you round if she likes. I've some work to do. I wonder what you think you are going to find?"

"There's a young lady," Bobby said. "A Miss Isobel Winlock. Do you know her? Is she here?"

There was a pause before Vea answered; and that sixth sense judges, lawyers, police officers, all claim they develop told Bobby she was going to lie. Nor was he much inclined to think that that was rare with her. She said slowly:

"Isobel who? Winlock, did you say?" She shook her head. "Who is she? There's been no one here all day that I've seen except one or two about the dance this morning. I've been in the supper-room most of the time, getting things ready for to-morrow. There's to be a dance and supper to-morrow. Grace said she saw some one—some man Jerry brought with him, I expect. Wasn't that what you said, Grace?"

It seemed the two women were allies now, for Grace nodded an agreement.

"I said I thought most likely," she agreed. "I've been busy all day with one thing and another. I saw a man I didn't know going into the supper-room. That's all. I thought it would be some one about the dance. There've been lots of them, goodness knows."

"Is that the man you spoke of just now?" Bobby asked. "The man whose hand I helped tie up, and you said walked like a cat."

"I thought it might be."

"You knew his voice?"

"I didn't know it. I heard him speak to some one as he went into the supper-room. I noticed because of its being so screechy like. That's all."

Bobby's sixth sense, already referred to, was telling him more and more plainly that this woman, too, was lying. He said sharply:

"If you didn't know him, why did you say he was false?"

"Because of the way he walked," Grace answered steadily, looking him full in the eyes—a method that habitual liars very often practice. "Just like a cat slinking into the pantry," she said.

"Had he any woman with him? Did you see anything of any woman?"

"I expect I would have taken more notice if I had," she answered. "I heard him speak to some one, though I didn't notice what he said. I thought Jerry must be there."

"Didn't you wonder how he got in?"

"Why should I? The door's often left open when men are bringing in stuff for any big do we have on. He might have come with Jerry. Nothing to do with me. I haven't had a moment to myself all day. Miss Burden and me have it all to do. No help—you can't get it—and everything to be just so, or Jerry carries on something dreadful."

"You said you heard a cry?" Bobby reminded her.

"That's right," Grace agreed. "It gave me quite a turn. Vea said there wasn't one—as good as called me a liar."

"Oh, Grace, I didn't," Vea protested. It was more than ever clear that now the two women were allies, even though allies only waiting to resume hostilities once a present danger had passed. Bobby assumed that he and his companion represented that danger. Vea was saying: "It might have been some one outside. I don't think it can possibly have been in the house."

"It might have been outside," Grace agreed. "Very likely it was."

"If it had been, I should have heard it," Long said. "I didn't." He went on: "If no one's been here, what about that car I saw being driven off at top speed about half an hour ago?"

"I don't know anything about that. I didn't know there had been any car," Vea answered. "It can't have been Jerry. He always comes by train. The station's not far."

"How long is it since the cry you heard?" Bobby asked Grace.

"I didn't take much notice," Grace answered. "About an hour, I think. I'm not sure."

"Who is the man you talked about?"

"I don't know, I told you," Grace repeated. "I was coming downstairs. I only saw his back for a minute. I didn't worry. I thought it must be some one come with Jerry. We were expecting him."

"I've got to get on," Vea interrupted abruptly. "If you think we've a girl hiding here, look all you want. Tell me if you find any one. Grace can take you round."

"So can you," Grace retorted. "I've got plenty to do without running round with nosey-parker police."

But Vea was already walking away, and she ignored this protest. Grace looked more sulky than ever.

"It's always me," she complained. "Thinks too much of herself, she does. Well, come on, if you have to." She pointed. "That's the ballroom. They must have had money to burn, putting that up. It's a fine floor—best ever. There's a platform at one end for the band, and Jerry's had it arranged for a stage when any one wants to put on a show. There's the drawing-room next to it. People who don't want to dance can play bridge there if they want. The dining-room's that side where supper's served now. We supply plate, linen, and chairs and tables and so on, but we've no catering licence, so if refreshments are wanted they have to see to that themselves. There's a shop in the High Street doing it for to-morrow. Want to look for yourselves?"

"I think we had better," Bobby said.

Vea, who had vanished into the back regions, reappeared in time to hear these last remarks. She called out:

"See they look under all the tables, Grace. Miss What's-her-name might be under one of them."

No one took any notice of this gibe. Vea vanished again, upstairs this time. Watching her go, Bobby asked:

"What's up there? Is it used for anything?"

"Cloak-rooms," Grace answered. "Some of it is shut up—dangerous. And two rooms Vea uses for herself. She lives here."

"By herself?" Bobby asked. "Is she married?"

"Better ask her," Grace said briefly. "If you want to look round, come along. I haven't all night to spare."

She led the way into the ballroom—a magnificent apartment with a first-class floor. It must, as Grace had said, have cost a very large sum of money. But then, in the early twenties many thought a kind of promised land of business had been entered wherein ever-increasing share values reflected ever-increasing dividends, so that all you had to do to grow rich was to buy a few shares, wait a few months, sell at an enormous profit, and then repeat as before. A dream of a kind of happy spiral of prosperity that has unfortunately turned into the reality of the vicious spiral now more familiar.

From the ballroom they crossed the spacious inner hall and came to the former dining-room. Grace went in first, turning on the electric light as she did so.

"There's a window open," she said, in a surprised tone. "I shut them all."

It was a fine, spacious room, facing west, with great windows reaching to the ground and affording a fine view in day-time across the bend of the river. It was one of these windows that was now wide open, admitting a fresh evening breeze that blew softly across the room. At one end was a long table, laden with plates and dishes, knives and forks, glasses, and so on. About the rest of the room stood many chairs and small tables. One of these tables, near the window, had been overturned; and the long, laden table at the end of the room seemed to have been disarranged at one end. Some of the glasses had been knocked off and had broken in falling.

"Look at that now," Grace exclaimed angrily. "I wish I knew who had opened that window. There's been a cat in."

"This is the room where you saw a man you say was a stranger to you go in?" Bobby asked. "Could he have left again by the window?"

"I suppose he could if he wanted to," Grace said. "Why should he? Jerry won't half create about those glasses being broken. I can't help it if people go opening windows and letting cats in." She went across to the scene of the breakage as she spoke, and suddenly she began to scream. "It's all blood," she cried—"all over everywhere."

CHAPTER V
"A KILLING FOR SURE"

IN A MOMENT Bobby and the sergeant were by Grace's side. There on the table-cloth, on the dishes and the plates near, were great, widespreading, crimson splashes, and on the floor beneath had collected a red and dreadful pool. At it the two men stared in horrified bewilderment, in appalled silence. Long spoke first. He said slowly:

"There's been a killing . . . a killing for sure. Look at it, all that. There's the knife."

Bobby was stooping over it. He did not touch it. It seemed an ordinary dinner-knife. He said to Grace:

"It's one of yours, isn't it? It looks like the others on the table."

Grace was in no condition to answer. She had collapsed on a chair near, and indeed seemed on the verge of fainting.

"An ordinary table-knife," Long confirmed. "Not very sharp either."

The door opened, and Vea came in.

"What's the matter now?" she asked. "I heard some one scream."

No one answered her. Grace, still pale and shaken, was muttering to herself over and over again: "Oh, my God! oh, my God!" Bobby picked up a woman's handbag he saw lying near. On it, too, that sad stream of death had run and splashed. He opened it. The first thing he saw was an envelope addressed to a Miss Margaret Kerr in a Thameside. Village street. He put the handbag down, wondering who Miss Kerr might be and how her handbag came to be there. Long, seeing it, said:

"That'll be the young lady's you were looking for, sir. Forgot it, they did. She must have seen something. She tumbled to it, saw what was up. But they couldn't let her go, and so they did her in—to stop her giving an alarm."

Bobby made no comment, nor did he say that the bag seemed to belong to some one else. No need for Grace to know that as yet. He went across to the open window. Grim traces showed that a body had been carried thither. Outside was a border of soft earth, now much overgrown by weeds and grass, though once brilliant with flowers. In the clear moonlight it showed trampled and with broken plants. Beyond it was a paved path, and beyond that again a neglected lawn that ran down to the river. Long came across to join Bobby. Vea, nearly as pale and shaken as Grace, was standing by Grace's side. She had just said something to her, but in a low tone, and Grace had not answered. Grace got unsteadily to her feet.

"I'm going to be sick," she said.

Vea said, loudly and angrily:

"Don't be a fool. That won't do any good." To Bobby she called: "We didn't know, we had no idea. Had we, Grace?"

Without replying, Grace made a bolt for the door and vanished. Vea began to walk away, as if inclined to follow her example. Bobby said to her:

"Is there a 'phone here?"

He had to repeat the question before she answered. She shook her head then and said:

"No. No. We asked for one, but they only put us on the waiting list. What's it all mean?" she asked. "What's happened?"

"We've got to find out," Bobby answered. "Don't leave the house. We shall have to ask you some questions presently. Look after your friend." Vea made no reply, but went away. To Sergeant Long Bobby said: "Find the nearest 'phone box. Report to Centre, and then get on to the D.D.I. Tell him to bring a doctor. I'm going to have a look outside."

Long went off accordingly. Bobby shut the room door behind him. There was no key, so he couldn't lock it, but he put one of the small tables with a chair balanced on top of it against the door so that it could hardly be opened without a noise being made that he would hear. He opened one of the other windows and stepped out. The sill was only a foot or two from the ground. He went round to the window that had been opened previously. It was here that plain traces of recent movements showed. Growing plants had been trampled on and the earth trodden. But also the earth where the footprints showed had been hurriedly—and efficiently—raked over, so that it did not seem likely any useful information would be gained from examining them.

The paved path showed nothing, but on the overgrown lawn beyond car-tracks were clearly visible.

Some one, man or woman, dead or alive, had evidently been carried out by this window and then removed in a car, probably the one Sergeant Long had seen departing at speed. Bobby contented himself with a brief look round. Little chance of the body having been left anywhere here, or deposited in the river, as he had first thought might possibly be the case. The garden would have to be searched, of course, and the riverbank closely examined. Not likely that anything would be found.

An unpremeditated murder, Bobby thought. A blow struck in sudden passion, or possibly in fear. Impossible to say which or exactly what had happened. Something seen, something said, some flash of understanding that had revealed the truth, and then a knife snatched from the table and a blow, deadly, fatal, dealt with all the fierce energy that passion gives—or fear. So Bobby reconstructed in his mind what had happened, and then reminded himself that very possibly it was all quite wrong. Quite possible the whole thing had been planned and intended from the start and all that blood merely some sort of elaborate laying of a false trail. But that was hardly likely; and Bobby did not believe it for a moment, though he never forgot that even the most improbable hypothesis must be considered.

One thing was sure, though. It was going to be difficult. His thoughts turned to the parents waiting anxiously for news, and to the unhappy girl herself, so suddenly, so unexpectedly involved in what seemed a strange labyrinth of crime. Bobby went back into the house by the window he had used before, and almost at once Sergeant Long returned. Instead of bothering to look for a 'phone-box he had run back to the police station, done his 'phoning from there, and had now brought with him the sub-inspector in charge, a uniformed constable, and the police surgeon, who by good luck had been there on some routine piece of business or another. Bobby had heard them coming, and he went into the hall to admit them. The women were not visible. The sub-inspector introduced the police surgeon as Dr James. Dr James, unaware of Bobby's identity, and taking him to be a resident of the house, said to him briskly:

"Where's the body? I hope you haven't touched it."

"There is no body," Bobby said.

"What? what's that?" snapped the doctor indignantly. "I thought it was a murder case. Eh?"

"I don't know what it is," Bobby answered.

"I understood there was a girl been done in," said the sub-inspector; and though he knew Bobby's identity, and so had to be respectful, his tone was nearly as indignant as had been the doctor's.

"Come and look for yourselves," Bobby said. "Then you can tell me what you think."

He led the way into the dining-room, and when they saw what he had to show them, tragic and strange in its contrast to the festive air the rest of the room displayed, they, too, stood staring and wondering in silence.

"Not much life left where all that came from," the doctor said presently. "No body, you said?"

"There are traces of blood all the way to the window over there," Bobby explained. "Outside there are car-tracks. Presumably a car was brought up, the body placed in it, the car driven off, and by this time can easily be fifty miles away. One was seen leaving. You don't know the make, sergeant, do you?"

"I couldn't say, it was going all out," Long answered. "It might have been a Bayard Twenty. Looked like it, anyhow. I couldn't see the number, either."

"Well, I don't know what I can do if there's no body," Dr James protested, and he sounded quite hurt, as if he felt he had been cheated.

"Do you think any one who lost so much blood could possibly survive?" Bobby asked.

"Hard to say," answered the doctor, who hated giving any one outside the profession any definite information. "Can't even measure the exact amount lost. I should doubt it. Prompt and efficient treatment might have saved the man's life. Nothing of the sort is likely, I suppose. Death would result almost certainly, in my opinion. Is that the knife used? Looks as if it had been snatched up from the table, doesn't it? It would hardly penetrate clothing, but a good hard jab at the throat might cut the interior jugular. If it was like that—and I don't see how else to account for so much hæmorrhage—you wouldn't live two minutes. That's about all I can say. Don't want me any more, do you?"

Bobby agreed that in the absence of a body there was no further help the doctor could give. He departed accordingly. Inspector Peate, the local C.I.D. officer, known throughout the Force as Daddy Peate because of a benevolent air and manner that was in fact slightly deceptive, now arrived, followed in quick succession by various specialists. Bobby told his story, and Mr Peate began to look more worried than benevolent.

"No body?" he said. "No proof what really happened? Nothing to show this Mark Monk fellow was here at all. Or the girl either, for that matter. And the man you saw in the road outside. Do you think he comes in?"

"Might," said Bobby cautiously. "Where does this come in?" He showed the handbag he had found. "Another woman's name in it," he said. "It's a Thameside address, so you can check up on her."

"Do you think it can be her done in?" Peate asked. "It's a good-class street—semi-detached."

He meant the houses, not the street, and Bobby remarked that anyhow they could soon clear that point up, as the street in question was not far from Bexley House.

"As for the chap I saw outside," he added, "at any rate he was on the spot. One of the women here says she saw a man she didn't know. Her description and what she said about his voice sounded like this other fellow. Not much to go on."

"He'll have to be traced," declared Peate. "If he's O.K., he'll come forward."

"We can't be sure of that," Bobby remarked. "Some people really dislike the idea of being mixed up in police cases, and some people have their own reasons for keeping as far away from the police as possible. Or he may never hear his help's wanted. Astonishing what some people never hear."

"He'll have to be traced, all the same," Peate asserted—"if any way possible," he added, in deference to one holding so exalted a rank as 'Commander', even if Peate was not yet quite sure what a Commander really was. "What about these two women in the house? They're still here, aren't they? Do you think they know anything?"

"I'm sure they do," Bobby answered; "but I'm not at all sure they will say anything. They may start telling lies, though," he added thoughtfully, "and that's always useful."

"I would rather have the truth," Peate remarked, and Bobby regarded him sadly, and asked him if he really thought he was likely to get it.

Peate, now looking not at all benevolent, said that anyhow he would have a jolly good try, but thought the first thing to do was to carry out a thorough search of the house. The murderer, if there were a murderer, or the corpse, if there were a corpse, might be still here. Not likely, perhaps, but one had to make sure, and in any case something useful might be found. Bobby agreed, and he, Peate, and Sergeant Long, who had been attached to 'O' division on his recent promotion, began it accordingly. Also a uniformed man—the only one who could be spared—was sent to search the garden, and was told to pay special attention to the river-bank and the decayed landing-stage.

"If there was a stiff," Peate remarked, "the river's handy."

Both searches were hasty and superficial, since there was so much to be done. Peate promised a much more thorough examination when time—and daylight—permitted. Vea Burden and Grace were found sitting together in one of the upstairs rooms. Grace wanted to know if she could go home. She was feeling ill, she said. Peate said they would appreciate it if she would stay for the time, as he thought she could help them in finding out what had really happened. He asked if either of them knew a Miss Margaret Kerr, a Thameside Village resident. They both denied it. The room in which they were sitting was one of three, including a small kitchen, occupied as a kind of flat or suite by Miss Burden, who lived on the premises. There were two very big front rooms in which, Peate told Bobby in a whispered aside, it was believed that poker, baccarat, and roulette were carried on at irregular intervals.

"They rather specialize in taking their chance when there's a show or a dance downstairs," he explained.

The whole of the upper floor of the house seemed both un-inhabitable and difficult of access. A fire caused by incendiary bombs had destroyed part of the roof and most of the stairs leading up from the first floor. A couple of anti-aircraft shells had on a subsequent occasion completed the damage. Bobby and Peate agreed that a search of these upper regions could be put off till the morning. Nor did they attempt to search the cellars. A pile of caterer's stuff in front of the only door leading to them gave proof no one could have been there since had happened whatever had happened in the supper-room.

"Next thing," announced Peate, "is to look up this Miss Margaret Kerr and see what she has to say, if she's there. If she isn't, then perhaps it's her been done in, and not the other one. What did you say her name was?"

"Isobel Winlock," Bobby answered, and his thoughts turned again to the quiet little mouse-like girl he remembered sitting in her inconspicuous corner at Mrs Barrett's party.

"Maybe they're the same," suggested Peate. "Isobel and Margaret using different names."

CHAPTER VI
"A NIGHT LIKE THIS"

THE HOUR was late by now, for all this had occupied much time. Bobby suggested that, as the distance was not great, it might be better to walk rather than take the car. No need to attract more attention than need be, he thought, and Peate agreed.

They set out accordingly on foot, pursuing their way through the silent, moonlit streets, the night more quiet by far here in town than ever it is in country districts. For here there were none of Nature's busy children of the darkness, hurrying about their private concerns. It was a night of extraordinary beauty. Even Peate, little susceptible to such things as a rule, remarked on it. Bobby did not reply. There was a memory in his mind of those other nights of the full moon when other things had happened. Presently he observed as they walked along:

"There seems to be some sort of idea that the Isobel Winlock girl may have gone off with a man named Mark Monk. Ever heard of him?"

"Not that I remember," Peate answered. "Any record?"

"It's possible he may have something to do with the Bexley House place," Bobby said. "Nothing much to go on. Only that Miss Winlock used to get 'phone messages from hereabouts, and told her parents once or twice that she was staying the night with a Thameside friend. This Miss Kerr may be the friend, though that wasn't the name. For that matter, there's nothing to show that whatever happened at Bexley House has any connection with Miss Winlock's disappearance. Bit of a coincidence, though, if it hasn't. Mark Monk has no record that I know of. Ever hear of Matt Myers?"

"Chap tried and acquitted for doing in his wife, wasn't he?" Peate answered. "I remember the case. Made a big sensation some years ago. The papers called it 'The Full Moon Murder'." He stood still suddenly. "Good God!" he said. "A night like this."

"Yes," said Bobby.

"The same initials—Matt Myers and Mark Monk?"

"Yes," said Bobby.

"You think it may be the same man?"

"Yes," said Bobby for the third time. Then he said: "Here we are."

They halted before a fair-sized, semi-detached house, standing back a little from the road. No light showed. Probably the inmates had long been in bed and asleep. Bobby and his companion walked up the short paved path leading to the front door. Peate said abruptly:

"I don't like it."

Bobby said he didn't either. He found the bell and pressed it, remarking that that would make less noise than an attack on the knocker. Fortunately, as is not always the case with electric bells, it was in working order. They heard plainly how its shrill clamour filled the house.

"We'll give them five minutes," he said. "If they haven't answered by then, we'll have a go at the knocker."

However, it only took three minutes for the bell's thin crying to take effect. Then a window above opened and a man's voice called:

"Who's there? What do you want? What's the matter?"

"Does Miss Margaret Kerr live here?" Bobby asked.

"What on earth—" said the voice indignantly.

"I'm more than sorry to disturb you so late," Bobby said. "We are police officers. There seems to have been a bad accident. Could we see Miss Kerr?"

"At this time of night? She's asleep in bed. Won't it do in the morning?"

"I assure you," Bobby said, "we shouldn't have dreamed of disturbing you at this hour if we hadn't felt it absolutely necessary. Miss Kerr may be able to give us vital information. It's a little difficult to explain—especially like this. If you could allow us a few moments talk in private?"

There was a moment's hesitation. Both Bobby and Peate had the impression that a brief consultation was going on above. Peate whispered that he was sure he heard a woman's voice suggesting that perhaps these two nocturnal visitors might really be burglars. The head appeared again at the window and the voice called:

"I'm coming down."

There was a brief delay. Then a sound of bolts withdrawn. The door opened. Still murmuring apologies, Bobby and Peate entered. An elderly man, sleepy, cross, puzzled, in dressing-gown, pyjamas, and slippers, led the way into a conventionally furnished dining-room. Switching on the light, he said:

"I knocked at Maggie's door. She's my daughter. She says she doesn't know anything about any accident. Why should you think she does? There must be some extraordinary mistake."

"That is what we want to clear up," Bobby said. "On the scene of the accident, or whatever it was, we found a handbag. Apparently it belongs to Miss Kerr. At any rate, it has her name and this address."

Mr Kerr blinked and looked more cross, more bewildered, but less sleepy than before.

"Maggie's bag?" he repeated. "Oh, that's impossible! I'm sure she would have told us if she had lost it. There must be some most extraordinary mistake," he insisted.

"I can assure you," Bobby said, "there is no mistake about a handbag having been found on the spot where an accident or something else equally serious appears to have happened. Nor any mistake about its containing Miss Kerr's name and address and other articles of hers."

"Well, I don't understand it, not at all," Mr Kerr protested.

"Nor do we," Bobby told him. "If we could have a few moments' chat with Miss Kerr, no doubt it could be all cleared up at once."

"At this time of night?" Mr Kerr asked doubtfully. "In the morning—"

"I am sorry," Bobby interrupted. "Accidents, or whatever it was, take no notice of the time."

"I'll ask her about her bag," Mr Kerr said.

He went away. Peate said:

"They aren't too keen on letting us see the girl."

"No," Bobby agreed. "Of course, it is late," he admitted.

There was some delay before Mr Kerr returned. This time he was accompanied by an elderly lady, who was looking not only sleepy and bewildered, but also very indignant. Mr Kerr hung back a little; and Bobby fancied he was now not so much angry and bewildered as uneasy, even afraid. But Mrs Kerr, as Bobby assumed the newcomer to be, showed only indignation as she snapped out:

"My daughter's in bed. I've told her to stay there. She doesn't know anything about any accident, and she hasn't lost her bag. It's there. I saw it. I don't think you've any business to disturb respectable people at this time of night. You can come back in the morning if you want to."

"I'm really awfully sorry," Bobby repeated patiently. "I do assure you that if we hadn't thought it absolutely necessary we shouldn't have troubled you. If the bag in our possession is not Miss Kerr's property, she may still be able to help us to find out how papers and other articles apparently belonging to her come to be in it."

"Not at this time of night," Mrs Kerr told him firmly. "I'm not going to have Maggie turned out of bed at this hour to talk to two strange men. I don't know if you really are police—though if you are, that's no excuse."

"Oh, you can see our authority—" Bobby began, but Mrs Kerr interrupted.

"I don't want to see anything," she announced, "and you aren't going to see Maggie, not at this time of night."

Her voice was loud and determined. Bobby began to wonder if there was some reason for such strong resistance. In the background Mr Kerr was looking nervous, unhappy, worried. It might, he supposed, be merely middle-class resentment at such an intrusion on privacy, such a suggestion of police intrusion on a rather stiff and starchy respectability. Or was there some stronger reason? Impossible to be sure as yet. Bobby tried a little more persuasion. Without effect. He decided reluctantly to fall back on a familiar and often successful manœuvre.

"I'm sorry you feel like that," he said. "Generally we find the public ready to help. We grow to depend on it. In this case we are not sure what has really happened—whether it was an accident or something else. It is necessary for us to know. So necessary that I shall feel obliged to place a constable on duty outside this house. I cannot run the risk of learning in the morning that Miss Kerr has had to go into the country for a rest or been called away on important business. And I must warn you that if Miss Kerr did wish to leave here before seeing us, it would be necessary for her to be what we call 'detained for questioning'."

This brought forth a torrent of protests, accompanied by threats to consult a lawyer, to write to the local Member of Parliament, and so on. Bobby picked up his hat, said it would be very wise to consult a lawyer, they had a perfect right to take any other steps they thought desirable, and what was the earliest hour when it would be convenient for him to call, and so relieve the officer on duty at their door? Mr Kerr said: 'Oh, well', and took his wife aside and then into the passage outside. He came back and said that under protest, but under protest only, her mother would ask Miss Kerr to dress and come down.

Bobby said how grateful they were; they quite understood how Mr and Mrs Kerr felt, but they always found that in the end they could rely on the full co-operation of the public. Mr Kerr gave a most unco-operative scowl and retired. Peate looked after him very doubtfully.

"They don't want us to see the girl," he said. "Why not? A bit fishy. Do you think they will try to smuggle her off?"

"Not likely, not at this time of night," Bobby said. "Too difficult."

They had again a little time to wait before at last Mr and Mrs Kerr returned, accompanied by their daughter, Maggie Kerr. She was a pretty, fair-haired girl of about twenty, with a small, oval face, well-matched features, and unusual grey speckled eyes that normally were bright and eager and direct, but now were restless and, Bobby thought, uneasy and alarmed. Not unnatural, perhaps. Most young girls would feel nervous at being hauled out of bed in the middle of the night to talk to two police officers. But Bobby noticed, too, that those grey speckled eyes showed red and swollen and there was a damp appearance under and around them that suggested they had recently been bathed in cold water. He was inclined to think that those eyes had shed many tears this night.

He began again his apologies for so late a visit. Maggie interrupted him in a high, excited voice.

"I hadn't the least idea it was her bag," she said. "I must have picked it up by mistake. I didn't know, not till now. Have you got mine? Do you mean she's been hurt?"

"We are trying to find out," Bobby said. "Some one has certainly been hurt—badly hurt. But we've no idea what really happened. Can you tell us where you saw Miss Winlock?"

"It was Bexley House," Maggie answered, and this was said with a slightly uneasy glance at her parents, as though she knew it would not be approved. "Mrs Winlock rang me up where I work at the Universal and General Bank in Cheapside. Miss Winlock works there, too, only she's in Foreign Exchange, so I don't see much of her. I knew she hadn't turned up that morning and there hadn't been any message, and Mrs Winlock sounded very worried. She said something about a friend living at

Thameside, and she thought it might be me, or I might know. I didn't, but I knew she went to Bexley House sometimes—Miss Winlock, I mean. So I said I would call and ask, and I did, and she was there."

"Are you friendly with Mr and Mrs Winlock?" Bobby asked.

"I've never met them. I hardly knew Miss Winlock, only to say good morning, and sometimes at lunch."

"What happened when you saw her at Bexley House?" Bobby asked.

"I told her Mrs Winlock had rung up at the office. She said her mother was always fussing and she would ring her up and tell her it was all right. She said she would have done it at once only they've no 'phone at Bexley House. I said there would be a row at the office when she went back and she said she jolly well wasn't going back. That's all."

"Not quite, I think," Bobby said. "There was more to it than that, wasn't there? What was the quarrel about?"

Maggie gave a little gasp, taken entirely by surprise.

"Oh, there wasn't," she exclaimed—"at least, I mean. . . . How do you know?" she demanded.

"My dear young lady," Bobby said. "I don't think any woman goes off with another woman's handbag without finding it out very quickly, unless she is in a state of considerable excitement—or should I say distress? And, if you'll excuse my saying so, I think something has happened to distress you very seriously. Haven't you been crying a good deal to-night?"

"Oh, I haven't, I haven't!" Maggie exclaimed—"at least, I mean . . . I mean . . . why shouldn't I? I've got a cold, that's all."

"More than that, I think," Bobby said. "I fancy if we could see your pillow . . . handkerchiefs as well."

Maggie was staring at him with undisguised terror. He tried to smile at her reassuringly. The effort wasn't very successful. She began to cry again. Mr and Mrs Kerr began to talk, both at once and very excitedly. Maggie went on crying. Bobby remained silent.

CHAPTER VII
"I'LL LIVE AS LONG AS YOU"

THEN MAGGIE brought this trying and confused scene to an end by turning suddenly and running out of the room. They heard the light patter of her feet as she ran up the stairs. Mrs Kerr followed her, though not so quickly but that she had time to throw a furious glance at Bobby. Mr Kerr stood staring after them. Peate said:

"Well, that's that."

Mr Kerr went to the door and stood listening. His wife called from the top of the stairs that Maggie had locked her door and wouldn't open it. Peate remarked again that 'that was that'. Bobby picked up his hat and said:

"Well, I suppose that will have to do for to-night. But I am afraid it can't stop here. I don't think Miss Kerr has been entirely frank with us. Probably a formal statement will have to be taken. You may think it advisable to get in touch with your solicitors. I would ask you to impress upon Miss Kerr the necessity of being absolutely and entirely frank. Even in the smallest details. The truth is bound to come out in the end. But meanwhile a lot of trouble may be caused, with rather unpleasant results occasionally. To every one concerned. One thing before we go. I take it Miss Kerr has Miss Winlock's handbag she picked up instead of her own. Will you let us have it, please?"

Mr Kerr hesitated, grumbled that it was Miss Winlock's property, and ought only to be handed over to her. However, he went away, and after more delay presently returned with it, Maggie having been persuaded to open her door and admit her mother. Bobby asked how she was; and Mr Kerr said resentfully that considering the way she had been cross-examined she was much calmer now, and it was a wonder she was, considering the way she had been bullied. Bobby said he resented very strongly the suggestion that Miss Kerr had been bullied. He must ask Mr Kerr to withdraw it. Bobby could both look and speak formidably when he wished to, and Mr Kerr looked rather scared, and complied. Bobby said again that it would be necessary for Miss Kerr to be questioned further, and Mr Kerr countered by demanding the return of her bag he supposed was in Bobby's possession.

"I am sorry," Bobby said in reply to this, "but it must remain in our hands for the present. I will see an acknowledgment is sent Miss Kerr with a list of contents."

"I don't see what right you have to keep it," Mr Kerr protested.

"It may be important evidence," Bobby told him. "There seem to be bloodstains on it."

"Bloodstains? Nonsense!" Mr Kerr retorted angrily. "What does all this mean? I insist upon knowing."

"I don't know myself, so how can I tell you?" Bobby retorted in his turn. "It may turn out to be nothing at all—a mare's nest. Or it may prove to be very serious indeed. That's all I can say. But I do think it is sufficiently serious to make it very necessary that Miss Kerr should keep nothing back. Not even the merest detail—nothing."

He moved towards the door, followed by Peate. Mr Kerr followed them into the hall. He went to open the door. With his hand on the latch, he said:

"There was something about an accident or whatever it was. What did you mean? . . . 'whatever it was'."

"Only what I said," Bobby answered.

"Is it . . . do you . . . well . . . murder?" Mr Kerr asked at last, bringing out the word with a rush.

"I have not said so, I do not know," Bobby answered.

He and Peate went away then. Peate spoke first:

"Tumbled to it pretty quick it might be murder, didn't he? What's he know?"

"No telling," Bobby said. "Mustn't jump to conclusions. Quite natural he should think of murder when I told him it was serious and that his daughter's handbag had blood on it. No, I don't think we can take much notice of that."

"The girl was pretty badly upset," Peate insisted. "There's a lot behind she doesn't mean to let out if she can help it. Do you think this Maggie girl can have outed the other one? There's never any telling what a woman won't do once she gets worked up."

"If it was that way," Bobby asked, "who removed the body? A girl like Miss Kerr could hardly have done it by herself."

"I should like to have a look in their garage," Peate remarked.

"There wasn't one," Bobby said. "Not at the house. They may have a lock-up somewhere. But I can't see that girl carrying dead bodies in and out of cars and garages."

"There was that fellow you saw," persisted Peate. "What about him? You said there was blood on his hand."

"He had given himself rather a bad cut," Bobby pointed out.

"In a struggle?"

"It was a clean cut, freshly done," Bobby said thoughtfully. "Razor blade could have done it."

"Or a dinner-knife?"

"If it were sharp enough," agreed Bobby.

"Well, looks to me as if there was a tie-up somewhere," declared Peate, and Bobby said he rather thought so, too.

"Only where?" he asked.

Peate left that question unanswered. They had nearly reached Bexley House when he remarked:

"The station sergeant said you were asking about a Miss Bella Brown, a journalist living in this part. We don't know her. Could it be Miss Kerr?"

"It might be, I suppose," Bobby admitted. "We can clear that up, though. I think Miss Winlock's parents met her once, and they should be able to describe her. She ought to be found."

"We'll find her," declared Peate confidently. "That is, if there is any such person and it wasn't all a put-up job."

"Quite possible," Bobby said; "but it does look as if there was another woman in it somewhere."

"Miss Maggie Kerr," declared Peate with conviction.

"Yes," agreed Bobby. "Or Miss Vea Burden? Oh Miss Grace Williams? We may be able to find one of the three is connected with Mark Monk. I meant to show the Kerr girl his photograph and see if she could identify it, only she did rather put a stopper on things, the way she ran off."

"First thing to do," declared Peate, "is to pick him up. You think so, sir?"

"Oh, yes, the obvious first step," Bobby agreed once more.

"Shouldn't be difficult," Peate said optimistically, and this time Bobby said nothing, but thought it might be very difficult—very difficult indeed.

They had reached Bexley House now. The constable on duty admitted them. The routine of an investigation was in full progress under the direction of Mr Ferris, the Divisional Detective Inspector, called away from fireside and slippers. Very likely it would go on till dawn or later. Every bloodstain was being examined, recorded, plotted on a plan of the room, photographed. Elaborate measurements were being taken. It would be possible, if necessary, to produce a model showing every detail down to the position of the most distant chair and table. Mr Ferris said gloomily that he expected it would all turn out waste time and labour. Somebody's nose had been bleeding a bit more freely than usual. That was very likely all there was to it. It was quite evident, however, that he did not really believe this. The finger-print specialist was equally gloomy, but for a different reason. He was a frustrated man. He had failed to find a single 'dab' of any significance.

"Must have been wearing gloves," he told Bobby.

"Oh, yes," Bobby said, and went into a trance, as they say at the bridge table. When he emerged from it he saw the finger-print man was watching him curiously, as if he thought Bobby couldn't be quite well. Bobby said: "You may have something there."

"Well, sir, people always wear gloves," said the other disgustedly, and walked away.

Bobby went back into the outer hall. He asked Long, whom he found there, about the two women, Vea Burden and Grace Williams. Long said he hadn't seen either. He thought they must be both in Vea's rooms upstairs. He was sure they had had no chance to slip away unseen. Bobby said he supposed not, not with so much going on. He and Long went into the inner or lounge hall, whence rose the great main stairway. Vea was sitting on the stairs. She watched them as they came in, but she did not move or speak. Only her great dark eyes, dark circles beneath them, straight, thin dark brows above, showed by their intent gaze that she was aware of their entrance. A figure of fate, she seemed, Bobby thought; for there was something brooding, patient, ominous in her motionless form. Bobby did not speak, nor did she, only watched them intently. Bobby had hoped she would be the first to break the silence. As she clearly did not intend to do so, he said:

"We are wondering if there is anything you or Miss Williams can tell us. Is she upstairs?"

"In bed and asleep," Vea answered. "No good waking her, either. She got so worked up about it all I told her to take a nip of whisky, and she did. Several."

"I see," Bobby said. "Of course, all this must be terribly upsetting for both of you."

This very conventional remark earned him, he was not sorry to notice, a glance of extreme scorn. It was always an advantage to be under-estimated, and he was already aware of a feeling that in Vea Burden he was face to face with a formidable personality—on which side, for or against, he was not sure. He was not even sure that she herself knew that as yet. He said:

"Well, perhaps there is something you can tell us. I am sure we can depend on your giving all the help you can."

She seemed to meditate on this, cupping her chin in one long, thin hand. Presently she said in her harsh, husky voice:

"You think there's been a murder here."

"I have not said so," Bobby answered as he had answered before.

"Well," she said. "Well!"

"What do you think?" Bobby asked.

"If there was," she said, "who was it? who?" and when she repeated this last word it was like a cry of terror and despair from the very depths of her being.

"Will you help us to find out?" Bobby asked, very gently. "Will you?"

But to that she made no answer. Only sat there very still and quiet, except for a faint swaying motion of the body so that her long pearl earrings swung slowly to and fro.

When she was still silent, Bobby took from his pocket the photograph of Mark Monk that Maggie Kerr's abrupt departure had prevented him from showing her. He showed it to Vea now, and she transferred to it her intent and hungry gaze.

"It's Mr Monk," she said at last. "How did you get it? Why? What about him?"

"Will you tell us what you know of him?"

"Very little," she answered. "He has something to do with Jerry. I think he has money in this place, but I don't know. Ask Jerry. He comes sometimes, but it's always Jerry who looks after things. He wouldn't murder any one, if that's what you're thinking."

"Every one keeps talking of murder except me," Bobby complained. "I'm only trying to find out what did happen. When Mr Monk came here, had he generally a girl with him?"

"I don't know about when he came," she answered slowly and carefully. "You never saw him without half a dozen little fools buzzing round. He couldn't help it." She paused and then, as if she had been searching for a Word, she said: "Glamour. That's what they would have called it in a girl. But it didn't mean a thing, he always—" She stopped abruptly, as if conscious she had been about to say too much. "Glamour," she repeated.

"He was a friend of yours, wasn't he?"

"No," she almost snarled, and then she began to cough. She put her handkerchief to her lips, and when she took it away Bobby thought there was a speck of blood on it. He waited gravely. She said: "What chance do you think I had against all those kids? He only had to look at them. It's all men want, a pretty young face and an empty head. Till—till—"

"Yes," Bobby said. "Yes. Till . . . till . . . ?"

"Till trouble blows up," she said. "Then it's different. Then they remember . . ." She cut her sentence short again and got to her feet. "I'm tired," she said. "Done in. I'm going to bed."

"One moment," Bobby said. "Did you notice if there was any one girl he seemed to be with more than another?"

"You mean that girl you were asking about? What was her name? Winlock? Isobel Winlock? A little devil for the men."

"Who? Miss Winlock?" Bobby asked, surprised.

"If that's the one you mean," Vea answered, and there was deep anger in her voice. "Took you in, very likely, if you ever met her. She used to sit in a corner and look shy and pathetic and lonely and lost. It always worked. Poor little shy girl!" she mocked. "And all the men feeling big and protective and running to fetch her things, and then she had 'em, she was so grateful and clinging—especially clinging." Bobby felt himself flush slightly. It did rather describe what had happened that day at Mrs Barrett's party. Did it also account for a certain readiness he supposed he had shewn to interfere on her behalf? But Olive had more or less felt the same. As if she had read his thoughts, Vea went on: "Women, too. Sometimes. If they were older and feeling motherly and kind. Never with girls. They knew. The others found out. Later." Her dead-white face blazed suddenly with a fierce, controlled passion. Her expression changed again. "When trouble blows up," she said, "then it's different." She got to her feet and stood looking down at them, pale, still, and upright. She lifted a hand and said something that startled considerably both Bobby and Sergeant Long. "They all think I'm going to die," she said, "but I'm not. Not yet. I'll live as long as you."

With that she turned and went swiftly away, up the stairs, and still after she was out of sight they heard her dry and distant cough.

CHAPTER VIII
"FAIR GIVES ME THE WILLIES"

BOBBY WENT again into a 'trance'. Above a door banged and the sound of coughing ceased. Sergeant Long said: "Well!" This producing no reply from the still meditative Bobby, he said:

"Well, sir, if you ask me, she's got a flap on—good and hard. She knows a lot."

Bobby, aware of a murmuring voice by his side, woke from his abstraction.

"It's jolly late," he said. "I think I'll be off home." Long was immediately consumed with envy and deep yearning for the day when he, too, would be senior enough to take himself off to bed whenever he chose. No bed this night, he knew well enough, for such small fry as sergeants. "Have to let Mr Ferris know about those two women," Bobby added. "What was that you were saying, sergeant? Got a flap on? You spotted that? But I don't think she knows a lot. What's troubling her is just the opposite—that she doesn't know. No more than we do. Something happened, yes. No telling what. And she can't tell either, and it's upsetting her pretty badly. No telling even whether Monk and Miss Winlock were in it. May be something quite different."

"She doesn't think so," Long remarked.

"No. That's why the flap's on," Bobby answered. "She's afraid. Looks to me as if what she called Mark Monk's glamour has worked on her all right. And I should guess she has a sort of hope that if he's mixed up in it, then he may turn to her for help."

"I was thinking," Long suggested, somewhat diffidently, for he knew sergeants should listen to the suggestions of their seniors, not make suggestions themselves—"I was thinking perhaps it might have been her used the knife on the Winlock girl, if all that about glamour meant she was jealous. A jealous woman—" said Long; and left it at that, thinking it enough.

"It might be that way," Bobby agreed. "Yes, it might be that way."

"What do you think all that meant about she wasn't going to die soon?" Long asked.

"I think it meant she knows she is, but she doesn't mean to," Bobby answered. "Perhaps she won't, either. I should say she's plenty of will-power—enough even for that. To keep off even old antic Death."

"Beg pardon, sir," said Long, puzzled.

"Meant for a quotation," Bobby explained apologetically, "but I think I got it wrong. Ought to be old Antic Law, not Death. Much the same, though—fatal in the long run. You know, Long, Vea Burden has me worried."

"Yes, sir," agreed Long, and thought to himself that it was time the Commander did take himself off to bed.

They went to find Ferris. He had established himself in one of the smaller rooms, leaving the technicians to get on with their job in the supper-room and elsewhere. When Bobby and Long entered he was in the act of examining the contents of Miss Winlock's handbag, recovered from Maggie Kerr. There was nothing in it of much interest—nothing more than the normal contents of a woman's handbag. Inspector Peate was there, sitting at a table and making a list of the various articles found. Ferris listened to what Bobby had to tell him. He did not seem much interested, but remarked that he supposed that in the morning he would have to put Miss Burden and the other woman 'through it'. Bobby thought, but did not say, that putting Vea 'through it' was not likely to have much result. He dropped a hint that he would be inclined to suggest not 'putting them through it' just yet, but rather 'going easy' with them both for the present. Of course, Mr Ferris must use his own judgment, and of course, too, there might be developments. But for the moment there was jolly little to go on. Ferris, who liked to go to American films, so as to study police technique in the United States, said:

"You're telling me."

He spoke with some bitterness. Bobby tried to cheer him up by remarking that possibly the whole thing would peter out. Might be a case of much ado about nothing instead of a last-act-in-Hamlet affair. Ferris, who was no Shakespearian, looked puzzled. Bobby said he was going home to bed, and Ferris remarked sadly that he didn't suppose he would see his bed that night, and a busy day to follow, too. Who wouldn't, he asked passionately, chuck the police and go for a sailor, if only it wasn't for being seasick?

He was, in fact, feeling nervous about his ability to handle the affair. He had only recently been appointed to the very responsible post of Divisional Detective Inspector in the famous 'O' division, one that had a reputation to preserve, and was, indeed, the first in which the present careful and elaborate C.I.D. organization had been set up. He had his hands full, he said, with at least half a dozen other important investigations, and he dropped a broad hint that 'off the record', so to speak, he would like to drop in now and then to ask what Bobby thought about any fresh development.

Bobby, drawn by any hint of a problem as is a woman by the suggestion of a new hat in the spring, remarked, with a careful suppression of any show of eagerness, that of course he would be always ready to give any help he could. Whatever else a Commander (Senior—unattached) was for—and on that he himself wasn't too clear—he was certainly there to be helpful.

With that he departed to snatch an hour or two of sleep before turning out again to attend a conference at the Yard on some far-reaching organization scheme, specially affecting, as it happened, 'O' Division.

Ferris ought to have been there, but wasn't, the 'O' Division superintendent explaining that Ferris had a difficult investigation on hand.

"You know something about it, Commander, don't you?" he asked Bobby, and Bobby admitted, reluctantly, that somehow or another he had got mixed up in it.

"A missing girl," he told the conference; "bloodstains or, rather, pools of it; mixed-up handbags; a man who hasn't a record, having been acquitted on a charge of murder; another man, unknown, who managed to give his hand a bad cut the same night; and a woman who says people think she is going to die, but she isn't—not her. And what all that adds up to may be anything or nothing. Ferris has a job on."

"I expect you are thankful it isn't your job," observed, with sarcastic intent, one of those present.

Bobby said, falsely, that he was indeed more than thankful, and was surprised to notice a smile go round the table. He couldn't imagine why.

In the afternoon, however, Ferris turned up in Bobby's room, arriving almost at the same time as the traditional cup of tea and bath-bun, which are, as every one else knows, the chief preoccupation of all public officials. So Bobby sent for another cup of tea and bath-bun and asked how Ferris was getting on.

"Getting on like an escalator in reverse," said Ferris gloomily. "No trace of either the man or the girl."

"Oh, well," Bobby said, "very likely they're quite happy in some remote village inn, all peace and roses and romance."

"Have to get the B.B.C. on the job," Ferris said. "Grace Williams says she knows nothing about anything. Vea Burden says she knows less. Close as a clam, both of them. Miss Williams has a small newsagent's and tobacconist's shop in Pimlico. She says it doesn't do very well, and she is glad to go to Bexley House, or anywhere else, to get a little extra money. She helps the Burden woman, who acts as housekeeper there, mistress of ceremonies, receptionist, and anything else, including, if you ask me, what goes on on the side; and, in my view, that's plenty."

"I shouldn't wonder," Bobby agreed. "To make it more difficult. The whole thing may have nothing much to do with the runaways."

"On the spot by a sort of coincidence?" Ferris asked doubtfully. "In that last lecture of yours you gave us you said never to put your trust in coincidence. Too much of a coincidence, you said, to trust to coincidence for an explanation."

"That's the worst of lectures," Bobby sighed: "always liable to rise up and hit you in the eye."

"Anyhow, we got the address of the shop," Ferris went on. "I rang up Centre and asked them for some one to keep an eye on the place. They gave me Miss Rice."

"Good!" said Bobby, for Miss Rice was known as one of the most efficient of the women police attached to the C.I.D.

"I asked her," Ferris continued, "to go first to the Universal and General Bank to see if she could pick up anything. She had Mr Winlock's card and their authority to make inquiries. She was to say it was feared there might have been an accident. Miss Rice says Miss Winlock seemed very popular with the male staff. Less so with the girls. Apparently she had the name of what one of them called 'pinching your boy' if she got half a chance. Miss Rice thinks some of them will feel a bit more sure of their own boys if she doesn't come back. There were hints that one of the sufferers from this boy-pinching act was Miss Maggie Kerr. You knew she worked at the same place?"

"Yes, she told us that last night," Bobby remarked. "Did Miss Rice get any details?"

"No, only that there had been some gossip that a boy who had occasionally been seen waiting for Miss Kerr after business had later on been seen with Miss Winlock."

"That might be worth following up," Bobby agreed. "Could it be Mark Monk?"

"I don't think so—much younger, apparently. But we could keep it in mind," Ferris answered. "The line the Winlock girl takes is that it isn't her fault, she can't be rude to people and, anyhow, if you can't keep a boy when you've got one, it's your own look-out. The head of her department couldn't understand such a nice, quiet little thing as Miss Winlock stopping away without saying anything. Not what you would expect, not from a timid little thing you would hardly think would dare say 'Boo' to a goose. Her work had always been quite satisfactory, though a little lacking in initiative. Not like Miss Kerr, for instance. She was the equal of any man, and better than most. Did you know she was the heroine of the bottle-of-ink affair?"

"What was that?" Bobby asked.

"It was in the papers at the time," Ferris said. "Just on closing time a man came in and tried to snatch a pile of notes a customer was counting. Miss Kerr made a grab, too, got some of them back, and then, as the fellow was making a bolt for it, chucked a bottle of ink at him. He didn't get very far. All over ink, and attracted attention. Miss Kerr had a letter of thanks from the bank. There was a sequel, too—a spot of jealousy, apparently—and a woman supervisor, or whatever they call it, made some sort of complaint against her. Miss Kerr went in off the deep end, and seemed inclined to repeat the bottle-of-ink stunt. In the end the supervisor lady was transferred to another branch and Miss Kerr was told to lay off bottles of ink for the future, as far as the staff was concerned, anyhow. Bit of a tartar, apparently."

"Little things like that," Bobby remarked thoughtfully, "are worth knowing. Show up character, and character means pretty well everything. I wonder if there's any chance that Miss Winlock made a dead set at Miss Kerr's boy to show that if she couldn't compete in handling bank robbers she could all right when it came to boys."

Ferris said possibly it might be like that. In tones as thoughtful as Bobby's, he remarked that some girls were catty enough. Plenty of scratch beneath the purr.

"From the bank," he continued, "Miss Rice went on to Pimlico. There she had a stroke of luck. Just as she got there she saw a man go into Grace Williams's shop and she noticed that his hand was bandaged—rather carefully, with a roller bandage, as if it had been done either by a doctor or by some one who knew something about first aid."

Bobby beamed. You might accuse him of being dull or plodding in his work, or tell him that an Oxford training had been wasted on him, or almost anything else you liked, and he would listen meekly. But you had to be very, very careful about showing any disrespect for his knowledge or ability in administering first aid.

"It wasn't such a bad job," he agreed, with a modest smirk. "Done practically in the dark, too."

"So Miss Rice," Ferris continued, "thought it might be a good idea to investigate further. She went into the shop. Probably thought it a good chance to buy a packet of cigarettes and put it through expenses."

"Won't come off," said Bobby firmly. "They'll snaffle the cigarettes for their canteen. Go on."

"The man wasn't there, but she could hear him 'phoning behind. Suggests he was known, not a chance customer. A girl came to serve. Miss Rice thinks she recognized her as a witness for the defence in a gangster case. Miss Rice went off with her cigarettes, but when the man reappeared she followed him to a flat in the King's Road, where he let himself in with a latchkey. She asked the locals what they knew. It seems his name is Harper—Alfred James Harper. He is an ex-service man—served with the commandos—and now has a small car-hire business—two private cars and one Realist lorry. Nothing against him; but the other day he was mixed up in a street row. Miss Rice got a copy of the report made. It didn't amount to anything. Here it is, if you like to look at it."

Bobby took it, glanced at it, agreed it didn't amount to much, and observed that Miss Rice had done a good bit of work and deserved a pat on the back.

"I rather think," he added, "I ought to call on Mr Harper and see if we recognize each other. What do you say?"

"I was going to ask," Ferris said, "if you would, only I thought it might be an idea to have another talk with Mr and Mrs Winlock first. They know we are taking it seriously. There may be something more they could tell us. Do you think the Miss Bella Brown they talked about—the journalist Miss Winlock is supposed to have stayed with at Thameside Village—could be Miss Burden?"

"Could be," agreed Bobby. "Has she said anything?"

"Her line is that she doesn't know a thing and why should she?" Ferris answered. "She does her job, asks no questions, gets her pay, and that's all she cares about. I can hardly get another word out of her, but the way she sits and stares and stares from those great eyes of hers, and her face like a corpse—well, it fair gives me the willies," said Ferris, and he looked it.

CHAPTER IX
"MY BANDAGE, I THINK"

THE BLOCK of flats where the Winlocks lived was not far from Scotland Yard. A police car took Bobby and Ferris there in a few minutes. They alighted at a little distance, since police cars are apt to attract an attention that is not always appreciated. Both Mr and Mrs Winlock were at home, both evidently in a state of considerable distress and apprehension, all the more so, indeed, as they had just been rung up by a neighbouring garage.

They had no car themselves, and, when they wanted one, had been in the habit of hiring from this garage. Neither of them drove, so when they were alone the garage provided a chauffeur. When, however, their daughter was with them, she always drove. The message they had just received was to the effect that she had taken out a car the day before—a Bayard Twenty. As the garage knew her, and Mr Winlock had a running account with them, there had been no difficulty about this. She had mentioned that it might be required the whole day, and had promised to ring up and let them know when to expect it back. But she had not done so, nor had the car been returned. The garage message was to ask when they were likely to hear, and this added complication had much increased the Winlocks' anxiety.

Bobby asked for the address of the garage, and said he would call there and get all particulars. He asked also a few more questions, but without much result. Ferris secured a list of the missing jewellery, though it was provided with some reluctance, and only on a promise given that the utmost discretion would be used in making any inquiry thought necessary. The missing articles were of no very great value: two hundred pounds in all, perhaps, or possibly a little more. The most valuable single piece was a gold snuff-box showing on the lid a portrait of Marshal Saxe. It was a family heirloom, and was supposed to have been presented to an ancestor by the Marshal himself. The value had been put at fifty pounds.

While Ferris was noting down these particulars, Bobby went on to explain that they were trying to trace Miss Bella Brown, the woman journalist of whom the missing Isobel had spoken and with whom she said she stayed at Thameside Village. Could, he asked, Mr or Mrs Winlock describe her? Too much to hope, he supposed, that Miss Isobel had possessed a photograph of her friend?

It was too much to hope for. Nor were the efforts Mr and Mrs Winlock made to give a verbal description much more successful than are in general those made by the untrained observer. Mrs Winlock was able to give a full and accurate account of the lady's frock, but that was not likely to be of much assistance—frocks are seldom permanent features of any woman's wardrobe. It did emerge, however, that Miss Bella Brown was tall and thin, with dark, shining eyes deep sunk in hollow cheeks. That agreed well enough with Bobby's vivid memory of Vea Burden. But, then, Miss Brown had been very heavily made up, and her coiffure had been in the latest and most elaborate style. Probably the removal of the make-up and a different style of hairdressing would make recognition difficult. In any case, the encounter had been brief, Mr Winlock was very short-sighted, and Mrs Winlock had clearly given most of her attention to Miss Brown's clothes. Bobby gave up hope of being able to obtain from them any proof of identity that he could rely on. Strong suspicion, perhaps, but that was all.

"Most likely precautions had been taken beforehand," he remarked as he and Ferris were on their way to the garage of which Mr Winlock had given them the address. "Plenty of make-up and a different hair-do, and you would never be sure it was the same woman, unless you were on the look-out."

At the garage they were given particulars of the missing car. It was a Bayard Twenty, No GADD 37. The garage foreman said he hoped it was all right, and Bobby said he hoped so, too. But the young lady's parents were growing anxious, and seemed to be afraid there might have been an accident. What sort of a driver, he asked, was Miss Winlock?

The foreman hesitated, and then permitted himself a discreet smile.

"A little devil," he said, half disapprovingly, wholly admiringly. "Class O.K. No. 1; but the risks she took! Enough to turn your hair white. The Bayard Twenty can do a hundred m.p.h. easy as nothing, and she jolly well saw it did. Been had up twice for dangerous driving, but got away with it both times. Her looking so small and scared like, and doing her 'please won't some one take care of little me' stunt, no jury was going to believe she had been up to tricks, as was said. You could see the whole court—judge, jury, lawyers, the whole blessed lot—wanting to buy her chocolates and take her home safe to her mother. A one-er," pronounced the foreman, no disapproval now mixed with his admiration, "a one-er if ever there was such. Wrists like wire, she had, and a nerve like—like—" He looked round, despairing of finding the appropriate word—"a nerve like hell," he concluded, doing his best. "Like hell and blazes," he added for confirmation.

As there seemed nothing more the foreman could tell them, Bobby and Ferris returned to their car. Ferris asked the driver to take them to the little street off the King's Road to which Miss Rice had traced the visitor to the tobacconist's shop.

"What that chap at the garage told us," he remarked, "doesn't sound much like no initiative and not being able to say 'Boo' to a goose."

"No," agreed Bobby, "no. Possibilities in that young woman—possibilities both ways. Sort of a zigzag, but always between two extremes. Either the daren't-say-'Boo' idea, or else she's a little devil. Either she sits shyly in a corner keeping out of the way, or else she's busy pinching other people's boys. Possibilities all the way round," he corrected his earlier remark. "She might go off with some one who saw her as the daren't-say-'Boo' young woman and found he had caught a 'little devil'. Or, again, she might carry her pinching act a bit too far one day. Or . . . or . . ."

He left the sentence unfinished—showing, indeed, signs of going into another bridge-table trance.

"If there's been an accident," Ferris said, "we ought to have heard by now."

"I don't quite see how any accident," observed Bobby, "is going to account for what we found at Bexley House. Something happened there. I suppose there might have been an accident later on. Long said the car he saw was being driven all out. You've got the number, and that's something to go on."

"Probably find it abandoned somewhere," Ferris prophesied. "Good thing you had that photo of Mark Monk. I've had the copies made you asked for." He gave Bobby one or two as he spoke, and Bobby accepted them with a word of thanks. "We ought to be able to get his address pretty soon," Ferris went on. "All the Bexley House lot swear they didn't know it."

"Jerry George?" Bobby asked.

"Gone away on a business trip," Ferris said disgustedly. "Left no address and didn't say when he would be back. Smells—stinks," he corrected himself and repeated: "Stinks."

"You have his home address," Bobby said. "But I expect you'll find Mr Monk has been living in an hotel. More likely a one-room flatlet and no questions asked. A bird of passage, I expect, and didn't leave much behind when he moved on."

They had reached their destination now. This time the car was left waiting on the spot. Just as well, perhaps, that curious neighbours should be aware of a certain police interest in this particular house. More likely, then, that any unusual incident would be noticed and remembered. Their luck was in, too; for, as they alighted, the door of the house opened and a man came out. He was under middle height and slight in build, but strong and active-looking. In appearance he was fair, with light brown hair and blue eyes, and strongly marked, prominent features. Beneath heavy eyebrows his eyes were lively and alert, and one hand was bandaged. He seemed in a hurry, and paid no attention to the two new arrivals or their car. Bobby stopped him as he was beginning to walk away.

"Excuse me," Bobby said. "Could you spare us a moment? You are Mr Harper, aren't you? Alfred James Harper? In the car-hire business? Two private cars and a small lorry you let out?"

"Well, what about it?" Harper asked. "I'm booked up, if that's what you want. Nothing wrong, is there?" He glanced from them to the car waiting near with a uniformed constable at the wheel. He looked startled. His expression changed, grew more alert and wary. "Police?" he asked.

"There are one or two points in an inquiry we are making," Bobby told him, "we are rather stuck at, and we think you may be able to help. It's difficult to explain in the street. Would you care to come back to Scotland Yard with us, or would it be better in your own place? You live here, I think? Lucky we caught you just as you were going out."

Harper had no air of thinking there had been any luck about it. His manner, indeed, had grown sullen and defiant, even truculent.

"What's it all about?" he demanded. "Can't an ex-service man try to get going again without having police on his door-step all the time—licence this and licence that and what did you do with half a pint of petrol you had standing in the corner the other day? Enough to make you turn the whole thing up."

"Oh, we can quite understand how you feel," Bobby answered, in his most dulcet tones. "No one loves a policeman—except when they want a spot of help. As does happen. But we don't want to interfere with you—not in the least. All we want is a little help to clear up one or two doubtful points. I'm sure we can depend on your co-operation. We find we always can—except, of course, from those who really have something to hide."

It was a remark that did nothing to charm away the scowl Harper had developed. For a moment or two he seemed to con-template a flat refusal. Then he said:

"Oh, all right. Come in, if you want to. The only way to get rid of you."

"Exactly," Bobby agreed, his tones more dulcet still. "I must admit we are stickers—the old bulldog breed, you know. Never let go. Regular limpets."

Harper received this remark with a grunt. Quite obviously, 'limpets' was not the word he would have chosen. He opened the door of the house with his latch-key. There was a dark, narrow passage within, and stairs covered with shabby linoleum. Harper ascended them, leaving Bobby and Ferris to follow as they liked. On the landing at the top of the stairs Harper unlocked a door and entered, still not troubling to look if Bobby and Ferris were following. The room was of a fair size, and seemed to serve at once as bedroom, sitting-room, kitchen, and office. There was a gas-fire with a gas-ring attached, and a half-open cupboard showed a glimpse of crockery, pans, and so on. An old roll-top desk with a battered typewriter standing on it and a telephone adjacent, occupied one corner. Against the inner wall was a small divan bed, and by the window were two rickety armchairs. The room nevertheless was clean and tidy and well cared for. Harper seated himself at the roll-top desk, turning the swivel chair to face his two visitors. A sulky gesture he made towards the two chairs by the window seemed intended as an invitation to be seated. He said:

"Well, what's it all about?"

"That's where we hope you may be able to help us," Bobby explained. "I think I saw you last night, didn't I?"

Harper looked at him quietly, reflectively. But for the dark anger in his eyes—and was there fear as well?—he might have been trying to remember, trying and failing.

"Not that I know," he said at last. "Where? At the local?"

Bobby pointed to the other's bandaged hand.

"My bandage, I think," he said.

CHAPTER X
"SHOPPED ME, DID SHE?"

HARPER MADE no answer to this, only his dark and angry eyes grew darker, angrier still. Bobby did not speak either. Ferris began to fidget. He did not understand this silence, did not understand that there was, as it were, a battle of wills going on, that much might hang on whether this silence was broken first by Harper or by Bobby. But it was very possibly the signs of impatience Ferris showed that induced Harper to speak. Fumbling in his pocket for a cigarette he produced but forgot to light, he muttered:

"Well, now then, what are you trying to pin on me?"

"We are inquiring into recent events at Bexley House," Bobby answered. "That's all. You were near there last night—in the road opposite. Your hand was bleeding from a nasty cut you had given it. I tied it up for you. A roller bandage. The one you have on now. Are you willing to tell us how you happened to be there and anything else you know or noticed?"

"I don't know what you are talking about," Harper retorted. "Trying it on, aren't you? I wasn't anywhere near Bexley House last night, and it wasn't you did up my hand for me. At least, not unless you are Lil in disguise," he added, grinning, as if he thought he had made a good joke.

"You deny," Bobby asked, "that it was you I spoke to last night or that I tied up your hand?"

"Absolutely," Harper answered, and favoured Bobby with another of those looks straight in the eye whereby a liar sometimes tries to carry conviction.

It had no such effect on Bobby, who knew the trick well enough, and regarded it as more a sign of lying than of truth-telling.

"Who is Lil?" Bobby asked. "Can you tell us where to find her?"

"I don't know where she lives, if that's what you mean," Harper answered. "And if I did I shouldn't tell you. Nice girl, but she doesn't like your sort."

"She may have her reasons—good reasons, perhaps," Bobby agreed. "Do you mind telling us where you were last night and how you hurt your hand?"

"I was here most of the time, doing my books," Harper answered. "Somewhere about nine I went out to get a drink. If you are interested, I did rather expect to meet Lil. I ran into her just outside the King's Head round the corner. I generally use the Bell and Bush, farther on. I said to come along there for a drink. She asked me to sharpen a pencil for her." He paused and stared at Bobby. He went on: "I expect she wanted to book a date. She gave me the pencil, and I got my knife, and just then a fellow came pelting along full speed as if all the devils in hell were after him—or else busies. Much the same, anyway. He bumped right into me, sent me sprawling, and I suppose I fell on my knife. It went pretty deep, but Lil tied it up for me. She knows how—been a nurse or something. Then I went home. Felt like it.”

“A very clear story,” Bobby commented, “full of convincing detail. I only wish—we are like that in the police—you could give us some independent confirmation. Miss Lil's address, for instance, or name some one who saw it happen. Or even your pocket-knife still showing traces of blood. Anything like that?”

“You needn't believe me if you don't want to,” Harper answered carelessly. “I'm not going to set you on Lil. Find her for yourselves if you want to. I haven't got the knife. I expect I dropped it when I got bowled over. It may have been picked up. Something for you to do—trace the missing knife.” He gave another of his half-sulky, half-defiant grins. “Well, now then, like to tell me what it's all about and why you want to pick on me?”

“I think I told you,” Bobby reminded him, “that last night I saw a man resembling you waiting outside Bexley House, and that I tied up his hand for him. He had cut it badly. I put on a roller bandage like the one you have on your hand you also have cut badly.”

“Can you produce any supporting evidence?” Harper asked, his grin broader than ever. “What proof have I you didn't invent that yarn so as to have an excuse for trying to fix something on me?”

“Look here,” began Ferris indignantly; but Bobby, in secret more than a little amused by Harper's rather boyish impudence and his evident pleasure in cheeking the police, made Ferris a sign to be silent.

“There is something else,” Bobby continued. “The man I spoke to outside Bexley House had a rather distinctive voice— harsh and penetrating, easily recognizable. You have the same sort of voice and the same build, and I think you are the same man. He kept very much in the shadow, and his cap was pulled down over his eyes. All the same, I think I recognize you.”

“The point is,” Harper said, “what supporting evidence can you produce?”

"Also," Bobby went on, without taking any notice of this question Harper asked, again with such an air of smug triumph and enjoyment, "Miss Grace Williams, who works at Bexley House, told us that a man answering your description, and whose harsh voice she mentioned particularly, had been seen at Bexley House. She did not know who he was, she said, and did not question him, as she thought he was there in connection with the preparations for a dance."

Harper's expression changed. The rather boyish, not wholly unattractive impudence it had shown when he thought he was, as he would have phrased it, 'getting a bit of his own back', changed slowly to the dark, smouldering anger that had been there before, only ten times intensified.

"She shopped me, did she?" he muttered through clenched teeth. "You wait, my dear, you wait."

As he spoke he slightly lifted his clenched right hand in a gesture that somehow conveyed an impression of an imminent and deadly threat. It was as though all at once the atmosphere became charged with a dangerous tension that might well issue at almost any moment into act. Ferris, startled, made as if to rise. Bobby said sharply:

"Steady, Mr Harper, steady."

Harper stared at him, but did not speak for a moment or two. He took out a handkerchief and wiped his lips.

"I could do with a drink," he said slowly, and his violent and threatening stare never changed or wavered or relaxed. "Shopped me, did she?"

"Is it 'shopping' you to say you were at Bexley House last night? And why do you deny it?" Bobby asked.

"So I wasn't," Harper snarled. "Telling lies, she was. That's her. Liar."

"Have you known Miss Williams long?" Bobby asked.

"Yes, worse luck," Harper answered, his manner a little more normal now, as if the strain and tension he had shown before were slowly lessening. "She and me palled up after I was de-mobbed. I was feeling so I would have palled up with any one. Lost like; demobbed after never knowing nothing but the Army, and all my folk wiped out. No one left. That was the blitz. I was glad enough to have some one to pal with. But not after I got to know her. Jealous as hell. I couldn't even look at another bit of skirt but she would start raising hell. Just passing the day with another young lady I was once, and up came Grace and smacked her face. Then she wanted us to marry. Nothing doing. Not me. It was her let me in for Bexley House. I might have guessed there was something crooked, and that's what she was after. Getting me mixed up so she could have a hold on me. I'll fix her."

"What can you tell us about Bexley House?" Bobby asked.

"It smelt," Harper answered. "That's all I know. Hired my lorry and paid double rates. Well, I ask you. Made me think. So next time I said the lorry was booked. Then a call came through from a firm I knew and if it was free could they send a man to the garage to collect it? I said O.K. Afterwards it turned out it wasn't them had rung me, only some one else using their name. But the lorry came back all right, so I hadn't any grouse—paid for and all. But Grace behind the whole thing most likely. You ask her."

"Yes, I think we shall have to," Bobby agreed. "You still deny you were at Bexley House last night. Have you ever been there?"

Harper took a long time to answer this question. Presently he said:

"I was trying to think. It's nearly a month ago I picked up a load for there. After dark. They rung up and said it was emergency. Lorry broke down and another wanted for transfer. I took my Realist along. Cases it was. I didn't ask what was in 'em, and they didn't say. Next day there was a bit in the paper about a lorry loaded with radio sets being missing. Same thing a week or so later. This time I did ask. They said as them that asked no questions heard no lies. I didn't argue. Tough, both of 'em, and no business of mine. And they paid double ordinary rates. Smelt. People don't pay double rates for nothing. So next time when rung up I said the lorry was booked, as I told you before. My idea is Grace was working it, trying to get me mixed up in it so she could have a hold on me. You can tell her that from me," he added viciously and again his eyes glowed with a dark, interior rage.

"Is that all you can say?" Bobby asked. "Have you been there at other times?"

"Well, Grace sent me tickets for a dance, and another time for a smoking concert. I didn't want any more trouble with her than I could help. So I went. Good shows, both of them. Nothing out of the way. Nothing for even the nosiest busy to smell at." He paused, and still that interior rage of his seemed to smoulder and glow within him as he muttered: "I'll have it out with her, 'shopping' me and all."

"What can you tell us about a man called Jerry George?" Bobby asked, shifting the subject suddenly.

"That little fat bloke?" Harper asked in return. "Runs the show, doesn't he? Keeps out of the way, but Grace told me he was the boss. Tells Vea what to do and sees she does it; but you wouldn't notice if you didn't know. I heard him once, though, having a row with another bloke there. Told him to watch his step or there'd be trouble. Sounded as if he meant it, too. The way he looked made me think of the way some of our Commando chaps looked when they were going out to get a Bosche sentry. The killer look."

"Who was the other bloke?" Bobby asked.

"Don't know. Didn't see him. And wouldn't tell you if I had. I don't shop blokes. Name of Mark, though, if that's any good to you." He grinned again, apparently thinking that a mere Christian name would be no great help. "In my idea," he added, "whoever the bloke was, he was in it and he was putting the screws on Jerry good and tight and Jerry didn't like it one little bit."

Bobby showed him one of the photographs of Mark Monk the Yard had had reproduced from that Mrs Barrett had supplied.

"Ever seen that man?" Bobby asked. "Recognize him at all?"

Harper looked at it long and intently, in silence. He showed no sign of recognition, and yet Bobby was convinced that it meant something to him. He handed it back to Bobby.

"Reminded me," he said slowly, "of a bloke in 'C' platoon. Name of Jones, I think, I'm not sure. Not the same, because the man I mean went west in Italy. We found him knifed near Naples. An Eye-tye had got him. In the throat. Bled it did like nothing else I've ever seen. There's a look of him about that photo of yours."

"Interesting coincidence," Bobby remarked. "We'll try to check up. It might be useful to know if he had a brother, for instance."

"I'm not sure his name was Jones," Harper said, rather hurriedly, and as if this suggestion of Bobby's was both unexpected and unwelcome.

"Just one thing more," Bobby went on. "Our information is that you were mixed up a week or two ago in a street quarrel. There was a scuffle, and you knocked a man down. The report of the constable on the beat says that the man concerned refused to make any complaint. His story was that you were showing him how to get in a left swing and his foot slipped and he fell and that was how he hurt his face. Obvious lie, but there it was. Nothing our man could do but move them all on and make sure that you and the other chap went different ways. Who was he?"

"Didn't know him from Adam," Harper answered promptly. "He had had a drop too much. Bumped up against me. Said it was my fault and wanted to fight. I had to put him down to keep him quiet. That's all."

"I suppose," Bobby said with a smile Harper did not much like, "what you mean is that that is all you intend to tell us. Any time you feel like telling us a bit more, let us know. Anyhow, I think we shall probably want another chat with you sooner or later. Oh, and just one word of advice. Keep away from Grace Williams. Somehow I didn't quite like the way you looked about her—not the killer look, of course. All the same, take my advice and keep away. And now I think we must be off. Good-bye—for the present."

This amiable farewell brought no response. It was a scowling, angry, rather frightened man who, his hands thrust deep in his pockets, watched them go.

CHAPTER XI
"YOU'RE POLICE, AREN'T YOU?"

On their way back to Scotland Yard neither Bobby nor Ferris spoke much. They were occupied with their own thoughts. Only when at their destination they alighted did Ferris say:

"I don't much like the way that fellow talked. My view is that he is in it up to the neck."

"Well, it's quite clear he knows more than he wants to say," Bobby agreed. "But he didn't impress me as a criminal type. Hot-tempered and reckless—and his war experience has left him a little confused about law and order. That's all."

"It's his sort," Ferris declared, "that's giving us all the trouble. Start with the black market they kid themselves is just another bit of excitement and ready to shoot if stopped."

"The raw material of a criminal," Bobby commented. "But I don't think Harper has quite got there yet. If we can stop him before it's too late . . ."

"In my view," Ferris said, "it's too late already. There's got to be some connection between Harper's cut hand and all that mess you found at Bexley House."

"I suppose so," Bobby admitted. "If you noticed, what he told us about his pal killed in Italy sounded very much as if he knew what had happened at Bexley House and it was so much on his mind he couldn't help it coming out."

"Means he's the murderer?" Ferris asked.

"Much too soon to say that," answered Bobby. "We don't even know if it was murder, or even what did happen. May have been an accident of some sort. Not likely, but possible. The thing is to find the Winlock girl."

"If she's there to find," remarked Ferris grimly. "I'm thinking of dropping a hint to Miss Williams to be on the look-out. I didn't like the way Harper looked—not one little bit I didn't."

"I expect it might be as well to keep them both under observation as far as you can," Bobby agreed.

"Jealous women," Ferris said, shaking his head gloomily. "Never know where you are with 'em. I've known a woman give a man away out of jealousy and then go rushing off to warn him, knowing jolly well she would get beaten up for her pains. There's no sense to women," and now the shake of his head was reproving rather than gloomy.

Bobby agreed that women had no sense, and refrained from quoting the celebrated dictum of Mrs Poyser's that that was because God had made them to match the men. He was in the act of bidding good-bye to Ferris when a constable came up to say that Mr Ferris was wanted on a 'phone call from his office in 'O' Division and that it was urgent.

Bobby waited to hear what it was all about. Ferris returned presently in some excitement. A report had come in to the effect that the previous evening a car, believed to be a Bayard Twenty, had crashed traffic lights in Reading about an hour after Sergeant Long had seen a Bayard Twenty leave Bexley House.

"If it's the same car," Ferris said, "they were in a hurry."

Yet another report, this time from Ilchester, said that a complaint of dangerous driving had been laid against a car, make unknown, but with a number in two figures and lettering that began with a 'G'. The accused car had overtaken on a narrow bridge, passing at what was described as a terrific speed, with hardly an inch to spare. The driver of the overtaken car had had a bad fright, and was sure that only his own skill and presence of mind had averted a crash. The time given was only about an hour later than the Reading incident.

"Some going," Ferris commented. "Ilchester must be seventy or eighty miles by road from Reading."

"Heading west," Bobby remarked.

Finally there was a third report from the other side of Exeter. No official report had been made at the time, and therefore the hour was not certain, but a constable on night duty had noticed a car travelling at a very high rate of speed in a westerly direction. The road at this point was good, clear, and straight, with no side turnings, so there had been no reason for any action to be taken. Nor had he made any attempt to observe the car's make or number—which would, indeed, have been difficult, considering the speed at which it was going. The incident had only returned to his mind when he heard that inquiries were being made.

"Good going!" Ferris commented again. "Exeter can't be far short of two hundred miles. If it's the same car it must have been doing an overall speed of between eighty and ninety miles an hour or thereabouts."

"Heading Cornwall way," Bobby remarked.

"You can understand a spot of hurry," Ferris went on, "if there was a murderer and a dead body in that car. Only what murderer and what dead body?"

"There's that," Bobby said; and both men were silent as to their minds came a vision of what seemed to have been a wild, fierce flight through the moonlit night and the silent country, the dead driven by one who knew his own life forfeit.

"If it's Cornwall," Ferris said, "it might be the idea to leave the car on Dartmoor and hope it wouldn't be found for months, maybe years. Or there's the sea. Send a car over some of those Cornish cliffs and no one would ever know."

"Dartmoor can be searched," Bobby remarked, "and it's not only the last day when the sea gives up its dead. I think there might be some other plan, though," he added with a somewhat troubled air.

With that they parted, and Bobby returned to his own quarters, there to become submerged in other business.

But he did not forget Bexley House or cease wondering what might or might not have happened there. Occupied as he was with the unexciting details of the new organization scheme, he felt at times a trifle envious of Ferris, busy, for his part, with as strange, as fascinating, as doubtful a problem—one so doubtful, indeed, that it was even doubtful if it was a problem at all—as the Yard has often found itself presented with. Incidentally, Ferris, much worried by a complete inability to make any progress towards a solution, often felt more than a trifle envious of Bobby. For Bobby at least had only to deal with a simple and straightforward problem of reorganization, and knew clearly both the object to be attained and the nature and value of all the pieces concerned.

But presently Ferris paid Bobby another visit.

"Thought," he explained apologetically, "you would like to know there's a fresh development just when everything seemed at a dead end."

"Traced the car?" Bobby asked hopefully.

"Not the car, the snuff-box," Ferris answered. "You remember? Family heirloom, or something of the sort: Miss Winlock was thought to have taken it with her when she went off. Well, now it's turned up. It was pawned at a place in the City for fifteen pounds. Name, David Pope. An address in Bloomsbury, and the date of the sale is the day after Miss Winlock was missed. I thought you might like to come along and see what Mr David Pope has to say for himself. If you can spare the time."

Bobby said, with a sigh, that he couldn't possibly spare the time, and, with determination, that he was jolly well going to all the same. It was an interesting and unusual case, and the missing girl's life might well depend upon prompt action. It could well be she had seen something it was necessary she should never tell. Not but that there were various other explanations, all equally likely, and none of them very pleasant. Anyhow, it was very good of Ferris to keep him informed. Especially as some of the other senior officers were inclined to think that more fuss than was necessary was being made. Nose-bleeding, for instance, was still occasionally suggested. But only by those who had not seen that grim spectacle in the supper-room all arrayed for pleasure and festivity.

Ferris made a polite reply to the effect that he was only too happy to avail himself of the help and advice of any officer so well known as Mr Owen. Probably what he really meant was that he knew how much Bobby would like to have a hand in the investigation, that he would be grateful for the opportunity offered, and that it would do no harm to any young officer, recently promoted, to keep himself under the notice of an influential senior. Why, Ferris told himself, if he did well in this affair he might some day be a commander himself. Dazzling thought, especially as this brand-new title in the police hierarchy carried a certain glamour of its own, as of the unknown.

The two men accordingly set off in Ferris's car for the Bloomsbury address supplied to them and there learned that Mr David Pope was at his City office. The address of this was given at once by an obliging landlady.

"You're police, aren't you?" she asked.

Bobby withered her with a glance, or at least that should have been the effect, if only the smiling little landlady had noticed. Few things annoyed him more than to be recognized as a policeman when he was so certain he bore none of the insignia of his profession. He was equally certain, by the way, that he could recognize the profession of any one else, no matter how well they thought it concealed. Ferris, however, admitted quite cheerfully that the guess was correct.

"What makes you think so?" he asked.

"About the accident, isn't it?" the landlady asked in her turn. "Real upset I was to see the poor young gentleman with his face in such a state—all bruised and swollen—and I always did say as them motor cars are nasty things as shouldn't ever have been allowed. Mr Pope said he would have the law on them if the police could trace the car that did it, and I only hope he will."

Ferris said he hoped so, too. Bobby said it would be only right, and could the landlady give them the exact date?

It seemed she could, and did, and it also seemed that this date coincided with that on which a report had been made of a scuffle between Harper and an unknown man outside a public-house in Pimlico. So they thanked her, said they would have to try to see Mr Pope another time, and when they were back in their car again Ferris asked, with some excitement, what Bobby thought of that.

"Got to try to find out first what the quarrel was about," Bobby remarked thoughtfully. "And where this David Pope comes in. New character altogether. Getting more and more complicated, isn't it?"

It was a proposition to which Ferris gave a gloomy and somewhat worried assent.

"If only we knew what it really was happened that night," he said, and went on more cheerfully, "Pope may be the man we want. Explanations needed when a woman disappears and next day some of her jewellery is pawned by a third party."

CHAPTER XII
"YOU SPOKE OF MURDER FIRST"

THE ADDRESS given by the obliging landlady proved to be that of a well-known engineering concern—Greater Engineering, Ltd. Here, when they asked to see Mr David Pope, they were shown into a waiting-room, where presently he joined them.

He proved to be a tall, good-looking youngster, fair-haired, blue-eyed, with a rather brusque, self-confident, yet slightly defiant manner, as if he felt the need to assert himself, or at least to be always on the defensive. Bobby's impression was that here was a youth faced too soon with responsibilities whereto he was not always sure that he was equal. It was an impression strengthened by a certain restlessness, a touch of unease, that seemed to show in those blue eyes of his, where but little appeared of the frankness and candour of youth.

Ferris began by explaining that they were police officers. Miss Winlock's parents had asked them to make inquiries about her. She had left home without explanation, and they were very anxious about her. Could Mr Pope give them any information?

"I don't know anything about it," Pope answered. "Why come to me?"

"We are going to every one we think might be able to help," Ferris explained. "Privately. There is no wish for undue publicity at present. But Mr and Mrs Winlock are uneasy. There are reasons that can't be gone into just now. When did you see Miss Winlock last?"

"Look," Pope said slowly, "I don't understand this. I don't know anything, and I don't quite see why I should say anything if I did. If Miss Winlock chooses to go off on her own for her own reasons, what's that got to do with any one else? I suppose it's natural enough for her people to be upset, but it's a bit thick, isn't it? to go to the police. What right have you to interfere?"

"Some jewellery disappeared at the same time," Ferris said.

"You're not accusing her of stealing it, are you?" demanded Pope indignantly.

"It's a point to be cleared up," Ferris told him. "One of the articles missing is a snuff-box."

"It belonged to her, left her by an aunt," Pope exclaimed. "She told me so herself." Evidently it had never even occurred to him that this statement might not be strictly accurate. "She wasn't very happy at home," he added. "They didn't understand her."

"How did the snuff-box come into your possession?" Ferris asked.

"I haven't said it did," Pope retorted.

"Our information is that you pawned it," was Ferris's brief reply.

"You seem to know a lot," grumbled Pope. "I don't see what business it is of yours. It's between Miss Winlock and me. Nothing to do with any one else."

"When a woman disappears," Ferris answered, "when there are curious and unexplained circumstances about her disappearance, and when jewellery belonging to her is pawned by a third party immediately afterwards, explanation seems called for."

"Good Lord!" Pope exclaimed impatiently, "you talk as if you think I might have murdered her."

Neither Bobby nor Ferris answered this, and slowly the young man's expression changed to one of a bewildered horror. He became very pale. The silence lasted perhaps for a couple of minutes, though to all three of them it seemed much longer. It was as though the air in the room grew heavy with the shadow of an unknown terror. At last Ferris said slowly and quietly:

"You spoke of murder first, not us."

Pope was still silent. He seemed incapable of speech, he could only stare at them with a kind of bewildered incredulity. They remained equally silent, waiting. At last, in a high, changed voice, he said:

"Oh, that's absurd! . . . It couldn't be . . . not that . . . I mean, it doesn't happen, does it?"

"Yes," Bobby answered. "Sometimes." The boy lapsed into silence again, but the doubt and terror in his eyes grew no less. Bobby said: "What made you think of murder so soon: murder that you think doesn't happen?—not to people you know, I expect you meant."

"It was what you said," Pope muttered. "I mean . . . there was a fellow with her once. I saw him look. I mean to say . . . well, of course it was only fancy. I dreamed of him, that's all. I suppose it made me remember—dreaming, I mean."

Bobby took from his pocket a copy of the Mark Monk photograph.

"Do you recognize it?" he asked.

"That's him," Pope said at once. "I saw him at a dance I went to."

"At Bexley House, Thameside Village?" Bobby asked, and when Pope nodded, he asked: "Who was he dancing with? Miss Winlock? Was that when you saw him 'look'? Was there any reason you noticed? any sort of disagreement? Was she refusing to dance with him or anything like that?"

"It wasn't during the dancing," Pope answered reluctantly, as if he regretted having said anything. "There were card-tables if you didn't dance, or wanted a change. Look, you can't possibly mean . . ." He started to mop at his forehead, where beads of sweat had begun to appear. Now, too, the deathly pallor of his complexion had become intensified. Quite plainly he had been terribly shaken by that word 'murder' he had been himself the first to pronounce. He muttered: "Well, now then, I'm not going to believe anything like that. I don't expect you do either. Not really. It's not . . . reasonable. Is it?"

"No," agreed Bobby, "not a bit. It never is." He did not say what 'it' meant, but they all three knew. He went on: "Anyhow, we shan't be satisfied till we've got in touch with Miss Winlock and made sure she is safe and well. About what you were saying. They weren't dancing, you said. Were they playing cards, then?"

"They were in the card-room, but they weren't playing: they were talking in a corner out of the way. It startled me, the way that fellow glared at her. I mean the chap you've got the photo of. I went towards them. But they started laughing, and I thought it was only my fancy. When I said something to her later on when I got a chance, she told me to mind my own business. She was ratty, did a glare on her own."

"Had you gone to the dance with her?"

"Oh, no."

"With Miss Maggie Kerr, then?"

Pope stared at him in a very disconcerted and surprised manner, and he hesitated for a moment or two before finally he muttered:

"Well, suppose I did? What about it? Look, what's the idea? What's all this got to do with it? All these questions!"

"It's very helpful in these cases," Bobby explained, as he had done before in similar circumstances, "if we can get an idea of the background. There's generally a sequence, and if we know that 'B' happened to-day because of 'A' yesterday, we can some-times get an idea of what sort of 'C' is likely to-morrow. That's all. But it would be helpful if you would be just a bit more can-did. I suggest there was more to the card-playing than you've told us. Bridge and whist or solo for penny points downstairs; but upstairs, roulette, and probably poker, for a good deal more than penny points. I daresay downstairs there wasn't much idea of what was going on upstairs. Isn't that so?"

"Oh, well, you know already, don't you?" Pope grumbled. "We were all asked to give our word not to say anything."

"Did you lose heavily?" Bobby asked.

"More than I liked," Pope admitted. "But not more than I can stand all right, if that's what you're after."

"I take it you work here?" Bobby asked next.

"I've a desk here at present, that's all. We're an independent firm, but we work in a lot with 'Greater' people—subcontracting mostly. I'm looking after our London end at present. My father is our managing director, and he's pally with some of the Great-er directors, so they let me have a desk here till we can get office accommodation without having to pay through the nose for it. Greater wants to take us over, but they aren't going to, not if I can help it."

He spoke these last words with an emphasis that made him look older, more responsible, gave him an air, in spite of his youth, of one who knew what he wanted and meant to have it against all odds. For the moment, too, he seemed to forget, as in thoughts of a hard fight before him, those deep terrors and alarms that this questioning had roused in him. But they re-turned again, and with increase, at Bobby's next question when he asked:

"About this snuff-box? How did you come to have it?"

"Miss Winlock rang me up and asked me to meet her. She said she was in a bit of a jam for ready money. She didn't say why, and I didn't ask; but I guessed, of course, she had been bitten at the Bexley House do. She showed me the snuff-box and asked me if I would buy it or sell it for her. Well, of course I couldn't buy the thing, and I didn't want to sell it for her, either. Family heirloom and all that. I turned up what I could manage—about thirty pounds. It left me jolly short. So I thought the best thing I could do was to pawn the thing. I knew it would be safe—as safe as in a bank. And I got some cash—fifteen pounds to carry on with."

It was a plausible story enough, and for the time, at least, Bobby felt it had to be accepted. He went on to ask how the young man had first met Miss Winlock. There was a certain hesitation about answering. Finally it came out that he had been in the habit of meeting Miss Kerr to have lunch with her. Not regularly by any means, because business claims didn't always permit, but fairly frequently. So, as Miss Winlock generally came out to lunch about the same time, she and Pope got to know each other by sight, to begin to say 'good day', even to exchange a word or two. It also began to appear that Maggie Kerr had not much approved of this growing friendship. Finally, when Pope was staying with his parents at a Cornish hotel, Miss Winlock arrived at the same hotel on a week's holiday.

"Maggie," said the young man ruefully, "wouldn't believe it was just an accident. It was. Miss Winlock was as much surprised to see us as I was to see her. Mother took rather a fancy to her. Said she was so different from the ordinary pushing, slangy modern girl—more like what girls were when she was young, Mother said. But Maggie wouldn't have it. Seemed to think we had fixed it up together. She didn't even want to believe I was just there on business because Dad wanted me to help. He had money in tin-mines, and during the war it wasn't so bad—except for the 'Round Table' Mine. That was always a wash-out. Everything always went wrong there. It's shut down and derelict now, and likely to stay so. Maggie said, why couldn't my dad see to things when he was there already? But he wanted me to help in clearing up. And I couldn't refuse when Miss Winlock asked if she might see over the 'Round Table'. Funny thing, but her people had owned it at one time and dropped a lot of money. Every one always did. Regular hoodoo. Queer stories about it as well, so the local people never go near if they can help. Miss Winlock said she did so want to see where half the family fortune had gone, and ghosts as well. One of her family had seen one there, she said. Well, I couldn't very well say I wouldn't take her along, could I? not when I was going."

"I suppose not," agreed Bobby, though suspecting the young man had had no very strong objection to the company of a pretty girl on the trip, even though that in his thought had implied no sort, or kind, or hint of preferring her to Miss Kerr, far away in London. "What was your business at the mine if it's shut down?" he asked.

"To see if there was anything worth salvaging," Pope answered. "There wasn't. Empty buildings, that's all."

"Are you engaged to Miss Kerr?" Bobby asked next.

"No," Pope answered, flushing slightly. "She said we must wait a little, till we knew each other better. And would my people approve? Because she wasn't going to upset things if they objected. She and Mother hadn't quite hit it off. Mother was a bit snuffy with her, not like she was with Miss Winlock. But I think really Maggie hadn't made up her mind. And then, when she cut up rough about Miss Winlock just happening to hit on the same hotel as us, well, there was a bit of a row."

"Thank you," said Bobby. "Now, could you tell us what you know about Miss Winlock—character, tastes, habits, disposition, anything to help us get in touch with her. Trifles often help. We traced one girl who had left her home because she generally smoked a rather unusual and expensive brand of cigarettes. Tobacconists were asked if they had sold any recently to a new customer, and we heard of her in that way. So we could tell her parents she was all right and safely married, even if to a man they didn't approve of."

"I don't know anything like that about her," Pope answered doubtfully. "She's just an ordinary, quiet, shy girl—jolly friendly and amusing if you know her. But if you don't, you don't get a word out of her. Rather lost in business—a home bird. That's what she used to get called. I don't think her people understood her. Pushed her out to work because they thought she wanted taking out of herself, they said. Wouldn't believe her when she said she would much rather stay at home. For one thing, she wasn't used to men. She always says girls are much nicer. You know some women hate each other, but she's just the opposite. She was awfully upset about Maggie not liking her being at that hotel in Cornwall. You know, I think men rather frighten her at first."

"Not quite the modern girl?" Bobby suggested.

"Oh, no, very much the old-fashioned sort."

"I see," Bobby said impassively. "Do you happen to know if she was a motorist? Could she drive?"

"I think she had her driving licence, but I know she didn't like driving if she could help it. She told me that once. She was always so afraid of doing something wrong."

"I see," Bobby said again, as impassively as before. "Now, can you tell us about your own movements on the evening when Miss Winlock left home. You saw her when she gave you the snuff-box. After that?"

"Well, I went back to the office to clear up. And then, after dinner, I went for a walk. I often do. You have to try to keep fit somehow. It was a lovely night."

"Where did you go? Was it Bexley House?"

"No, it wasn't," Pope retorted. "I started out thinking I might. I was wondering a bit about that snuff-box business. But then I turned back. If she was gambling too much, it wasn't my affair, and I thought I should only make a fool of myself if I tried to do anything. Besides, there was Maggie."

"Could you say what time it was when you got back?"

"It was pretty late. I don't know exactly. After twelve." He hesitated, looking even more pale and troubled than before. "Is this some sort of alibi idea?" he asked uneasily.

"Merely that we like confirmation, when possible, of anything we are told," Bobby explained. "For instance, did any one see or hear you when you came in?"

"I don't know; I don't suppose so. Why should they? Mrs Hands leaves the door on the latch, and I lock up. They're all in bed, and I don't make any more noise than I can help."

"Thank you," said Bobby again. "One thing more. What can you tell us about your quarrel with Mr Harper?"

"Oh, that," Pope said, his manner no less uneasy and dismayed. "I suppose he's been telling you. We had a bit of a turn up, that's all. Why?"

"What was it about?" Bobby asked, ignoring the 'why?'

"Oh, I don't know. Nothing much. He was a bit offensive. That's all."

"Anything to do with Miss Winlock?" Bobby asked. "Come, Mr Pope, I've asked you once already to try to be more candid. When two young men, comparative strangers, get fighting, it's a fairly safe guess that there's a girl in it somewhere. Harper has given us his version. We would like your side of it, too."

"It was my dance all right," Pope said sulkily, "but I couldn't find Miss Winlock at first, and then I saw her dancing with Harper. He told her he had seen me with another girl. When I tackled him afterwards, he said he hadn't. So I told him he was a liar and a few other things as well, and he asked me to meet him at a pub in Pimlico. That's all."

With that, with only one or two other questions asked of but minor importance, Bobby and Ferris departed, leaving a very disturbed and frightened youth to return to his desk.

CHAPTER XIII
"YOU MUST FIND HER"

DRIVING SLOWLY and carefully through the crowded City streets, Ferris was silent till they reached the Embankment. Then he said:

"That young man. What do you make of him? Is he the chap we want? Is he deep as hell or is he just the prize mug he lets on he is?"

"Eh?" said Bobby, wakening abruptly from his own thoughts. "What's that? Oh, no, I shouldn't say he was a prize mug exactly. Young and a bit unformed as yet, and innocent as a babe when it comes to girls. Takes 'em at face value—literally. A mistake. But plenty of guts at bottom. Put him in a corner and I should say he would fight tooth and nail. Greater Engineering won't have an easy job taking him over. And he's not the only mug when it's a pretty girl, you know."

"Tooth and nail if in a corner," Ferris repeated. "Well, suppose he was? In a corner, I mean. And no alibi."

"First thing a guilty bloke thinks of," Bobby remarked, "is faking an alibi. He didn't try."

"Some are too smart," Ferris retorted. "According to him, he swallowed everything she said the way a cat laps up cream. Let her palm off the snuff-box on him with a yarn about needing the cash when we know she had drawn five hundred pounds out of the P.O."

"We must remember that," Bobby remarked, and Ferris gave him a quick glance.

"Plenty been done in for less," he said. "It's a point to remember all right, though it's apt to get overlooked with all this chatter about girls and what not."

"Especially what not," agreed Bobby.

"Suppose," said Ferris, slowly, "suppose both of 'em—Mark Monk and the girl—were scuppered for the cash? Five hundred pounds is quite a bit, and odds and ends of jewellery as well." They had reached the Yard by now, and Ferris was carefully backing the car into place. "Harper," he said suddenly.

"It couldn't have been Harper driving the car Sergeant Long saw and that we've heard of going all out Cornwall way," Bobby observed.

"Might have been Jerry George or some one we haven't heard of yet. This thing goes deep."

"So it does," agreed Bobby.

"Talk about making bricks without straw," Ferris complained. "How can you carry on with an investigation when you don't even know what you've got to investigate?" he asked bitterly. "Take Mark Monk—murderer or murdered? Why should he do in a girl who was eating out of his hand? All he had to do was get what he wanted out of her and then ditch her. Much simpler than cutting her throat."

"I know," Bobby agreed again. "That's another point to remember. I always believe in simplicity," he added thoughtfully.

"Simplicity?" Ferris exclaimed. "If this is your idea of simplicity, it isn't mine. Simplicity all right, though, if that Pope young man really believed the girl turned up at the same hotel in Cornwall by pure chance. And if it's between Harper—not that I think much of him—but if it's between him and her which of 'em lied when Pope was done out of his dance, then my money's on her."

"So is mine," Bobby told him. "A dangerous young woman. Remember how Pope told us she did a glare on her own? Shook him for the moment. And it's odd how every one tells us a different tale about her—a home bird, this time. Why Pope's mother liked her. The right sort of daughter-in-law."

"Huh," said Ferris.

"Infinite variety all right," Bobby remarked. "Always trust a poet to know. Clear enough, though, that she's a kind of Autolycus."

"A what?"

"A picker up of unconsidered trifles in the way of anything wearing trousers, either attached or unattached," Bobby explained. "Was it like that with Mark Monk?"

"If it was, it rather looks as if she got more than she bargained for," Ferris commented.

"Looks like it," Bobby said. "Notice, by the way, how Cornwall keeps turning up—investments in Cornish tin-mines on the part of the elder Pope, Miss Winlock's holiday in Cornwall, this car we hear of pelting through the night Cornwall way."

"That reminds me," said Ferris. "There's been another report in about that car. A couple of girl hikers. On a walking tour—Devon and Cornwall. They thought it was such a lovely night they would do a moonlight hike. It was the other side of Exeter, on the Truro road. They say a car passed them hell for leather, and if they hadn't jumped into the hedge they would both have been killed. One of the county police who knew we were asking heard they had been talking and questioned them. Asked them if they wanted to make a complaint, and, if so, could they give the car's number? They had been much too busy jumping into the hedge to notice."

"Cornwall again," was Bobby's comment as they parted, Ferris to return to his 'O' divisional head-quarters, and Bobby to his desk, where for once the ever-flowing tide of paper work was well under control.

So he was able to get home at an unusually early hour, to be greeted by Olive with the news that a woman giving her name as Vea Burden had rung up shortly before. She had wanted to know when she could see Mr Owen, and Olive had told her to ring up again later on. She hadn't said what she wanted, but had sounded excited, Olive thought, and she had rung off very abruptly when told Bobby was not there. As Bexley House had no telephone, there was no way of communicating with her, and Bobby had to content himself with passing the news on to Ferris. His call to 'O' division was, however, answered by the information that Mr Ferris had been obliged to hurry off on some other case and would not be back till late. So all Bobby could do was to ask that Mr Ferris should be informed as soon as possible, and had scarcely hung up when once again he was called by 'O' Division to tell him they had just learned that Harper had sold up and vanished. It seemed he had disposed of his assets—lorry, cars, good will and all—to a bigger concern for cash down and with no undue haggling as to the price. He had given his landlady a week's rent in lieu of notice, asked her to keep any letters until he called for them, and so departed 'without trace'.

"Given us the slip and gone underground, ten to one," the voice over the 'phone said disconsolately. "Mr Ferris won't like it. Where are we to look for him now?"

"Try Cornwall," Bobby said and hung up.

"Do you think that's why Miss Burden wanted to see you?" Olive asked.

"It was Grace Williams who was supposed to be his young woman," Bobby remarked. "My impression is that it was Mark Monk who was Vea Burden's meat."

Olive took some pains to make it clear that in her opinion this was a most vulgar expression. Bobby was suitably contrite.

"But all the same," he tried to excuse himself, "this sort of thing does rather get you down. Groping in the dark," he complained, "and not even sure there is anything to grope for. The proverbial black cat in a coal cellar at midnight, and not sure whether there is either a cat or a coal cellar. Or even if it's midnight."

"There's poor little Isobel Winlock," Olive reminded him. "You have to make sure about her."

"Might as well try to be sure about a will-o'-the-wisp," Bobby grumbled. "As soon as you think you have an idea of what she is really like, you get handed an entirely different picture. If we knew what she was in fact, we could form some notion of her probable actions. Is it, on the whole, an affair of glamour boy meets glamour girl and what happens then? Well, what does?"

"Just anything," was all Olive could say.

"Exactly," agreed Bobby. "Take all these people and what we know about them. First, Mark Monk. Glamour boy with a record of a wife dead in suspicious circumstances and a girl friend not heard of since. And there's always a background of a moonlit night of unusual beauty. So does a kind of suggestive memory come into the picture?"

"There have been a lot of full moons," Olive pointed out. "Why this one more than any other?"

"Why should one cigarette end cause a fire and others die out harmlessly?" Bobby asked in return. "Then there's Harper's story that Mark Monk was trying to blackmail Jerry George, and Jerry didn't like it. He wouldn't, and blackmail isn't always a very safe game to play. We'll come to Harper later. Take young Pope next. How far had he gone with the new love after he was off with Maggie Kerr? Possibly he knew, or suspected, that Isobel was going away with Monk, and tried to stop her. If he did, what was the result? On the one hand, Monk, a suspected killer, and, on the other, young Pope. It's the fact that he is the only one of all those we know who could possibly have driven the car we've heard of making all out for Cornwall."

"Could he?" Olive asked doubtfully. "And be back in London in time next morning?"

"Quite possible," answered Bobby. "If he had enough petrol. Exeter is only about two hundred miles, and that car would do up to a hundred miles per hour. Tough, but it could be done, though counsel for defence would try to persuade a jury it couldn't. But you can do a lot when you have to. Some one drove that car, and drove it recklessly. Or, again, money may have come into it. Pope admitted he had been gambling, and his losses may have been higher than he said. There's always that five hundred pounds the Isobel girl had with her. Has she got it still, or who has it? Another unknown factor. Let's leave him and go on to Harper."

"Can you believe his story about how he cut his hand?" Olive asked.

"I suppose you can, but I don't," Bobby answered. "But I can't quite see where it works in. And now he has gone underground, as 'O' Division says. And in a hurry. He and Pope had been fighting. How does that tie up? Or need it? Clearly he wasn't the driver of the car, but did he know what was in it? He has a lot to explain—if and when we find him. Meanwhile, there's Jerry George."

"But he was still at Bexley House after it all happened," Olive said.

"So he was—and before as well, whatever 'it' was," Bobby agreed. "Take this for a theory. We know he was running Bexley House. We suspect black market of a bad type, stolen goods probably, and we know heavy gambling was going on. It would have been raided before now, only for the hope of catching bigger fish than fools getting rid of their money. If they don't do it one way, they will another. But there's nothing so profitable as running a gambling-show. Witness football pools and greyhound racing. Only they operate within the law, and poker and roulette outside it. Quaint, but there it is. Suppose they were partners, and Jerry George was keeping rather a bigger share than Mark Monk liked. Or even that there was a suspicion of double-crossing, and Monk was going to try to make Jerry pay up, preparatory to going abroad with Isobel. Jerry is no fighter, but he might have got Harper and some other tough for protection. In the argument Monk gets his. But the Isobel girl was there, and saw, and so had to be got out of the way. So she may have been bustled off to Cornwall till it is decided what to do with her, or till it is felt she is sufficiently compromised to be trusted."

"You must find her," Olive declared. "At once."

"But it mayn't have been like that at all," Bobby reminded her. "For that matter, there may have been two victims: Mark Monk himself as well as the girl."

"Is that possible?" Olive asked.

"If you had seen that room," Bobby told her grimly, "you would think two killings more likely than one. Then there's another girl—Maggie Kerr."

"But there's nothing to show—" Olive began and stopped.

"Her handbag was there, and she had Miss Winlock's," Bobby said slowly. "Not too convincing an explanation, either. Unless she was in such a state of excitement and agitation she wasn't in a condition to notice. If she was, why was she? It rather looks as if she thought she had lost the man she loved to Isobel. She may have got a hint that Isobel was running away with a man, and taken it that that man was David Pope. Isobel may have encouraged the idea. Out of pure devilry, perhaps. Or possibly she really hadn't made up her mind which one she was going to favour. She may have thought it would be fun to keep two strings to her bow till the very last minute. Even with the idea of seeing how they took it, and then going off home again, leaving them both in the lurch. Only more happened than she expected, and that may have been because Maggie turned up and took a hand. Is it possible that in a fit of jealous rage Miss Kerr snatched up a knife and did what was done in the supper-room that moonlit night?"

"But the men would be there?"

"Only Mark Monk, perhaps, and it may be he had no time to interfere. And then he may have thought the best thing to do was to try to hush it up or he would come under suspicion himself, with his record. Or Miss Kerr may have threatened to accuse him. If so, he was the driver of the car we've heard so much about. And Isobel's body was in it. By this time, it, and the girl's dead body with it, may have been driven over the Cornish cliffs into the sea. Even if they are recovered, it will probably be too late to get any reliable evidence."

Olive was silent, in her mind a vivid picture of a car hurtling down the moonlit roads, conveying the dead at such wild, dreadful speed through the loveliness of that exquisite night, through a sleeping land, to its destination in the lost loneliness of the sea. In Bobby's mind, too, that picture was clear, insistent. Nor, indeed, had it ever been long absent from his thoughts since the first reports had been received. Presently he went on:

"There are the two Bexley House women as well. They may very well come into it—Grace Williams and Vea Burden. As she's been ringing up, she may have something to say. She is a striking personality. You could tell that much. Interested in Monk, I think. I hope, if she turns up here later on, I shall get a better idea of what she is really like. And Grace Williams. A more commonplace sort of person more easily understood—at least, as far as it's possible to say that of any woman."

"Or man," retorted Olive, and then added: "What have you been scribbling? Doodling?"

For answer Bobby handed her the tabulated notes he had been jotting down.

"Rather a neat job, don't you think?" Bobby remarked with some satisfaction as Olive, looking slightly bewildered, presently put the notes down. "I shall get a good mark when I hand that in. Except that there's no red ink."

"What good is it?" Olive asked in her matter-of-fact, womanly way. "It's all 'ifs' and 'ans'. You can't just put down a lot of doubts and guesses and expect them to add up to certainty."

"Oh, well," Bobby protested, slightly hurt that his effort had not received warmer appreciation, "a tabulated statement like that always makes an impression. Besides, when all the doubts and guesses have cancelled each other out, then a kind of probability may begin to show. I think it would show there, only you interrupted me before I had finished. You can see at once that as it stands there's a pretty big omission."

"Why do you think Vea Burden wants to see you?" Olive asked.

"I'm waiting for her to tell me," Bobby answered, and as he spoke the bell rang. "I expect that's the lady," he said.

CHAPTER XIV
"THEN THE SIRENS WENT"

OLIVE GLANCED at Bobby, expecting him to open the door, but he nodded a request to her to do so. He wanted their visitor to know there was some one else in the flat, and he wished also to know what impression she made on Olive. For he was still not very sure what impression she had made on him himself. He had a good deal of faith in Olive's judgment, especially of another woman, more especially still of her first, swift judgment before she had had time to let her quick and ready sympathies run away with her. She came back now after taking Vea into the room Bobby used as a kind of office or study.

"It's Miss Burden," she said. "Or Mrs. I'm sure she wears a wedding ring sometimes."

"I know," Bobby agreed. "They said 'Mrs' Burden sometimes at Bexley House. But wearing a ring is no proof of marriage. What did you think of her?"

"She looks ill," Olive answered. She paused. "Hungry," she said, and then corrected herself, "No, not that exactly. I don't know." Her voice was troubled and hesitant. She went on: "I think I mean she looked as if she knew there wasn't much time, and so she had to hurry, and so she didn't care."

"Much time for what?" Bobby asked, but Olive did not reply, nor did he repeat his question.

He supposed that on the whole what Olive had said represented more or less what he himself felt the first time he saw Vea. And yet he felt also there was something else that neither he nor Olive had divined, and he felt that that something was of importance. He went to the room where Vea was waiting, sitting by the window, her back to it. He thought she had probably chosen the position on purpose. But that was something he never objected to. People could often control their facial expression more easily than they could—or perhaps thought to do—their gestures, their tone of voice, all the other 'imponderables' that tell so much to the trained observer. There was, too, the additional advantage that, seated thus, they acquired a certain sense of ease or self-confidence—even over-confidence—and so became more willing to talk more freely. There is only one really difficult witness, and that is the silent witness. But they are rare, almost non-existent, for probably the greatest of all human urges is the urge to talk. He noticed she had on the same close-fitting black frock he had seen her in before. She was wearing neither hat nor gloves, and her long pearl earrings still swung to and fro with every movement of her head. Bobby greeted her pleasantly, and sat down opposite. He made some banal remark about the weather and offered a cigarette. She shook her head and shifted her position abruptly, so that the light from the window fell full upon her face. Bobby supposed she had either forgotten about the light or else that she had simply never thought of it and had taken up her first position without design. He guessed this probably meant that she was too absorbed in her errand, and what it meant to her, to have any thought to spare for minor details. Her uneasy glance was wandering up and down the room, flickering from one object to another, but now and again it fixed itself for a moment or two upon Bobby with a strange and almost troubling intensity, as if both in defiance and appeal. And then he was aware of what Olive had first of all called her 'hungry' look, and yet somehow he felt in it, too—or, at least, so he thought—a kind of excited fear that had mingled with it a great longing. He would have given much to know what was in her mind, though he imagined also that that she hardly knew herself. He waited patiently for her to speak, and the idea came to him that though he had seen and known many strange phases of human nature, now he was facing the strangest yet. She said suddenly:

"I suppose you are wondering what I've come for?"

"I am waiting for you to tell me," he answered.

"Oh, well, now then," she muttered. She turned her head to stare out of the window, but not for long. Soon her uneasy and troubled gaze was wandering again, hither and thither, never resting long anywhere, always avoiding looking directly at Bobby. He even found himself wondering if she were not afraid that if she did so she might betray to him hidden thoughts that above all things she wished to keep secret—even, it might be, secret from herself.

He still waited silently and patiently, fairly certain that presently she would speak, and that this long delay might well serve to make her talk more freely once she made up her mind to begin. She jumped suddenly to her feet.

"I'll go," she said, and repeated defiantly: "Well, I'm going."

"If you wish to," Bobby said, though making no effort to rise, for that she should, in fact, depart without speaking was the last thing that he desired.

"Oh, well, now then," she muttered again, standing uncertainly, but without making any definite movement towards the door.

"I would like you to believe this," Bobby said, speaking slowly and carefully. "The duty of the police is as much to help any one in trouble or difficulty, or tell them where they can get that help, as it is to bring to justice any one who is up to mischief. I mean, of course, when it is of a criminal nature. And bringing to justice doesn't mean that we have anything to do with punishments. Our job is simply to say that some one seems to have done something more or less serious, perhaps very serious indeed, and this is why we think so. Then the court decides."

"The cop your best friend," she sneered. "I've heard that one before." All the same, after a moment of hesitation, she sat down again. "I'm not in trouble," she announced in the same defiant manner, and when Bobby did not answer, but still waited patiently and in silence, she burst out suddenly, "Is it true Alf Harper's done a bunk?"

"I don't think we can quite say that," Bobby answered. "There is reason to believe he was near Bexley House that evening, and he was asked if there was any information he could give. He denied having been there and said he knew nothing. Now I'm told he has sold his business and gone away. But I don't think we can call that doing a bunk. What makes you think so?"

"Grace"—and Vea snapped out the name with vigour, indeed with venom—"says he has. She's scared."

"Why?"

"He's her boy. At least unless this Winlock girl has got him for keeps. Grace tried to get him in, and now she wants to try to get him out. She's a fool. She thinks you think it was him. Do you?"

Before Bobby could reply she began to cough—a hard, dry, racking cough that shook her from head to foot, and left her exhausted. Bobby went to get her a glass of water, but she would not touch it. When she was a little recovered, she said again:

"Well, do you?"

"If we did, we certainly should not tell you so," Bobby answered smilingly. "Hardly our line to answer questions, you know. It's our job to ask them."

"You think there was murder done that night at Bexley House," she said, but more as a statement than as a question.

"That is a word we have never used in connection with this case," Bobby answered formally. "Others have used it. We never have. But we do think it our duty to find out what did happen, and Miss Winlock's parents have asked us to try to get in touch with her. We mean to do both these things. If you can help us in any way, please do. You know, of course, that keeping back information may be a serious offence, involving penalties. You are a woman, and Isobel Winlock is a young girl—"

She interrupted him with a snarl in her voice and an angry gesture with her long, thin hands.

"Young girl my foot!" she exclaimed. "She knows it all and then some. If I were a man I would sooner go to bed with a viper than her. If she's had it, she asked for it."

"Has she had it?" Bobby asked.

At that Vea began to laugh, no pleasant laugh, and then the laughter turned into one of her fits of coughing. He noticed that she looked a little anxiously at her handkerchief, as if to be sure it showed no sign of blood. Recovering, she said:

"How should I know? At least, unless perhaps you think it was me?"

"Well, why not?" Bobby asked, quite pleasantly, but watching her closely. "Women have killed before to-day. A blow with a knife. It is easily done. And I gather you don't much like Miss Winlock. Yet I don't think you know her very well. What has she done?"

Vea seemed to be about to answer, but then checked herself. Perhaps her eyes, the snarl that showed her white and pointed teeth, her flushed cheeks that changed again so quickly to a deathly pallor, were answer sufficient. When she did speak, what she said startled Bobby considerably.

"Killing isn't always murdering," she muttered, almost whispered. "Sometimes it has to be—it happens."

"Well, that's a theory," Bobby answered. "It was put forward three hundred years ago, wasn't it? And a good many people seem to think so still and be willing to call any murderer a hero. I don't think we can go into that now. If any one was killed that evening, then the word 'murder' will be used. As soon as we know."

"It wasn't me," she said slowly. "More likely to be Grace, if it comes to that. Alf Harper was her boy till that girl pinched him—and pinched him casual like. That made it worse. To see her lift a finger, in a manner of speaking, and your boy you think was yours go off without a word. Well, you don't like it, and

Grace didn't, either. But now she's scared, and she's gone chasing after him."

"Where?" Bobby asked.

"All worked up, she is," Vea said, without answering directly, and Bobby did not press the question, for he thought he knew.

But he did not like that remark about Grace being 'all worked up'. It seemed to presage fresh trouble, and from a new quarter. He had too often had reason to know of what a jealous woman 'all worked up' is capable. He said:

"Don't you think that if you would tell me plainly what is in your mind and why you've come that it might help?"

She shook her head again, and once more her gaze grew restless and wandering.

"I must be going," she said, and began to cough, though this time not so badly as before. "Excuse me," she said, and added, after a moment's pause, and in a quiet, meditative tone, "I reckon there's different ways, and one's much like another."

"Different ways of what?" Bobby asked.

"Of pegging out," she answered flippantly. "Might as well be quick and sudden as coughing yourself away in bed years after. I don't mean me," she explained. "I've got a chest, that's all. I must be going. Grace—she's no friend of mine, but she's a fool. Nothing in Alf Harper, and her half out of her mind and rushing off to find him because she says she's got to know or else she'll go crazy. She's that already, if you ask me. More do I."

"More do you what?" Bobby asked.

"There was a car," she said, ignoring this. "Some one drove it all through the night—top speed. Wasn't there?"

"Who told you that?" Bobby asked.

"Every one knows," she answered vaguely. "Some one drove it," she repeated. "Top speed. It was a night like day. Was there— was there something in it?"

"I think there was," Bobby answered. "Do you?"

"No," she answered quickly. "Why should I? No, I don't." She said this with emphasis. But they both knew it was not the truth. "There's Grace now—scared. Because she thinks Alf may be for it if you think it's him. Or her perhaps? Only you won't say. And then she thinks he may be for it, too, if he starts meddling. So he may, if he doesn't watch his step. There's times it's wiser to keep out."

"And times when it's necessary to get in," Bobby remarked, wondering a little if this had been in any way intended as a threat.

"Not for him, not for her," Vea declared. "What's she got to worry about? Nothing much to Alf Harper. Just another boy, and there's plenty of them. Nothing in him to tear at your guts—to tear you whether you like it or don't, whether you want it or not."

"Is that what Mark Monk does to you?" Bobby asked.

"Him?" she said, more than a little taken aback, or so he thought. "What's he do with it? I wasn't thinking of him."

"Are you sure?" Bobby said. "Have you been thinking of any one else all the time you've been talking?" His voice grew harder, sterner. "Miss Burden," he said—"Or should it be Mrs Burden?—you have been careful to tell me nothing. That means you have told me a lot. What people don't want to say is always more important than what they do say. Now it is my turn to ask you something. What do you know of Mark Monk, and what is your connection with him?"

"I don't know what you're getting at," she answered, very much on the defensive now, and even a little afraid, he thought. "He comes to Bexley House. He's pals with Jerry George. I've seen him there. That's all."

"Do you know that his real name is Matthew Myers, and that under that name he was charged some years ago with the murder of his wife?"

"He was acquitted," she answered quickly. "It didn't happen. Not like that."

"Do you know that later on a girl who had gone away with him disappeared and has never been heard of since?"

"Well, what about it?" Vea retorted. "If she got scared and wanted to get out, why shouldn't she? Her affair. I'll be going."

"Are you married to him?" Bobby asked.

"Never you mind," she said. "That's my affair. You leave me alone. I must go."

"Not yet," Bobby said. He was on his feet now, and he waved her back. "If you married him, have you left him? If you've left him, why?"

"I haven't," she muttered—"I mean—I never did," and now she was very pale, and she was trying to moisten her dry lips with her tongue.

"If you've left him," Bobby said again, "was it because he tried to kill you, too?"

She too was on her feet now. They were standing facing each other. Very slowly, almost unconsciously, as if impelled by a force or a memory beyond her control, she raised her hands till they encircled her neck, one finger of each hand pressed hard against the throat below each ear. Through Bobby ran a chill horror and great fear, such as he had never known before, and in her eyes there gleamed against the deathly pallor of her countenance a kind of dreadful and voluptuous terror of anticipation.

"Then the sirens went," she whispered; and suddenly she turned and rushed away, nor this time did he make any attempt to stop her.

CHAPTER XV
"THE GREAT DEEPS DRAW"

THE FIRST thing Bobby did next morning, immediately on his arrival at his office, was to ring up Greater Engineering and ask to speak to Mr David Pope. In reply he learned that Mr Pope had been unexpectedly called away and would not be back for a day or two. No, he had not said exactly when he would return, nor had he left any address. Letters were to be kept till he returned. All he had said was that he had heard of a chance of bringing off something rather good and he didn't want to miss it, even though there was only a slender chance of success.

Thoughtfully Bobby put down the receiver. Did this mean, he asked himself uneasily, that the young man had thought it best to disappear? If so, did that imply guilt? Did it mean that an uneasy conscience had taken alarm as a result of the questions he had been asked? But, then, of course, perfectly innocent people sometimes get into a panic, and bring needless suspicion on themselves by trying to keep out of the way.

As possible an explanation as any other, he supposed; but, all the same, he felt more than a little worried as he went to talk the case over with his immediate superior, Sir Henry Smith, the newly appointed Second Commissioner, who, in the press and bustle of taking over his new duties, had not so far heard much about what was indeed so strangely vague and indefinite an affair, and who had asked to be told more about it.

"It may," he told Bobby now, "as far as I can see, turn out to mean nothing at all serious. A ghost case. There's so little you can lay hold of in the whole thing, except that a girl has run away with a man her parents don't like. It happens."

"There is also," Bobby reminded him quietly, "what we all, including the doctor, saw that evening in the room at Bexley House where supper had been laid. Not a pretty sight."

"Yes, yes," agreed Sir Henry. "Yes. But it may have nothing to do with this girl. Nothing at all. There may be some quite simple explanation. You can't assume murder's been done just because there are some bloodstains. Might not be human blood at all, for that matter. All very indefinite. If you hadn't been on the spot at that exact moment we should never have had any reason to think it was anything but an ordinary girl-runs-away case." His voice sounded regretful, though he had not meant it to do so; "I don't quite understand how it was you came to be there," he added.

"I didn't much like the set-up," Bobby explained. "Then I knew Mark Monk's record when he was Matt Myers, and I didn't like that either. Or the full moon."

"Oh, yes, the full moon," Sir Henry repeated, and told himself Senior Commander Bobby Owen was a queer chap. Quite ordinary to all appearance in every possible way. No one ever called him brilliant. And yet with a—something—call it a flair, perhaps—for being on the right spot at the right moment and for asking the right questions of the right people. Useful things—flairs. And unaccountable. Only this full-moon business. Surely that was a bit thick—decidedly a bit thick. "You don't really believe that the moon—do you?" he asked.

"I do believe very strongly that suggestion is one of the strongest forces affecting us all," Bobby answered. "And I don't think it matters much whether it comes from a full moon or anything else."

"Yes, yes, I see your point," agreed Sir Henry. "Still, the full moon! A lovely night," he said. "I remember saying so. Yes, yes. Well, now then, this woman who came to see you—what's her name? Oh, yes. Yes. Vea Burden. What do you think she was really after?"

"I think," Bobby answered slowly, in a voice more doubtful than confident—"I think for two entirely contradictory reasons that ought to have cancelled each other out, but didn't. First, because she thinks Mark Monk is in trouble or worse, and she wants to help him. She as good as claimed to be his wife—though whether legally or what some people call unofficially I don't know. Anyhow, she still—well, remembers. The expression she used was that he tore at your guts. I don't know whether you can call that being in love. But I'm sure he is one of those people who have an extraordinary influence over women. He has only to whistle, and they come running. In Vea Burden's case I think she is held by a fascination that is more than half fear, and at the same time she is repelled by a fear that is more than half fascination. But now he's in danger, she thinks, or trouble, and she wants to know and wants to be able to help him, or to be in a position to do so. If she could find out how things really stood, then she would be. She may reckon that if she can help him, save him, then he may return to her and need her so badly that she will be able to depend on him. A poor hope, probably, but I think it's there. The driving force."

"Quite a psychological study," Sir Henry said. "I'm not sure I follow you all the way."

"I don't know that I follow myself, for that matter," Bobby answered frankly. "On the other hand, I also feel pretty sure that she came for protection."

"Protection?"

"As from a tiger you knew was running loose," Bobby said. "She as good as told me he had tried to strangle her, and that only the sounding of the air-raid sirens saved her. I felt that in a way she wants to be kept away from him, in case he tries again and—and succeeds. I imagine she thought, unconsciously very likely, that we might put her under restraint of some sort. Detain her, perhaps, or set a watch on her so that she would know there was always help at hand.”

“Isn’t all that getting a bit complicated?” Sir Henry asked.

“Women are complicated,” said Bobby.

“I’m a married man,” said Sir Henry simply. “All the same—”

“Vea Burden more than most,” Bobby said. “For one thing, she knows she hasn’t long to live, though she won’t admit it, even to herself. I imagine that makes a difference in the way you look at things.”

“Yes,” agreed Sir Henry. “Yes. Very likely. There’s another possibility, don’t you think? There’ve been cases of guilty persons coming of their own accord to talk it over. Sometimes very likely, as you suggested, in the hope of finding out how things are going, and sometimes because they feel so superior and clever they want to find expression for their superiority—to show off to themselves in a way. I’ve known that happen—and in murder cases.”

“I’ve known it myself in at least one case,” Bobby agreed in his turn.

“There’s the motive all right,” Sir Henry said. “This Winlock girl seems to have been a kind of professional kidnapper of eligible young men. Apparently she played the same trick on all the women mentioned so far. She got young Pope away from Maggie Kerr, this Harper person from Grace Williams, and I suppose Mark Monk from your last night’s visitor. Or, at any rate, stepped into her shoes. You think Vea Burden is still inclined to run after Monk and likely to be resentful of any other woman taking her place with him.”

“I’m fairly sure that’s so,” Bobby told him.

“Although he may have tried to kill her?”

“I’m wondering if that isn’t a driving force as well as a repelling one,” Bobby replied, though still with some hesitation. “The sort of feeling some people have in looking down at great depths. The Great Deeps draw. And not least the great abyss of death. Draws irresistibly sometimes, just as it may be the memory of his hands about her throat, hard and firm, draws her.”

"God!" said Sir Henry. "Morbid," he exclaimed angrily. "Like that full-moon business," he added, glaring at Bobby as if he were responsible for it.

"Very morbid," agreed Bobby. "But I think it would be wise for us to be specially alert at the next full-moon period. If we can, that is, if we see our way, and if we've managed to trace either of the two of them—Monk or Miss Winlock."

"I don't know what more we can do," Sir Henry said. "Ferris is taking all possible steps. There's nothing I've been able to suggest. Ferris has been in touch with all the Cornish police. He has asked them to keep a look out both for the girl and for the car she went off in. There's been no sign of it, has there? not since it was seen by those two girl hikers?"

"None whatever."

"Ferris suggests it may have been driven over the Cornish cliffs; or abandoned somewhere on Dartmoor where it'll never be found. He has asked for a general check-up at Cornish hotels and garages. Take some time. Anything else you can suggest? I take it you consider it's gone far enough to need special attention? Even though it may still well turn out to be all a mare's nest?"

"I certainly don't think that's in any way likely," Bobby answered with decision, and Sir Henry supposed ruefully that here was the 'flair' coming back into action again. "And I don't think," Bobby went on, "that almost every one concerned would be hareing off to Cornwall on the track of that midnight car unless they all felt—or knew—that it was pretty serious. I don't see a man like Harper selling up what seems to have been quite a good little business and vanishing in this way except for a very pressing reason. Even if he isn't actually guilty, I'm certain he has knowledge of some sort."

"You think that cut hand of his means a connection?"

"There was blood on his hand and blood on the supper-table in the house," Bobby replied. "If there isn't any connection, it's an odd coincidence. And I don't like coincidences, never did. The razor blade story isn't too convincing, either. I'm inclined to suggest that he knows who drove that midnight car and what was in it, and why there was such desperate need for such reckless speed. The implication seems plain."

"Accomplice?" Sir Henry asked. "Or guilt?"

"A readiness to help, at least," Bobby answered. "I think there's a deduction to be drawn."

"Yes," Sir Henry agreed, but not till after a long pause. "Yes, I see what you mean. All very complicated."

"Vea Burden says Grace Williams," Bobby continued, "has gone to find Harper—though whether to save him from the gallows or from Isobel Winlock, isn't very clear. Possibly not even to herself. Vea gave me the impression that she's going, too. In her case, though, it's Mark Monk she wants."

"General Cornish exodus," commented Sir Henry. "Yes. Well?"

"Again," Bobby went on, "when I tried to ring up David Pope this morning, I was told he had been called away on business and hadn't said where. Or when he would be back."

"Does that mean he's run for it?" Sir Henry asked. "Or merely that he has joined the Cornish procession?"

"Either is possible," Bobby said. "But it does look to me as if all the characters are drawing together for the final showdown."

"Yes," Sir Henry agreed. "Yes. The last act in the drama. Do they know it, I wonder? Puppets being driven by events to an end they have never dreamed of. Are puppets driven? And do they dream? Well, is there anything to be done except look on and wait developments."

"I think we must try," Bobby answered gravely. "I think there may well be a life at stake—or lives."

"Yes, I suppose so. Yes," Sir Henry agreed once more. "Difficult to see what we can do, though, with so little to go on. One good thing," he added, with much feeling. "We haven't got the Press on our heels. You can't interest Press or Public unless you have a corpse to show."

"I only hope we shan't have more than one to show before long," Bobby remarked gloomily.

Sir Henry was consulting some of the papers on his desk.

"There's the Maggie Kerr young woman," he observed. "Nothing been said about her. Do you think she's faded out of the picture?"

"Oh, no," Bobby answered. "She is still there. And not far from the centre. There has been no fresh development. Anyhow, she seems to be staying put. That's something."

"Looks," Sir Henry went on, "as if it ought to have a meaning that the only two material exhibits seem to be her bag found on the spot and the snuff-box Pope admits pawning, and that they seem to have been intimate. At any rate, at one time. The bag, the snuff-box. Yes. To use," said Sir Henry with distaste, "an expressive and vulgar Americanism—it stinks."

Bobby said he thought so, too, but wasn't sure what of. The 'phone rang. Sir Henry answered it. He hung up and said to Bobby:

"Well, that seems to wipe out one possibility. The Winlock girl has been found at a small hotel in Cornwall. Newquay district. Ferris is hinting, without actually asking, that he would like you to run down there and see if you can get her to talk. His idea is that, as you've met her, she might be more willing to talk to you. Ferris says he has such a lot on his hands at present."

"And I suppose he thinks," said Bobby bitterly, "that I've nothing on at all."

"Oh, well," Sir Henry remarked. "All D.D.I's—all the rest of 'em, for that matter—believe all seniors live in a perpetual lotus land of eternal afternoon. All the same, I think it might be useful."

"Oh, well, I suppose I had better," Bobby said, with a sigh of resignation, which was perfectly genuine, but would have been a much deeper sigh of disappointment had he been obliged for any reason to say No.

"Have to go cautiously, if only for the girl's sake," Sir Henry observed. "That is, until we know more. It's still possible the whole thing may come to nothing. If she won't talk, though, what about charging her with something—theft of the car, perhaps, or anything you can think of—and bringing her back to town?"

"I think that might have to be done," Bobby answered.

BOBBY, TAKING the train to Cornwall, tried to put out of his mind all thoughts of the 'Ghost Case', as it was beginning to be called, not without a faint touch of mockery, by some of his colleagues. Useless, he told himself, to speculate and theorize until he heard what Miss Winlock had to say. All the same, he remained troubled, even fearful of what might lie behind the 'Cornish exodus,' as Sir Henry called it. It might well be that a climax was approaching, one that he could neither foresee nor control, but that might turn this doubtful, indefinite, and hidden affair into open tragedy.

Of course, what was possible was being done. Efforts, for instance, to trace, and to keep under observation, all concerned. But that was a task difficult, perhaps impossible. For one thing, everything would have to be done with great discretion, since the grounds for action were so slender. Hotel registers could be looked at, and that might be helpful, but many hotels and boarding-houses are lax in keeping records, and false names and addresses can be given. Then, too, there are cottages and farmhouses where a bed can be secured, and where regulations about keeping records have not even been heard of. Other ways, too, and many of them, whereby those who wish to avoid leaving traces of themselves can easily avoid so doing.

Bobby had brought a good deal of paper work with him, but presently, with so many thoughts crowding in upon his mind, he put it aside. In some ways Miss Winlock's reappearance seemed to support the theory that had been slowly developing in his mind, founded though it had been until now on such details of doubtful import as the absence of finger-prints on the knife used at Bexley House, on Harper's conduct and his answers to the questions put to him, on the reckless speed at which the fleeing car had been driven along those moonlit roads. Well, Miss Winlock would have to be questioned very closely, and Bobby set himself to jot down the questions he would like to ask and the points he wanted more especially to see cleared up.

At his destination a police car was, by arrangement, waiting for him. The local superintendent was there, too—a tribute to Bobby's reputation, for the local police had seen no reason to suppose that the suggested inquiry was of any very pressing importance.

"Just the Yard wanting to fuss about outside London," some of them had been saying with a sort of good-humoured impatience. "Girls are always running away with boys—and both of them soon wishing they hadn't, nine times in ten."

A reminder that the Yard had seemed to think the case might develop unexpectedly did not attract much attention. And if an important executive like a Senior Commander—whatever that new-fangled expression might mean—was arriving in person, did that suggest much more than that Londoners liked a breath of fresh air at times, just as in the provinces an occasional trip to London was not without its attractions.

But now here was the superintendent to meet Bobby. Moreover, he had news to give after greetings had been exchanged.

"We've booked a room for you as you wanted," he said, "at the hotel where Miss Winlock is staying. But I've just rung up, and they say she's been out all day and is not back yet."

"Isn't she, though?" Bobby said. "I hope that doesn't mean she has taken alarm and disappeared. You don't think she suspected that inquiries were being made, do you?"

"I think we took adequate precautions," said the superintendent, a little stiffly.

"Of course, I didn't mean that," Bobby explained, not quite truthfully, for that was exactly what he had meant. "I only thought it just possible she might have noticed some one she thought looked like a plain-clothes man near the hotel."

"We always take care," said the superintendent, still more stiffly, "that our men are trained never to look as if they had any connection with police work. It is an angle we lay great stress on."

"Very wise indeed," Bobby approved, realizing, though, that the superintendent himself was inclined to be a trifle—well, angular. "I might rub that in a bit more vigorously, perhaps, when I'm talking to our chaps."

This time the superintendent was pleased. He seemed to hear Senior Commander Bobby Owen, in the next of those lectures of his, of which some had been circulated by the Home Office for 'general perusal', referring to a point to whose importance his attention had been drawn by—the superintendent, a modest man, did not allow himself, even in his thoughts, to be more specific. Instead he remarked:

"There's another bit of information I've just heard. The Mr Monk you wanted to interview is reported as having booked a room at a small hotel in Redruth."

"Has he, though?" exclaimed Bobby, wondering if this meant that the whole case was dissolving into nothingness, if he had been worrying himself unnecessarily, if the 'ghost' in the 'Ghost Case' was now to be finally laid. He very much hoped so, even though it would show that for once, at any rate, he had allowed his imagination—or what had been called his 'flair'—to run away with him. And yet—and yet—why, for example, that frantic dash all through the night? "Which of the two of them has the car?" he asked. "Do you know?"

"Well, no," the superintendent admitted. "We've made inquiries, but no result. Miss Winlock arrived in a taxi. I should say she probably began to get frightened, and ran away from Monk, leaving him with the car. She may be on her way back to London and mamma by now."

"I hope so," Bobby said. "If we can wash it all out, there'll be one less thing to worry about. Any sign of the car at Redruth?"

"Can't say," answered the superintendent. "I only heard about Monk as I was starting out to meet you. Hasn't taken the two of them long to split up, has it?"

"No, indeed," agreed Bobby. "How far is Redruth? I think I should like a word or two with Mr Monk, and it's no use going to see Miss Winlock if she hasn't got back yet."

"I could run you over to Redruth in less than an hour," offered the superintendent, who liked motoring, and was still feeling genial over the anticipated acknowledgment in Bobby's next lecture.

Alas! he now feels a little bitter over what he calls the tendency of some people at the Yard to suck the brains of provincial men and make no acknowledgment. As for Bobby, one fears he forgot all about it in the stress of later developments.

But now he expressed grateful thanks for the superintendent's offer, and they started off accordingly. It was a pleasant run to Redruth, though Redruth itself has perhaps sacrificed attractiveness to efficiency. The small hotel before which the superintendent presently drew up was of the type generally patronized by the less prosperous commercial traveller. There seemed to be no one about, but after a few moments there appeared a busy young woman who acted as receptionist as well as in various other capacities. Yes, she said, a Mr Mark Monk had booked a room. He had left his suit-case and a deposit, but he had gone away then and had not yet returned. No, she had not seen him. It must have been the porter, she supposed, who received suit-case and deposit. No, the porter wasn't there. It was his time off. All she could say was that the suit-case was in one of the bedrooms and the deposit in the hotel safe. And now they must please excuse her. She had a lot to attend to, with dinner so near and the gentlemen beginning to come in. If they wished to see Mr Monk they could wait for him or return later. Or they could leave a message. With that she retired. The superintendent said:

"Well, what next? Like to have a try for the young lady now, or do you want to wait till this bird returns?"

"I'm wondering," Bobby said, "if they've split only to join again?"

"Why should they?"

"I've no idea," Bobby confessed; "but, then, I've no idea what the whole thing means. All the same, I can't help feeling there is something queer going on."

"Always is," pronounced the superintendent, "when it's this run-away business—girl don't know her own mind, and the boy don't either."

"Mr Monk is hardly a boy," Bobby explained. "I'm not sure if you knew. Some years ago he was charged with the murder of his wife."

"Oh," said the superintendent blankly. "Oh." And then he repeated "Oh."

"The Matt Myers case," Bobby said. "You may remember it."

The superintendent said he did, which wasn't quite true. He said thoughtfully that it made a difference. Bobby agreed. The superintendent said:

"Acquitted, I suppose? Not much doubt he did it, though, was there?"

"Enough to make the jury bring in 'not guilty'," Bobby said. "The benefit of the doubt, perhaps. I've looked up the case recently. There were holes all right. No complete proof. Later on, another girl he was associated with disappeared. No case against him at all that time. But the girl has never been heard of since."

"Strikes me," said the superintendent, "the sooner this Miss Winlock is back with her mother, the better."

"I've been thinking that for some time," Bobby said.

"Well, how about getting her back?" asked the superintendent. "I'll take a chance and run her up to London myself to-night if she's agreeable. You, too."

"That's very good of you," said Bobby warmly.

"I've got a daughter," said the superintendent.

This time in less than an hour—for the superintendent drove fast, urged by the sense of apprehension Bobby's words had wakened in him—they reached the little hotel where Isobel Winlock had been reported as staying. It was no bigger than the one in Redruth, and possibly no more comfortable or better equipped, but it certainly had a much more attractive appearance. It stood in pleasant country surroundings, in its own well-cared-for garden. The sea was not far distant, reached either directly by road or by a winding path through woods. This time they were in luck. Miss Winlock had returned, they were told, and was having dinner. Bobby, conscious of a growing appetite—conscious, rather, of one already grown to full size—asked if he and his friend could have dinner, too. They were accordingly shown to a table, one in a sheltered corner the waitress believed she chose for them, since she had no idea of how discreetly Bobby directed her thereto. At another table, by herself, near a window, a girl sat. Her back turned to the door, she had not noticed their entrance. She was apparently absorbed either in her dinner or in her thoughts. Possibly in both. The waitress said:

"That's the young lady you were asking about, at the table by the window."

She went away, and the superintendent said:

"Well, she's all right, so far, anyhow. Not joined up again with Mr Monk, as you thought might be."

"No," agreed Bobby. "No, she hasn't, has she? Only that isn't Isobel Winlock. That's Maggie Kerr."

CHAPTER XVII
"SHE'LL BE ALL RIGHT"

THIS INFORMATION was received by the superintendent in puzzled silence. Bobby continued his dinner. The superintendent thought this at least was a good idea, and followed the example so set. Maggie Kerr went on with hers, too, though her appetite seemed small and she sent away untasted half or more of what was on her plate.

When it came to the coffee stage Bobby got up and went across to her table. She looked up, and when she saw him, half rose from her chair, something like panic in her startled eyes. Indeed, for a moment Bobby almost thought that she was going to try to run away, but she sat down again, her breath coming in quick gasps.

"I see you remember me," Bobby said quietly. "A surprise for us both, meeting again here. I wonder if you would mind joining us at our table so that we could all have our coffee together."

"What do you want? why have you followed me here?" she asked.

"Well, that's one thing we could talk about, isn't it?" Bobby suggested. "Allow me." He picked up her coffee-cup. "That table over there, in the corner. Please."

The 'please' had a note of authority, of compulsion, in it. Maggie, though she hesitated, yielded. She went slowly across to the other table. Bobby followed. He said to the superintendent:

"This is Miss Maggie Kerr. So far as we know, she is the last person to have seen Miss Winlock."

"Evening, miss," said the superintendent and pulled out a chair for her.

She remained standing. Bobby looked at her gravely. She was staring at him defiantly, angrily. He said:

"I wouldn't make a scene if I were you, Miss Kerr. People are beginning to look already."

A potent phrase, this last. Especially to a young woman with Miss Kerr's upbringing and background. She sat down, but her expression remained defiant. More sullen now, perhaps.

"Why are you following me about?" she demanded again. "You've no right."

"We are police officers," Bobby said. "We have every right—duty, rather—to call on all good citizens to help us." He offered her a cigarette. When he saw she was about to refuse it, he said, "Better have it. People here might as well think this is a friendly chat. No reason why it shouldn't be, for that matter. Or is there?" She did not answer this, but she did take the proffered cigarette, though still with only half-concealed hostility. Bobby continued, "As a matter of fact, we haven't been following you. It was a great surprise to find you here. We were expecting to see Miss Winlock, not you. Apparently you registered under her name. Why was that?" When she remained silent, he said, "Please, Miss Kerr. It is important we should know."

"It was the first name that came into my head," she answered then. "That's all."

"Why not your own?"

"I didn't want," she answered. "If you must know," she added, though reluctantly, when she saw that he still waited, "I stayed away from the office that morning after you woke us all up. I felt so upset. Mother would get our doctor in, and he said I had better stay at home, so Mother asked him to ring up the office and say I was too unwell to come, and he did. Then I got Mother to ring up and say it might be two or three days before I was well again, so would that be all right, and they said 'Yes', because they have to. If they don't you may give up altogether and get another job. They don't want that when they're so awfully short of staff. And it was quite true. I couldn't have settled with you keeping my bag and Father saying you had no right. He wanted to see the lawyers, but Mother said, 'Not yet', and I thought perhaps if I could find Isobel, it would be all right again."

"Yes; I see," said Bobby. "But why use her name?"

"Oh, well," she answered, "I hadn't thought of it before, but one of the girls in my section belongs here. It's her mother who is the manager here, and she writes every week and tells all about the office and the work, and if she said I was away ill, or if she heard I was here when I was too ill to show at the office, I thought there would be a frightful fuss and every one would think I was just slacking. So I used Isobel's name."

The superintendent grunted. He didn't much believe this explanation. Also he very strongly disapproved of such behaviour. Putting it across superiors! What about discipline? In his opinion, if you could do that, you could do a lot worse, and probably had. Bobby was more inclined to accept Maggie's story. He thought it rather weak and silly, and therefore probably true. Lies are generally clear, simple, straightforward—until tested. He asked next:

"Had you any reason for thinking it was likely Miss Winlock might be in Cornwall?"

"I don't see why you keep asking me things," Maggie exclaimed angrily. "Why can't you leave me alone? You've no right to keep on at me like this."

"I said before," Bobby reminded her, "that we have every right to ask questions. You have an equal right to refuse to answer. But if you do, we shall have to take a very serious view. You remember where your bag was found? You remember there were bloodstains on it? And, as you know, all trace of Miss Winlock has been lost since that night."

"You can't think—you can't possibly think," she muttered, and her hand was trembling so violently that she let fall the cigarette she was holding. "Well, do you?" she asked.

"You haven't told us yet," Bobby said, "why you thought of Cornwall?"

"She was always saying how much she liked it, and she didn't know why, when her people had lost all their money there. In tin-mines or something. She made a sort of joke about it. She said they had lost their money there, and if she went often enough perhaps she would find it again. Of course, it wasn't that at all."

"What was it, then?"

"She liked talking, that's all," Maggie answered, but more reservedly, and Bobby felt she was holding back something.

Then he remembered.

"A coincidence," he remarked. "Mr Pope's father also lost a good deal of money in Cornish tin-mines, didn't he?" Maggie's flushed cheeks told him he had touched a sensitive spot. He went on: "I expect she used that as a sort of bond between them, a kind of common experience?"

"She made him take her to see one that belonged to his father," Maggie said. "She said it was the same, and then she said it wasn't, and he had to take her to another as well."

"A kind of personally conducted tour," Bobby remarked; and lapsed into another of his bridge-table 'trances', for he thought that this information might prove of value.

Anyhow, it explained Maggie's dislike—or was it more?—of Isobel, who seemed easily and triumphantly to have carried off young Pope under Maggie's very eyes. Not a pleasant experience for any girl; and how far could it lead one like Maggie Kerr, with her strong though suppressed feelings and with that capacity for sudden, violent action the incident at the bank seemed to show. He put the question aside for the time. Maggie's voice broke in upon his thoughts.

"Can I go now?" she asked.

"Oh, sorry," Bobby said, rousing himself. He looked round. The room was nearly empty. "Shall we go and sit in the lounge?" he asked. "You started a train of thought, Miss Kerr. Nothing in it, perhaps. Coincidence. Well, I don't much believe in coincidence, but sometimes it's useful. One or two other little points I would like to clear up, if possible. Until we find Miss Winlock and can tell her parents she is safe and well, we shall have to go on worrying a lot of people. You, too, I'm afraid."

"I don't see why," Maggie complained when they had reached the lounge. "I don't know what you're worrying about. You can be quite sure she's all right. She knows how to take care of herself. Whoever gets hurt, it's not Isobel Winlock. She sees to that."

"Yes," agreed Bobby. "Yes, I did rather gather that much, though it's difficult to get a correct idea of some one you know only at third hand so to speak. A shadowy, illusive figure."

"Fiddlesticks!" flashed Maggie, suddenly angry again. "There isn't anything shadowy or illusive about Isobel. She's—" But then she stopped, either unable or unwilling to express herself more clearly. "She'll be all right," she concluded.

"Still," Bobby remarked, "there's the old proverb, you know— the pitcher that goes oft to the well gets broken at last."

"Not Isobel," repeated Maggie. "It's others get hurt, not her. Suppose there was some blood on my bag you won't let me have back? Can't people cut their fingers or something? When I was a child my nose used to bleed."

"But you didn't disappear afterwards," Bobby pointed out. "About Mr David Pope. You are engaged to him, I think?"

"No, I'm not," she exclaimed. "I never was. Never!"

"I understood—"

"Well, you understood wrong," she interrupted. "We never were. We did talk about it," she admitted reluctantly, "but we never settled anything. I wouldn't. The nearest we ever got to it was saying what a nice little hotel this was and it would be a lovely place for a honeymoon. And that was only a joke."

"Did you know Mr Pope had left London?"

"They told me he wasn't there when I rang up," she admitted, though with some hesitation.

Bobby lapsed into yet another trance, but one this time of only brief duration. What Maggie had said might prove of the highest importance, but it would need much thinking over. Confirmation, too. Her presence here and her use of Isobel's name might bear the comparatively simple and innocent, though muddled, explanation she gave. Or it might mean that she suspected her lover and Isobel had gone off together, had thought she might find them here at this little out-of-the-way hotel, and had written Isobel's name in the hotel register as a gesture of defiance for them to read when and if they arrived. Or it might mean that she and David Pope, who had left London at much the same time, had arranged to meet here and that she was waiting for him? That was the least pleasant theory of all, Bobby thought, for it suggested a grim possibility. Could she, then, have used Isobel's name in obedience to that dark primeval urge which tells us still that the dead are there, are watching, need to be appeased? And was this use of the name an attempt to placate the dead by, as it were, sharing the living? A far-fetched theory perhaps, but Bobby had known other cases when, under the dreadful stress of the shedding of blood, old strange beliefs, deep rooted in what is now called the unconscious, leapt suddenly into being.

Maggie broke in upon his thoughts by asking once again if that was all or did they want to go on asking a lot more questions when she had long ago told them all she could? Bobby said he was very sorry to have had to trouble her. He hoped it would not be necessary again, but what was necessary—absolutely necessary—was that Miss Isobel Winlock should be found. That had to be done.

"You needn't worry," Maggie repeated. "She'll be all right. She always is. You don't really think anything has happened to her, do you?" She got to her feet. She said suddenly: "Do you think it was me?"

"What was you?"

"Oh, you know," she answered. "Or David?" she asked.

Bobby did not answer. He went towards the door to open it for her. She followed, and at the door she paused and looked at him.

"I suppose you'll never give up?" she said.

"No," he answered.

She went out quickly. He went back to join the superintendent, who said it was getting late, and he must be off.

"Make anything of all that?" he asked.

"Got to think it over," Bobby replied.

"Cautious bloke, aren't you?" the superintendent said. "One thing. She kept saying the Isobel girl was all right, but it didn't sound as if she was so sure as all that."

"No, not by what she said last," Bobby agreed.

"Perhaps she knows it's the other way," suggested the superintendent. "You going to stop here to-night?"

"I thought of going back to Redruth and getting a room where Monk is staying," Bobby answered. "I want a chat with him."

"Give you a lift that far if you like," said the superintendent.

Before Bobby could answer Maggie appeared again. Standing there at the door, she said:

"Vea Burden is here. She has been in my room. What does she want?"

CHAPTER XVIII
"WHEN GLAMOUR MEETS GLAMOUR . . . ?"

MAGGIE REMAINED standing there, quite still, her hands pressed closely together, her eyes full of fear and disquiet. It was as though she were appealing for help and protection, and it was evident that she was very deeply disturbed. The one or two other occupants of the room stared at her, wondering what it all meant. Bobby went quickly across to where she stood by the door.

"Do you mean Miss Burden is staying here?" he asked. "Where is she?"

"She's gone," Maggie said, and repeated: "What does she want?" Then she said again: "Now she's gone."

"Had she a car?" Bobby asked. "Did you see?"

"I don't know," Maggie answered. "I didn't see her. She's been in my room. She was looking in my suit case and drawers and everywhere. What for?"

"How do you know it was her if you didn't see her?" Bobby asked next.

Maggie held out a handkerchief, one she had been clasping in a tightly closed hand.

"It's hers," she said. "There's her initials. There's blood on it. That's when she coughs sometimes. Look. It was on the bed. For me to see. She wanted me to see. To warn me."

"You say you didn't see her?"

"No. As soon as I went in I knew some one had been. I asked the maid. She hadn't seen any one, but she had heard some one coughing, only she thought it was me. Then I saw her handkerchief, and I knew she had left it there for me to see. With the blood on it."

Bobby did not quite know what this meant, but he did not wait to ask. He hurried away to question the hotel staff. None of them knew anything. No one had noticed any stranger either in the hotel or near it. Of course, various people had passed up and down the road on their way to or from neighbouring houses. Any of these might have slipped across the hotel garden and so into the hotel itself. But none of the staff would admit that this was very likely. Some of them were openly incredulous. They suggested that the young lady had been letting her imagination run away with her. They shrugged their shoulders at the handkerchief, material evidence though it was. Anyhow, if nothing was missing, it didn't matter very much, did it? But that was a point on which Bobby was not so sure. He thought it might matter a good deal. However, he agreed there was nothing much to be done. If Vea had been there, she had come and gone unperceived, and was by now far out of reach of any immediate pursuit.

Bobby went back to the lounge, where Maggie was still waiting, as if she felt safer there. He told her he had asked the management to see that a sharp look-out was kept. If Vea returned, he was to be informed immediately. He did not think there was any reason for Maggie to be alarmed.

"Can you suggest what she wanted or why she came?" he asked. "Or why she should want you to see her handkerchief?"

"There was blood on it," Maggie said in a low voice.

"You mean she wanted to remind you there was blood on the supper-table at Bexley House and that you had been there?" Maggie did not answer, but her eyes and the pallor of her cheeks showed that that indeed was what was in her mind. Bobby went on: "Miss Winlock had been there, too, and Mark Monk." Maggie, sitting there, pale and tortured, still did not speak. "Do you know in what relation Vea Burden stood to Mr Monk?"

"There was a story they were married," Maggie answered now.

"It's an odd thing," Bobby mused aloud, partly for the sake of giving Maggie more time to recover from what had clearly been a considerable shock, "that marriage—just a few words mumbled in a church never otherwise entered, or gabbled over in a registry office—does make a sort of tie-up nothing ever quite breaks. Our intellectuals don't understand that. I suppose it's outside intellect. Doesn't apply to a mistress—but, then, there aren't any nowadays, only unofficial wives, just as there are no more criminal lunatics, only Broadmoor patients. The smell of the rose depends to-day on what you call it. One in the eye for Shakespeare. Oh, well." He saw that though Maggie had hardly been listening, his flow of words had in some way helped to calm her. He went on: "If she is really his wife, do you think she is afraid of what may have happened to him?"

"Or to Bella," Maggie answered, using for the first time the familiar abbreviation by which most of Miss Winlock's friends knew her.

"Yes, I suppose there's that," Bobby agreed. "Does she think it may have been you?"

"I don't know," Maggie said.

"Or does she think it might have been David Pope?" And this time, though Maggie did not answer, he was sure that that was what she had been thinking. "Do you think so, too?" he asked.

"No, of course not; it's wicked, wicked—" she exclaimed, but did not finish the sentence, stammering a little as if she could not find the words.

Bobby thought it better not to press her further on that point. He was afraid she might break down altogether, and, besides, all this had given him much to think about. He hoped, too, that what he had said might help to make her realize her position and that of others more clearly, and even possibly make her more willing to speak. For he thought it certain there was much she was holding back. But, then, that, he knew, was true of all of them. True, for that matter, of all witnesses, of whom it is invariably the case that half won't say all they know, and the other half say a great deal more. He offered her a cigarette, and when she shook her head he lighted one for himself. He hoped this would help again to break the tension. Then he said:

"Do you know if there was any particular reason why Miss Vea Burden was supposed to be really Mrs Mark Monk?"

"I think it was only talk," Maggie answered, more readily this time, and as if a little relieved by the change of subject. "I thought at first she was just frightened of him. She looked like death if he came near, and slipped off at once. But she didn't keep away, and if he even crooked a finger at her, she almost ran to him. Almost like a dog. And then sometimes they would start quarrelling again, and she would rush away. But he laughed. It was rather horrid the way he laughed; and yet, somehow, you couldn't help . . ."

"Couldn't help what?" Bobby asked, but when Maggie was again silent he did not press that point either. For he thought he knew, and he did not much suppose that she could put it into words. He said: "I take it she didn't much like seeing him paying too much attention to other women?"

"She hated it," Maggie said. "She couldn't bear it. Only it was funny about that, too. If you danced with him too much, she would look at you as if she wanted to kill you, and then she would look ever so different, as if she were only sorry for you. I know she told one girl she had better keep away from him. But, of course, they only thought that was jealousy. So did Bella. Jealousy, I mean."

"Did you often dance with him?"

"I never wanted to," Maggie declared. "Only somehow—you can't be rude, can you? and he never would listen. You couldn't help. Of course, he was a lovely dancer." She paused and added abruptly: "Lots of the girls hated it. I did. Only—"

Bobby thought that that 'only' was significant. It seemed to symbolize the partly fearful, partly resentful, wholly powerful attraction the man appeared to be able to exercise at will. After a pause, he asked:

"Did Mr Pope ever say anything about your dancing with him?"

"It hadn't anything to do with David," Maggie declared with spirit. "I never did any more than I could help."

"Is it possible," Bobby asked, "that as you and Mr Monk both left London about the same time, Vea may think that you and he have arranged to meet here?"

"Oh, she couldn't," Maggie exclaimed. "I never thought. . . . Besides, I haven't. It couldn't be that, I'm sure it couldn't."

But Bobby thought that this idea, though it seemed to be one that had not occurred to her, was yet in some way a relief, and he wondered why. Was it, he asked himself, because that would imply that Vea was not in any way thinking of, or concerned with, David Pope? He said:

"Or do you think she may suspect you have come to join Mr Pope?"

"Well, I haven't."

"Or to try to help him?"

"I don't know what you mean," Maggie said, at once on the defensive. "What help? what for?"

"Well," suggested Bobby, "if he were in fact mixed up in the Bexley House happening—"

"He wasn't, he never was," she cried passionately.

"Or that you were . . .?"

He left the sentence unfinished.

"I don't even know," she told him, "what you mean or what did happen. I don't know anything," she cried again, "except what I said before. Bella was there, but I didn't see any one else, and I picked up her bag by mistake, and that's all. Why won't you tell me what it's all about?"

"You know very well," Bobby answered quietly, "that something took place at Bexley House, but we aren't sure what. Since then Mr Monk and Miss Winlock have not been heard of, but her bag has been traced to you, and some of her jewellery to Mr Pope. Now he's missing, too, and I find you registering under her name. And what does all that add up to?"

"David had nothing to do with it," she repeated. "I know he hadn't."

"How do you know?"

"Well, I just do," she answered, but her voice was less assured than her words.

There was no more to be got from her, and, after a few more questions of no great importance, their talk ended. Maggie went back to her room. The superintendent, who had taken no part in the talk, but had listened with close attention, remarked that he had his doubts of that young woman. Bobby said he had, too, but also he had doubts about all the rest of them as well. Then they both went to find their car. They started off, and once they were out on the main road with a clear run before them the superintendent said:

"I'm wondering if you can make any sense of all this. Because I can't. Can you?"

"Precious little," Bobby admitted. "But it's never easy to make sense of what people do when they're in love. If no one has ever said that love is the antithesis of common sense, they've been sadly neglecting their opportunities. Worse still when a glamour girl like Isobel Winlock meets a glamour boy like Mark Monk. *L'homme fatal.*"

"Eh?" said the superintendent. "What's that?"

"So what happens," Bobby continued, unheeding this question, "when they do meet—the woman with an irresistible attraction for men, and the man with an irresistible attraction for women? When glamour meets glamour . . .?"

"Lummy," said the superintendent.

"Never heard," Bobby said, "of anything like it before."

"Well, what does happen?" asked the superintendent.

"That," answered Bobby, "is the question, as some one said once. Complicated by the emotions and reactions of those whose love affairs have been broken up. This Maggie Kerr, for example. Plain enough that she is head over ears in love with David Pope. Goodness knows why, but clearly he's the man for her, and that's that. If she has lost him through Isobel Winlock, or was afraid she was going to, she may have expressed her feelings in violent action."

"Done in the Isobel girl, you mean?"

"It's a possibility. If so, she must have had some one to help get rid of the body, and that may have been Pope. A possibility, but no more at present. But he admits he set out for Bexley House, and there's nothing to show what time he got home again. So there you are. Or, again, it's possible she thinks David Pope knew Isobel was in a fix and went tearing off to help her, and so Maggie only wants to try to get her David back again. Or she may be afraid Pope and Monk quarrelled over Isobel, Monk got done in, and David's on the run with Isobel to help him.

I should imagine she could bear anything rather than that. So there you are."

"Not me," said the superintendent fervently. "Anything but. And where do you go from there?"

"To bed," answered Bobby, not without longing. "At least, unless when we get to Redruth we find Monk there."

"Regular wild-goose chase," grunted the superintendent, who was beginning to remember his own bed.

Bobby agreed that it did look like that, though he wouldn't, speaking for himself, be much inclined to put Mark Monk in the goose class.

In fact, when they arrived at the Redruth hotel, they were at once told that Mr Monk had not yet put in an appearance. His room was waiting for him, but at present his suit-case he had left was its only occupant. Bobby's hint that he would like to have a look at the contents of the suit-case was received coldly, and Bobby did not try to insist. He had no right to. The hall porter was on duty now. But he was old, very deaf, and nearly blind without the spectacles he was always losing. He remembered the arrival of the gentleman who had left a suit-case and a deposit. A half-crown tip had helped greatly to impress the event upon his memory. But he could give no reasonable description of the gentleman's appearance. For one thing, it had happened during one of the periodic disappearances of his spectacles. The one fact that emerged was that the gentleman had been youngish or thereabouts. Nor had he signed the register. He had been asked to, but had said he was in a hurry and would attend to the register on his return.

So Bobby said good-night to the superintendent, whose thoughts were turning more and more bedward, and then he booked a room at the hotel for himself. He was anxious to meet Mr Monk, he explained, and would stay the night in the hope of seeing him next morning. The porter, taking more interest in a guest, and therefore prospective dispenser of tips, now remembered that there was another gentleman who had been asking for Mr Monk. He, too, had taken a room for the night, but had not yet gone up to bed. He would be in the smoking-room most likely, or perhaps in the bar. Bobby said most likely it was a mutual friend and he would have a look to make sure. He wandered first into the smoking-room, where two or three games of cards were in progress. But there was no one he recognized. He went on to the bar, where the first thing he saw was the large, flat face of Mr Jerry George almost eclipsed behind a large mug of beer he was in the act of lifting to his lips.

"And that," said Bobby to himself resignedly—"that, I suppose, makes the Cornish exodus complete."

CHAPTER XIX
". . . THE DOUBLE-CROSSING SWINE!"

IN JERRY'S small, close-set eyes, barely visible above the rim of his mug of beer, there showed in equal measure surprise, dismay, and fear. Untasted—untasted, which shows the strength of his emotion—he set down his beer. Bobby went over to the bar and gave his own order. Jerry George, abandoning his still-untasted beer, came across to him.

"It is Mr Owen, isn't it?" he asked, as with a faint, lingering hope that possibly he had been mistaken.

"It is," agreed Bobby. "Met at Bexley House, didn't we?"

"That's right," Jerry agreed in his turn. "Costing me a fiver."

"What is?" asked Bobby.

"You," said Jerry sadly.

"How's that?" asked Bobby again.

"Fellow bet me half a dollar to a fiver the first person I'd see would be you. Seemed safe. I reckoned you would be tied up in town. And now here you are."

"So I am," said Bobby.

"Always nosey," sighed Jerry.

"That's me," agreed Bobby once again.

"Looking for Mark?"

"Among other things," Bobby said. "So are you, aren't you?"

"That's right," Jerry admitted. "He's booked his room here all right, but he hasn't shown up yet. Maybe he won't if he knows you are out trailing him."

"Or if he knows that you are?" suggested Bobby.

"Oh, we're pals—do business together," Jerry explained.

"So I've heard," said Bobby, and Jerry didn't look pleased. "Did you expect to find Monk here?" Bobby asked next.

"That's right," Jerry repeated. "It's where he said."

"He gave you this address?"

"That's right."

"When?"

"Before he left, it was. Said I could always hear of him here."

"Did you know he was taking Miss Winlock with him?"

"No, I didn't. Nothing to do with me if he was. Though I don't hold with it. Not bringing skirts into business. Have your fun with 'em if you want to, but don't mix 'em with business. Fun and business don't go together."

"Quite an aphorism," remarked Bobby.

"I never said nothing like that," protested Jerry in a very injured voice. "And never would, respecting the ladies same as I do."

"My mistake," apologized Bobby. "Why do you want to find Monk? It must be rather pressing to bring you all the way from town."

"Business deal," explained Jerry. "I can't get on with it till I know what he's done. I want his signature, too. Whole thing being held up."

"Is that all?"

"Quite enough, and too much too," Jerry declared. "Four thou. of the best going down the drain, like as not. That's money. Mr Owen, is it true there was bad doings that night at Bexley House?"

"It's to be sure about that we want to find Monk," Bobby told him.

"If there was," Jerry said, "it was after I left."

"Can you prove that?" Bobby asked.

"Now, Mr Owen, be fair," Jerry entreated him. "How can I prove anything when I don't know nothing?"

"It does sound difficult," Bobby admitted.

"You can't think," Jerry urged, "I had anything to do with it. Now can you, Mr Owen? Be fair. Can you?"

"Why not?" asked Bobby; and Jerry took out a handkerchief and began to polish his high forehead, where tiny beads of sweat were beginning to show.

"Stands to reason," he said. "Four thou. it means to me to find him. If I don't—it's enough to sink me. Means that much to me to find him. I'd stand ten per and say thank you for a tip where he was—or likely to be."

"As important as all that?" Bobby asked, ignoring what he took to be a hint of a proffered bribe.

"Well, I ask you," Jerry said. "Four thou. That's not chicken feed."

"No, it isn't," agreed Bobby. "Cigarettes?" he asked.

Jerry jumped and gasped.

"What cigarettes?" he asked when he had recovered a little.

"I was thinking," Bobby explained, "of a load of cigarettes that disappeared the other day. Valued at four thousand pounds. Four 'thou.', as you say."

"I don't know what you're getting at, Mr Owen," Jerry protested. "Just some of your fun?"

"I never mix fun and business," Bobby assured him. "Have another drink?"

"I never mix drink and business," Jerry retorted. "Not when I'm talking to a busy, not me."

"Very prudent," Bobby applauded. "There are some in gaol who might never have gone there if they had remembered that. What about those cigarettes?"

"I do seem to remember," Jerry answered, frowning heavily as he searched the depths of his memory, "a par. in the papers about a load of cigarettes being missing. Those lorry-drivers," he said reprovingly, and shook at them a reproachful head. "Nothing to do with me. I don't mix up with that sort of thing. Plenty of straight deals a bloke can handle."

"So there are," said Bobby, always pleased to be in agreement when possible.

"Now, this one," Jerry continued, encouraged to find the conversation running on such harmonious lines, "was Government stores Mark heard of. Not direct. A bloke had overbought. Mark offered to take the stuff off his hands. For cash. That was the point. Cash. The bloke had to have it, or he might be sold up. Monk said could I put it down. In Treasury notes. Which I did, scraping and borrowing and one thing and another. But I did it. And now there's Monk gone missing, and all I know is he rang up to say he had paid up and taken delivery. And there I am high and dry, not knowing where the stuff is or anything, believe it or not."

"Especially not," said Bobby, and Jerry looked at him with sad rebuke. "Know anything about Miss Winlock?" Bobby asked.

"Is that the girl that's missing, too?" Jerry asked. "Gone off with him? I don't know anything about it. I saw him once or twice with a nice, quiet-looking little thing. Not the sort of skirt he had generally."

"Vea Burden is really Mrs Monk, isn't she?" Bobby asked.

"Not knowing, can't say. If she is, you'd better look out for squalls. Vicious, she is. Vicious. Any little thing, and she's up at you like murder." Jerry spoke with feeling, and Bobby suspected that some 'little thing' he had attempted had been received in a manner he had found somewhat alarming. Jerry went on: "Mr Owen, is Alf Harper in this? Is he in these parts?"

"What makes you think he may be?"

"Well, he's sold up where he was," Jerry pointed out. "He hasn't done that for nothing. Stands to reason."

"He did some work for you at Bexley House, didn't he?" Bobby remarked. "You mean you think this time he may have been working in with Monk. Transport? Moving away the stuff you're looking for?"

"That's right," Jerry said sullenly. "Putting it across, the two of 'em together, the double-crossing swine!"

Bobby became thoughtful. It was an idea not altogether novel, but disturbing, in that it gave so little explanation of the role played or not played by the missing girl. Mark Monk might possibly have simply been engaged in securing for his own sole benefit the stolen cigarettes—for that these were the 'Government stores' Jerry had been talking about seemed certain. If so, Harper might have been a more or less unconscious assistant. And, possibly, the 'bad doings', as Jerry had called it, at Bexley House, was a result. Possibly, too, Isobel Winlock had become involved unintentionally, had seen too much, was being for the time kept out of the way for fear of what she might tell. Bobby began to feel depressed. It did not seem to him he had ever been engaged on a more complicated or difficult case, with so many doubtful and distracting side issues. Cigarettes? Or a case which at the same time it was more urgent to solve, since a girl's life might well be in question, and more difficult to make any progress in, or indeed to decide which path to follow. From the very beginning everything, everything, had been hidden in a thick cloud of doubt and uncertainty. Jerry, too, had seemed lost in his own black thoughts and now, abruptly, he spoke:

"If the two of 'em," he said—"Alf Harper and Mark—are trying to do me down, they're altogether liable to get hurt;" and as he spoke all the latent evil in the man seemed to show in his scowling, contorted features. He saw Bobby watching him. He added hurriedly: "I mean I'll see my lawyers. Damages. Break 'em—heavy damages I'll ask for. Smash 'em. I'll see what the law has to say."

"That," observed Bobby dryly, "is what any good citizen would do at once, if he felt he had been wronged."

"I'm going to bed," Jerry said. "I'm not waiting for Mark any longer. No good if he's not on the square. 'Night, Mr Owen."

"Good-night," Bobby answered. "See you in the morning."

Jerry did not look as if this prospect afforded him any great pleasure. He went off muttering to himself. Soon Bobby followed his example, though leaving strict instructions, reinforced by a liberal tip, that he was to be informed at once if Mr Monk did put in an appearance. Also he put through a 'phone message to his superintendent friend, asking if arrangements could possibly be made for observation to be kept on Jerry's movements. There might, he explained, be mischief brewing from an entirely new quarter. A gangster feud. Clear, Bobby said, that Jerry suspected Monk of treachery, and gangsters have a way of replying to that with the bullet or the knife. Jerry evidently feared that Monk had disposed of the stolen load of cigarettes for his own benefit. In order, perhaps, to be well in funds for his adventure with Miss Winlock. Upsetting, Bobby agreed, in answer to the superintendent's comments, if the thing were changing abruptly from a tangle of emotional relationships, with all the possibilities of sudden explosion that emotional relationships imply, to a more commonplace gangster feud with its more commonplace emotions and procedure. Including a likelihood of cold-blooded, deliberate killings. Anyhow, this new development had to be taken into account and further fresh developments guarded against. As far as that could be done.

But Bobby was not at all happy as he hung up the receiver. He could not feel that the emotional reaction theory had been entirely eliminated. How would Vea feel, for instance, if it turned out that the profits of a joint enterprise, in which most likely she had played a part, were being taken possession of by her husband for the benefit of her rival? A disturbing thought, if, that is, Bobby told himself, his estimate of Vea's character was in any way correct.

Gloomily assuring himself he would probably stay awake all night worrying, unable to sleep a wink, he retired to his room. And was in fact fast asleep before he was much more than well between the sheets. He had asked for a cup of tea to be brought him at an early hour next morning, and when it arrived he learned also that Mr Monk had not appeared, and that Mr George had already departed.

This last piece of news did not greatly surprise Bobby. He hoped that the unobtrusive watch he had asked might be set on Jerry's movements might at least help to give some indication of where the missing Mark Monk was most likely to be found. Even if Jerry, as was probable enough, managed to elude observation at present, it was very certain he would turn up again somewhere some time.

So Bobby went to sleep again. After a leisurely and very good breakfast—commercial hotels have to watch the quality of their food, for commercial travellers are a vocal and a communicative race—he presented himself at the local police station, where he had arranged for the loan of a motor-cycle: the Yard, of course, to pay for all petrol used. There was also waiting for him a message to say that there had now been traced the three girl hikers who had talked about the car they had seen thundering by them through the moonlit night at so fierce and reckless a speed. By a coincidence, they were all three named Mary—Mary Tiler, Mary Unsworth, and Mary Vent.

"Another little coincidence," Bobby said to himself, and considered them thoughtfully, wondering how they distinguished themselves from each other.

One, he supposed, could be Polly and one keep to Mary, and perhaps the third could use a second name—if she had one. He thought it would be amusing to know, but this suggestion, when he made it to the station sergeant, was evidently regarded as most unbecomingly frivolous. Besides, the three young ladies had gone home. Their names and addresses were on record, of course, but they quite plainly knew nothing of any interest. When you have to jump into a hedge to save your life, remarked the sergeant, you have no time to note details. Oh, yes, they had been asked for their identity cards, but two of the young ladies had not got theirs with them. Few people, in fact, troubled to carry them on their persons in these days. The other young lady had mislaid hers. She had thought it was in her handbag, but it wasn't there, and she supposed she must have left it at her home. In any case, there was surely no reason for troubling the young ladies any further in the matter?

Bobby accepted meekly enough the implied rebuke, and returned to the hotel for lunch, testing his borrowed motor-cycle on the way and assuring himself that it was a powerful machine and in good running order. One never knew. On such details life might depend—had sometimes depended in the past. It was still too early for lunch, so he selected a comfortable chair in the smoking-room and devoted himself to hard thought—with his eyes closed. Presently, feeling much refreshed, and lunch-time being still distant, he devoted himself to the study of a large-scale ordnance map of Cornwall till he began to feel as if he would be able to find his way in the dark all over the county.

A friendly 'commercial'—he was a Mr Saggers—gave him some information about the state of the roads and about the trade conditions in the county. Concerning these, Mr Saggers was professionally pessimistic—the worse you can show conditions to be, the greater your credit if you can also show a well-filled order book. Mr Saggers modestly admitted that he himself hadn't done so badly. China clay was booming, of course, but that was not a line in which Mr Saggers was much interested. No orders for him there. Tin? Mr Saggers was mildly amused by an innocence that imagined tin was still a living issue in the county. Cornish tin, said Mr Saggers, had been killed in Bolivia, buried in the Malay peninsula, and both killed and buried in Rhodesia. There was, of course, tin still in Cornwall, and probably plenty of it. More mines had been worked during the war; but sometimes at a heavy loss. But, then, war itself was a heavy loss—a total loss, indeed. Bobby agreed with this truism, and Mr Saggers said most of the reopened mines had been closed again. Now no one went near them from year's end to year's end. Just stood there with machinery rusting and buildings falling down. All marked on the big ordnance map, of course. As Mr Owen— was that the name?—could see for himself if he wanted to.

Bobby said, well, that might be one way of passing a day, and they both laughed a good deal at this, and Mr Saggers said he wasn't nosey, but he did wonder, in an entirely disinterested way, if Bobby were on the look-out for scrap iron? Bobby looked impressed, and said Mr Saggers ought to have been a detective. Mr Saggers beamed, and said he had often felt he could give Scotland Yard a tip or two. Bobby said he thought that more than likely and, still beaming, and even more so, Mr Saggers said he didn't think there was much in the scrap-iron idea. Rusting, and not enough to pay for collection and transport. But Bobby could see for himself. Bobby said perhaps he would, and so they parted on excellent terms, Bobby returning to the study of his ordnance map with even renewed interest.

CHAPTER XX
"THAT OLD DEVIL?"

LATER ON, after lunch, Bobby again went round to the local police, where he spent a good deal of time acquiring local knowledge, finding out all he could about tin-mines in the neighbourhood—Redruth is, of course, the centre, or rather former centre, of the nearly dead Cornish mining industry—and conducting various telephone conversations. Getting through to London, he asked that the names and addresses given by the three girl hikers—the three Marys, as he called them to himself—might be checked. Also he asked for renewed requests to be made to the heads of the various Cornish county and borough police for observation to be kept as far as practicable on the various persons concerned in what had been called the 'Cornish Exodus'. In this, however, the difficulty had to be faced that there was no certain knowledge that any crime had in fact been committed. All that could be considered clearly established was that a girl and a man had run away together and that neither of them had since been heard of. Vague suspicions certainly that somewhere or another in the story a killing had occurred. And now a tale of a load of stolen cigarettes over which it seemed a gang feud might be developing—developing, perhaps, as gang feuds do at times, into another killing. And had that earlier killing—if killing there had really been—had that also been a gangster feud, in no way connected with, or resulting from, the elopement?

Bobby did not think so. The gang-feud theory left too much unaccounted for. But the Cornish police, like all other police forces all over the country, were over-worked, under-manned, and not too anxious to go hunting what, it seemed to them, was very likely to turn out a mare's nest. Too much guess-work—'deduction' was the polite word—about it all, or so it seemed to them.

"Precious little to get our teeth into," said one police chief, and that was what most of them thought.

Bobby would not admit for a moment that there was much guess-work about it. But, then, he had seen what he had seen at Bexley House, and always there is the widest of gaps between what you see yourself and what you are told by others. What the soldier saw is no more evidence than what he said. Bobby was, however, assured that of course everything possible would be done. That—equally of course—meant, he knew, that everything would be done according to routine, and that he had entirely failed to impress on others the driving sense of urgency, as of fresh, impending tragedy, that drove him onwards, though with so little knowledge either of the destination to aim at or of the road to follow.

He returned to his hotel, and there he noticed that he was becoming an object of interest not only to others of the guests, but also to the management. Clearly he was not a tourist, for Redruth is hardly a tourist centre; he was equally clearly not a 'commercial'. So what was he? An opinion on the point had, however, evidently now been arrived at, for presently the hotel manager made an excuse to talk to him, and then asked him outright if he were not connected with the police?

"Mr Saggers," explained the manager, "saw a policeman saluting you, and it made him think."

Bobby remembered the incident, though he had had no idea that it had been witnessed by his new friend, Mr Saggers. He had been slightly annoyed at the time, though he supposed the policeman could hardly be blamed. Probably he had seen Bobby at the police station, had heard of the borrowed motorcycle, and had realized that only to some one of importance would such a favour be granted.

Not that it mattered much, and Bobby agreed that he was on official business, but he didn't want it talked about. The manager said he wouldn't dream of mentioning it to any one. He hoped it wasn't connected with any of his staff. One had to take any one one could get. Only the day before they had engaged a girl who said she was a private secretary waiting to take up a new job with a Redruth firm and obliged to take temporary work to carry her over the interval. She had been given work in the kitchen, as she disliked the idea of the dining-room or the bar.

"Didn't want to be recognized by any of the people she may be working with when she gets going," the manager explained. "And already smashed as much crockery as she's worth. That's staff these days," he added gloomily.

Bobby sympathized. His business wasn't concerned with hotel staff, he said, and the manager said he hoped anyhow it wasn't anything to do with the black market either. His guests were regulars, responsible people employed by well-known firms. All the same, things being what they were, you couldn't be sure of anything or any one.

Bobby was inclined to think all this was a sign of an uneasy conscience. Not all hotel-keepers can resist an offer of extra butter or cooking-fat on the quiet, a load of chickens at a little above controlled price, or a few cigarettes to be disposed of in the bar—a magnet, that, to attract new customers from far and wide. However, he thought it as well to try to put the manager's mind at ease by saying that, so far as he knew, black market came into what he was dealing with no more than it came into at least three-quarters of present-day police work. Of course, one never knew. Black-market activities might at any moment prove to be at the root of almost anything. What he was more especially concerned with at present was the Mr Mark Monk who had paid for a room he had never occupied. His suit-case was still there, wasn't it? What about letting Bobby have a look at it. He would, he said reassuringly, take all responsibility if Mr Monk appeared and made any complaint. Bobby added that he didn't think that was very likely to happen. Of course, one never knew. But the matter might prove to be serious, though there, again, one never knew.

After some protestations and doubts and hesitations—for if you are going to give consent, you might as well make it as big a favour as you can—the manager agreed. He produced the suit-case. It bore the initials 'M. M.' Bobby's police training—entirely unofficial and 'off the record' in this respect—had included a course on how to open locks 'without trace'. Though for this very ordinary suit-case lock no special skill was required. One of Bobby's own keys opened it without any trouble. The result was disappointing—or enlightening, whichever way you chose to look at it. The contents consisted solely of such articles of toilet and attire as any man would be likely to take with him on a brief holiday. There was a wallet with some money in it and one or two letters and bills, but that was all.

"Enough to show it really is Mr Monk's," Bobby remarked, and the manager looked surprised, and asked had Bobby thought it belonged to some one else.

Bobby repeated the platitude that 'one never knew'. He replaced everything as he had found it, and told the manager that the local police must be informed immediately if the suitcase were claimed. Nothing else, Bobby decided, he could do for the time, so he went out for a sharp walk to get up an appetite for dinner. He got as far as St. Day, turned and came back, deciding that an industrial town in the extreme south of the country was very like an industrial town in the extreme north, and returned to the hotel, where he was informed that a lady was waiting to see him.

He expected Maggie Kerr, he thought it might be Vea Burden, but found instead Grace Williams, looking pale and agitated. Bobby greeted her pleasantly and suggested a drink—a suggestion she did not even seem to notice.

"Vea's here," she said. "Did you know?"

"Every one seems to be here," Bobby answered cheerfully. "Including you and me. I wonder why. Any idea? You, for example."

"It's Vea," Grace repeated, her large, pale face strained with anxiety—or fear. "She thinks she's going to die. She says she won't. She puts all her will to living, but she knows, all the same. It makes her so she doesn't care."

"Doesn't care what?"

"What happens. She scares me stiff. It's like talking to some one already gone, so what does it matter? Why should she care?"

"I should have thought it would have made her care a lot more," Bobby remarked.

"All she wants is to have Mark back while there is still time. I don't think she used to feel the same way, but now she knows: she wants him with all she has, before—"

"Before what?" Bobby asked. But Grace did not reply, nor was it necessary, for both she and Bobby knew well the answer.

Abruptly and surprisingly, she said:

"Was it him?"

"Why do you ask?" Bobby said, watching her closely.

"I'm not a fool," she retorted angrily. "Everyone knows you think something happened that night at Bexley House. That's why you're here. Was it Mark?"

"I'm trying to find out," Bobby told her. "As yet we are sure of nothing. His suit-case is here. No one has been to claim the room booked at the same time—or the suit-case either."

"Well, he wouldn't, would he?" Grace said. "Not if it was him and he spotted you were here. Was it him, though? If he got his at Bexley House that night, if that's what you think . . ."

"I haven't said so," Bobby answered. "What can you tell me? I think we shall have to ask you to make a statement, if you will."

But at that she looked both sullen and alarmed.

"I don't know anything, nothing for me to make a statement about," she declared. "I didn't know anything about anything— till I heard you shouting and all. Why should I?"

"If you don't, why are you here?" Bobby asked. "Plain you expected you might find some one you knew. Was it Monk? Or was it Mr Harper?"

"If you think it was him," she said angrily—"if you think Mark got his that night, it wasn't Alf. How could it be? He had nothing to do with any of it."

"Oh, yes, he had; he's told us so," Bobby answered. "Then he took himself off. I rather think perhaps Jerry George is looking for him."

"Him?" Grace exclaimed, dismayed. "That old devil? What's that for?"

"Something about a lorry load of cigarettes apparently," Bobby said. "What do you know about it?"

"I never knew anything about anything," she protested, once more sullen again. "They never said and I never asked." She paused and then broke out: "I don't like it, not him being here and Vea and all."

"I don't like any of you being here," retorted Bobby, stronger than ever within him his feeling that there was approaching a climax that he could not foresee, that he could take no steps to anticipate or prevent. "You say Vea Burden wanted more than anything to get Mark back, even if only for the short time that may be left her. Do you think she wanted it so badly that if she found she couldn't have it, she might want to make sure that no one else should?"

"You mean it might be her knifed him?" Grace asked, and seemed surprised by what was apparently an entirely fresh idea. "I never thought of that," she said, and then inconsequently: "She frightens me. I dream of her sometimes—her and those earrings of hers, swinging all the time."

"If Monk was killed that night," Bobby went on, "and Vea thinks Alf Harper had anything to do with it, I agree with you

Harper may be in danger. If, again, Harper is mixed up with this lost load of cigarettes, then I think he may be in danger from Mr Jerry George. I think you had better be on our side, Miss Williams, if you take any interest in Mr Harper."

"Yes, but I don't know on whose side Alf is," she retorted with unexpected shrewdness—and candour.

"You knew," asked Bobby, "that Monk had a young girl with him. Miss Isobel Winlock. Did you see her?"

"Not that night," Grace answered. "I didn't see any one. If it's the girl I think, she's nothing to do with it. Just one of the fool kids he could pick up whenever he liked."

"She has not been heard of since that night, and her parents are anxious."

"Keeping out of the way," Grace answered indifferently. "If she saw anything, told she had better, unless she wanted trouble. She may have been parked somewhere safe and told to hold her tongue. She'll run away back to mamma as soon as she can, but you'll never get anything out of her."

"Perhaps not," agreed Bobby.

"Unless Vea gets after her," Grace said, and then dismissed the idea. "Vea won't. Why should she? Any one could see the girl was just one of the kids he was always picking up and forgetting next day. She don't matter one way or the other."

"Unless," Bobby suggested, "there happens to be some one who doesn't feel that way—who thinks she does matter, or did."

"You mean young David Pope?" Grace asked. "Oh, him! He's too respectable to make trouble. Office every morning nine sharp, that's him. You don't mean he's here, too?"

"If he is, and you hear of him, let me know," Bobby said. "I want to have a chat. And if you meet Harper, tell him his best plan is to come to us. Safest, too."

"If Alf isn't here," she repeated, "I don't know where he can be."

Bobby asked her where she was staying. She gave an address in the town, and promised to let him know if she made a move. But he had no great expectation that she would keep her word, nor was he much surprised to learn that she only returned to the address she had mentioned to pay her bill and depart, explaining that she had met a friend who wanted her to join her and that they had to catch a train.

CHAPTER XXI
"IF IT'S THAT POOR GIRL . . ."

IT WAS a talk that left Bobby with much to think over. Not that it seemed to give him much guidance, but rather to have increased his sense of doubt and of confusion. He was not even sure that Grace might not have been sent to him for the very purpose of misleading him. In any case, he did not see that for the moment there was very much he could do, beyond carrying out that tour of Cornish tin-mines which he contemplated, but of which, he feared, Centre might not wholly approve. Such a tour, if complete, would occupy much time, and the result was doubtful. There was plenty of work needing his attention at Scotland Yard. Nor did he wish to give further opportunity for the criticism he knew was sometimes made that he was far too apt to neglect the daily, hum-drum work of administration—the bread and butter, so to say, of all police work—for the heady wine of crime investigation.

Of course, too, this watch upon, and examination of, derelict tin-mines that he had in view, ought by all rule and precedent to be carried out by the local police. That certainly would be done, if an official request were made. But they could hardly be expected to perform that duty among all their many others, with the eagerness, the sense of urgency, the intense conviction now grown up in Bobby's mind, that whatever it was had happened at Bexley House was but a prelude to worse things to come. To them it would just appear as a vague routine inquiry not likely to lead anywhere and to be got over as soon as possible, so that more pressing and immediate matters could be dealt with.

Such misgivings as to how far or for how long he would be permitted to follow a trail doubtful even to himself and, as it seemed, invisible to others, were increased when next morning on the breakfast table he found waiting for him a letter from Centre, quite friendly in tone, no doubt, but hinting sufficiently plainly that the sooner a Senior Commander, even though still unattached, returned to his desk, the warmer would be his welcome.

"Which," said Bobby to himself, "about puts the lid on it."

There was something else, though. This was a brief official report to say that the names and addresses given by the three girl hikers—the three Marys, as Bobby called them—had been checked as requested, and had in each case been found to be false. In one case there was no such number in the street named. In another there was no such street. In the third case, though street and number were found, nothing was known of any Mary Tyler, or of any other Mary.

Bobby was interested. He was also aware that Centre would be less so. Centre would remind him that many people dislike extremely being mixed up with the police. They do not think it quite respectable. And of course the three Marys might have been indulging in some innocent little escapade to which they had no desire to draw the attention of their friends and relatives. Their parents might not approve of girls going hiking on their own, and might have believed them to be spending their holiday in some quiet, respectable boarding-house at Eastbourne or Bournemouth, not wandering alone about Devon or Cornwall. Or again, they might, like Maggie Kerr, be absent from work for given reasons not compatible with Cornish hiking.

All the same, Bobby spent a little time writing a memorandum explaining why he thought it desirable that these three girls should be traced and identified, and suggesting that an appeal might be made by radio for them to come forward. He wrote, too, another memorandum giving a brief account of his talks with Jerry George and with Grace Williams, and offering two or three different and conflicting theories for what had been called the Cornish exodus. He thought it probable that Centre would be a good deal more interested in the possible recovery of a stolen lorry load of cigarettes, with it perhaps evidence to convict the gang concerned, than so far it had seemed to be in the exact whereabouts of an eloping couple.

But scarcely had he got these safely in the post when he was called to the 'phone. His friend, the superintendent, was at the other end of the line, and sounded for once quite excited. For there was news. On the edge of the cliffs, at Gurnards Head, had been found a motor rug, some tools, a cushion, and a Michelin guide. Further investigation had shown plain indications that here a vehicle of some kind had been driven straight over the cliff edge at full speed. Also it had been found that both on rug and cushion were stains that looked like blood. These would be submitted for expert examination. Arrangements were being made to recover, if possible, what might be left of any car that here had taken the dreadful plunge these signs seemed to indicate.

Would Mr Owen, the superintendent asked, like to come along and see for himself what was going on?

Bobby, a little excited, too, said he would indeed. It really did look, he said, as though things were beginning to move at last. The superintendent remarked that it seemed a good easy way of disposing of an inconvenient corpse. The murderer's perennial difficulty. Corpses have an awkward way of turning up again, no matter how carefully hidden, even after the lapse of many months—or years. Fifteen years, for instance, between the murder and the discovery of the skeleton that had brought Eugene Aram to the gallows.

"No telling if it will ever be found," said the superintendent. "It may very well get washed right out to sea. Or, for that matter, into some cave or crevice of the rocks. Impossible to search them all. And if it can't be found—well, where are we?"

Bobby said he didn't know, and the superintendent said:

"Besides, whose body?"

Bobby did not attempt to answer. He was putting the same question to himself. The superintendent said:

"If it's that poor girl . . . hardly bears thinking of, does it?"

Bobby said it was a bad business altogether, and difficult to know what could be done until it was clearly established who it was was missing. Indeed, there was still no proof that any one was missing in any but a purely temporary sense. A case so difficult it was even yet not certain there was any case at all. He supposed the locating of the actual spot where the car lay beneath the sea, and then its recovery, would take some time. The superintendent agreed, and said it would depend on the weather. If the weather broke—as well it might, since that was its normal habit and procedure—then recovery might prove impossible. Wave and cliff and rock between the three of them were well capable, along that coast, of pounding any work of man into unrecognizable fragments.

That ended their talk. Bobby hung up the receiver, and as he left the 'phone box he thought he saw some one hurriedly scuttling away. It was only an impression. He had seen nothing clearly. There had just been a feeling of movement in the air, of a changing shadow on the wall, of a faint echo of a sound of swift, departing footsteps. He did not attach much importance to it. He was well aware he had become an object of interest in the hotel, and in any case he was sure nothing he had said could have been overheard. Nor would it, he thought, have mattered very much if there had been eavesdropping. The papers would soon be proclaiming at the top of their extremely clamant voices 'Tragic Discovery on Cornish Cliff'.

Plainly some considerable time would have to elapse before arrangements could be made for the locating and recovery of the wrecked car, even if the weather remained good. No use therefore in hurrying to the scene, so Bobby decided he might as well carry out his plan for visiting as many of the derelict tin-mines in the neighbourhood as he could in the time available. Especially that known as the 'Round Table' Mine—the one David Pope had mentioned as that in which his father had lost money, and which apparently he had visited in the company of the vanished Isobel Winlock.

He started, accordingly, and found his visits interesting and a little melancholy, such clear proof there was of human effort now for ever lost and abandoned. The mines seemed in various stages of neglect. One or two looked as if no living creature had been near them for years. The buildings were merely heaps of ruins, the machinery no more than rusty debris. For those were days in which the nation had been too rich and busy to bother its collective head about waste or scrap. In one case the entrance to the workings had been boarded over, but in the course of years the boarding had rotted and given way in part, so that a gaping hole showed deep below a sullen, dark surface of water. Bobby stood looking at it. The sea might give up its dead, he thought, but never that dark, subterranean pool, fed by perennial, hidden springs. He turned away with a faint shudder. He spent some time examining with close attention the approaches to this sinister and gaping hole, but could find no sign or trace of any recent visits.

One or two other mines had clearly been worked more recently when, under the stress of war conditions, the cost of securing tin had not been allowed to weigh against the desperate need for it, the still more desperate need for saving shipping space.

In these mines the buildings were in good repair, but the machinery, more modern, and therefore more in demand, had in general been removed. Here, too, the entrance to the workings had been closed with greater care—possibly from a genuine wish to guard against accidents, and possibly from a lively fear of actions for damages.

This was specially the case at the Round Table Mine. This he did not reach till late in the day—so late that he was beginning to think of turning back and postponing his visit to another day. It was a lonely district, too, and his memory of the sandwiches he had had for lunch, as of the tea he had managed to get at a wayside cottage, had grown both faint and thin. However, he decided to continue. The entrance to the mine premises was secured by a padlocked gate. But padlocks are less secure than they seem, and can generally be dealt with. This one offered little trouble, and Bobby soon had it opened. He sounded his horn once or twice, on the chance of there being a watchman in charge. There was no response—as, indeed, he had not supposed there would be—so he wheeled his motor cycle through the open gate and on up to the mine buildings. There he leaned it against a convenient support and proceeded on his tour of investigation. It seemed at first likely to yield small result. The buildings he looked at were still securely fastened, doors locked and windows boarded up. The sealed opening to the workings had certainly not been disturbed, and he saw no such open, direct access to unplumbed depths below as he had noticed elsewhere.

It was raining now, and low clouds suggested a stormy night. Bobby supposed that the work on the cliffs near Gurnards Head would probably be stopped before it had even begun. He noticed several heaps of refuse near, piles of mingled earth, ashes, and other debris that would presumably be cleared away at intervals when the mine was being worked, but whose removal since the stoppage no one had bothered about. Almost the last building he went to look at was one near the engine-house—probably a toolshed or something of the sort. The window was boarded up as usual, but the work had this time either been done carelessly or else the boards had been forced apart, for a gap showed several inches wide. Not enough for any one to enter by, but enough to supply a modicum within of air and light. Bobby examined the door, secured as always by a padlock. Not difficult to see that the staple had recently been withdrawn and then re-inserted.

So some one else had been here who knew how to deal with padlocks. For few think to make the staple secure by spread-eagling its ends, and yet if that is not done it is easy to force out the staple on which, of course, the padlock depends. Bobby repeated the process, easier now that it had been effected previously. Within there was clear evidence that some one had passed the night here. Plain to see where a rough bed had been made up. There was a tin that still held some dirty water, and on a spread-out paper were a few crumbs and an egg-shell to show it had served as a table-cloth during a meal.

Nothing could Bobby find, though, long and carefully as he looked, to show the identity of this recent visitor. But, then, the light was bad and his time short. Detailed examination by experts, including a finger-print expert—or 'dabs' man—might be able to find something. Difficult, indeed impossible, for any living creature not to leave behind distinctive traces of even the briefest, most transitory sojourn. That would have to wait for morning, however, and Bobby went to find his motor-cycle where he had left it leaning against the wall of the first shed he had come to. He found it with the tyres slashed to ribbons and the petrol tank opened and drained of its contents.

"With which they might have been content," he thought ruefully, "without ruining perfectly good tyres. A work of supererogation."

He was still contemplating the now useless machine when he heard the sharp report of a pistol and the whang of a bullet as it embedded itself, though at some distance away, in the wall of the building by which he was standing.

CHAPTER XXII
"THERE'S TIMES HE KNOWS"

BOBBY HAD many little prejudices of his own, and one of the most marked was an extreme dislike to acting as a target for pistol practice. He removed himself, therefore, with very considerable speed from where he stood to the farther side of the shed.

The rain was growing heavier, the darkness greater, and of these conditions he took advantage to slip away, he hoped unseen, to the shelter of other buildings. Thence he got behind one of the piles of ash and other debris he had noticed before. There he crouched, listening intently, trying to peer through the gloom to see if he could distinguish any sign of his assailant. Visibility, however, as the air people say, was now only some ten or fifteen yards. Cautiously he began to edge his way in the direction whence that shot had seemed to come.

Still nothing, and now there was no more shelter, neither for him nor for any lurking assassin. Only a wire fence that ran between the mine property and the bare moor beyond, where it sloped up to the summit of a hill into which the mine workings penetrated deeply. Beyond, as he knew, on the other side of the hill, about half-way down it, was a by-road that a few miles farther on joined the main highway.

He went forward more boldly now, the rain and the darkness giving him, he felt, good protection. When he reached the wire fence he found it broken down in several places, so that here access to the mine was easy and the formidably padlocked gate at the principal entrance of little value. Had he known, he might have saved himself the trouble of removing and replacing that first padlock. He stood for a moment hesitating what to do next, and then he saw a light show at a distance on the brow of the hill. It moved away, disappearing behind the hill, and he thought this meant that whoever had fired the pistol shot had had a bicycle, had wheeled it up the rough hillside, and now had lighted its lamp, mounted it, and was riding away to safety—not to mention, Bobby reflected ruefully, food, shelter, and a bed, triple desiderata which seemed to be becoming somewhat doubtful prospects for himself.

So far as he could remember, on the road he had traversed so swiftly and so easily on his motor-cycle, and that now in retrospect seemed to stretch away for such endless miles, he had passed neither farm nor cottage. No doubt, lonely and remote as was the district, there would be some human habitation not too far away. But how to find it in this darkness, in this increasing rain?

Nothing for it, he supposed, but to tramp the whole distance to the main highway. No pleasing prospect, but no alternative. He went back to his useless motor-cycle, got the waterproof cape he, having some knowledge of Cornish weather, had been careful to provide himself with, and started off, musing the while very bitterly on the malign fate that had made him a policeman.

"Some," he told himself, "are born unlucky, some have bad luck thrust upon them, and some achieve it by joining the police. Oh, well."

On and on he walked, at the best speed the darkness, the rain, and a rising wind permitted. Then fortune relented, and allowed him a glimpse of a lighted window at a little distance from the road. It vanished almost at once. Some one had apparently pushed aside a curtain or blind for a moment to look out into the night and then let it fall again. Bobby found a narrow lane that led in the direction where that welcome light had shown, and followed it. Before very long the loud barking of a dog announced that he was nearing a house of some sort, and then a beam of light shot out into the darkness as a door opened and a man's voice called:

"Any one there?"

Bobby responded and went forward, explaining his plight, and was invited inside, nor did he think that he had ever seen a more comforting sight than this cottage interior, at any rate by contrast with the wind and the rain and the night without. The inmates were a young man—the one who had opened the door to him—a young woman, presumably his wife; a baby sleeping in a cot, and an old, old man dozing by a small fire of brushwood in the kitchen grate. Bobby apologized for the mess he was making as the wet poured from his dripping clothes, and the young woman threw some more brushwood on the fire and told him to come nearer and dry himself.

"It was grand-dad told us," she said. "He said as there was some one out there as was lost, and I must draw the curtain to look out. So I did, though we don't most often take notice of what he says and him so old. But there's times he knows, though all knows how."

"Well, I'm glad he knew this time," Bobby said, surveying the ancient man with gratitude. "Saved me a long tramp."

"None too safe neither in this weather," the young man added. "There's the old road where it forks leads into Deep-side Pond that's all weeds and mud, and no seeing the danger sign at night, when it's dark and raining, too."

The young woman offered him refreshment, and he was glad to accept a cup of hot tea, though he refrained from any further inroad on rations not too liberal for hard-working farm labourers. He asked a few questions, and received no comforting information. There was a village not too far away, but not easy to get to in this weather. A farm or two as well, including the one where his host worked. To this the young man undertook to make his way, Bobby promising ample reward. There was a telephone there, and certainly they would be willing to ring up the police and convey Mr Owen's request that a car should be sent for him.

"Which they won't much like—not this night same as it is, with raining and blowing all out," observed the young man doubtfully, as if he felt by no means sure how this imperious request would be received.

Bobby remarked that indeed he knew very well they wouldn't like it. He pointed out that the police only existed to be at the beck and call of every one who managed to get into a mess from which he couldn't get out without their help. He made this observation with some feeling, and it was so unexpected and novel a point of view to his auditors that conversation died abruptly.

The young man completed his preparations and departed. Bobby, who had noticed during his talk with the two young people that once at least the old man by the fire had looked up with a sudden light in his ancient eyes, tried to speak to him. But the curtain of the years had enveloped him again. He took no notice, and the young woman said:

"There's times he notices and times he don't. No good saying nothing to him when he don't."

"It was he told you I was out there?" Bobby asked.

"Aye," the woman answered. "Most times I take no notice, but to-night I did."

"Good thing for me you did," Bobby said. "Or I should still be tramping along that road and perhaps walking straight into the pond you spoke of."

"And if you had, odds you would never have got out again," she told him.

Bobby asked one or two questions about the Round Table Mine. It had, it seemed, a bad reputation. A wicked mine. More accidents there than in any other mine in all the length and breadth of Cornwall. Three men had died there the very last day before the mine last closed down, and the body of one of them had never been found, in spite of prolonged search. The mine claiming its own! Again, the very day the mine had been reopened under the stress of war three others had been killed in a boiler explosion. That was the threat and menace of the mine in reply to the return of men to rob it of its treasure. And there was the story of one man who had gone back to fetch some tool or something he had forgotten and had never since been heard of.

"But there was some as said as that was only him getting off quiet like so as he wouldn't be called up for the Army," added the young woman.

From the fireside, his voice small and thin but clear, as though heard from an immense distance, the old man said:

"There's the unburied dead there still, waiting to be found."

"Now, dad," the young woman protested, and to Bobby she said: "We don't heed him much, he's that old no one knows for sure."

To the old man, Bobby said:

"Why do you say that? Tell me more."

But once again the curtain of the years had fallen, and the ancient did not seem even to hear, as he sank back to follow where his spirit roamed, in memory of the past or in knowledge of the future, in realms where perhaps, or so it seemed just then to Bobby, those two—the future and the past—might be as one in eternity.

"There's times he's took like that," explained the young woman apologetically. "It's on his mind seemingly about him as was killed and his body never found. Goodness knows what set him off, but ever since a day or two he's spoke of it, off and on. Remembering like."

"I suppose so," Bobby agreed. "What was it he said exactly? Can you tell me?"

"Only same all the time about him as wasn't ever found," the young woman answered; and repeated, even more apologetically than before: "He's that old—a hundred some says—and if you ask he says it's too long anyhow and time he went. So I tell him who'll keep baby quiet when I'm at the washing or such like if he isn't there? He's wonderful with baby, seems like as if they knew, both of them."

The old man looked up at the word 'baby', as though it recalled to him a self now but tenuously connected with a physical body. And yet Bobby was not sure but that all that passed, all that was said and done around him, was not in some obscure way noted and registered, there to be called upon at need. Now he said suddenly, and said it with a sort of half-concealed chuckle:

"Start and end and same for every job."

"Whose body is it that lies unburied at the Round Table Mine?" Bobby asked.

"It's there for them as looks to find," the old man answered in the same clear, high, and distant voice. "A bad thing," he said, "and bad'll come of it."

"Fair worrying of him," the young woman interposed. "Now dad, it's nothing you can't help, so let it be."

"Where would you begin to look?" Bobby asked.

But now the old man sank again into that state of coma, or rather of a deep and hidden abstraction, from which for the moment he had seemed to awaken. Bobby sat down at his side and took the old, chill, wrinkled hands in his, young and strong, holding them gently.

"Will you tell me more?" he asked.

"There ain't a thing he can know," the young woman said, a faint suspicion in her tone, as though, while she did not know what Bobby meant, she yet disliked it and distrusted it, as all of us dislike and distrust the unfamiliar.

"I suppose not," Bobby agreed, and from the old man he had no response.

It was, he was inclined to think, the presence, the interruptions, well meant and kindly in intention as they were, that kept coming from his grand-daughter, which had broken the continuity of whatever thought or dream or knowledge had been working in that old, almost departed mind. No use, Bobby felt, hoping or trying or expecting that he would say more. The young woman, apologetically, defensively, suspiciously, all three of these fully apparent in her tone and manner, repeated that he was very old, and when people got that way they couldn't help it, could they? Bobby said that indeed they couldn't, and nearly, but not quite, asked, why should they? The young woman added that he was wonderful little trouble and never ate more than half his rations, if as much. Or his tobacco either. They would miss him a lot when he went.

She put some more brushwood on the fire. Bobby devoted himself afresh to his interrupted task of getting himself as dry as possible. The young woman returned to the sewing she had been busy with. The old man dozed. Outside, the sound of wind and rain increased. Bobby supposed there would be small hope for the time of any progress being made in the task of recovering the crashed motor-car.

Presently the young man returned. Bobby's message had gone through, and a car was being sent immediately. Bobby sighed again as once more he thought ruefully of how that item would show up in his expense sheet. Not to mention that other little item about new tyres for a motor-cycle. The young woman said:

"Grand-dad's been rambling on again about the mine and him as was killed there and never found."

"Up at farm," her husband said, "they're telling there was a light there one night. Two saw it. They think it must have been a tramp, now there's a few on the road again with the war being over. Or it might be a hiker lost his way same as you, sir."

"I daresay it might be that," Bobby agreed.

"There was that lady you saw," remarked the young woman, looking up from her sewing.

"It was well on in the day when I saw her," her husband answered. "If she had put up there for the night, she would have been off early like. Stands to reason. Nothing to keep her or no one hanging about."

"What did she look like?" Bobby asked.

His efforts to get a description did not meet with much success. There had only been a casual, passing glance as she rode by on a bicycle, and no special notice had been taken. Nor had she answered the greeting given her in friendly country fashion.

"Uncivil like," the young man said, and added a detail: "Long, swinging earrings she had, swinging as if they might swing off. Swinging," he repeated, as if this had impressed itself upon his memory.

"Swinging," Bobby repeated, thinking at once of Vea Burden.

"Swinging," the old man said, returning suddenly and unexpectedly to common intercourse. "That's how it was once. My dad's told me how he had seen them himself—swinging in the wind up there on the hill. Murderers they were."

"Now, grand-dad," the young woman said, "that's long ago."

"Same as yesterday," the old man said.

"It's the hill beyond the mine," the young woman explained to Bobby. "Where there was a gallows once, folk say. But it's long ago."

The conversation died. It was not long before hooting outside told of the arrival of the car Bobby was expecting.

CHAPTER XXIII
"THEY FOUND THE BODY IMMEDIATELY"

BOBBY STILL had much to do even after he was back in his little Redruth hotel. Arrangements had to be made over the 'phone for a thorough search to be carried out next morning of the Round Table Mine. This involved disturbing a sleepy superintendent at the very moment when he was hopefully donning his pyjamas. Bobby was a bit vague about the reasons he said he had for believing that just possibly a dead body might be hidden there. He did not think the superintendent would be impressed if he knew those reasons were founded on the murmured wanderings of an old, old man. So he didn't go into details; and the superintendent grumbled, but agreed that the search requested should be made. All the same, Bobby became aware that his popularity with the Cornish police was a rapidly diminishing quantity, so he thought he might as well complete the job by adding that possibly he might have to ask that all the old deserted tin-mines in Cornwall might also be thoroughly searched. To which the superintendent replied with bitter irony that probably Bobby would next be asking him to bail out Dozmary Pool with a leaking limpet shell. But this left quite unmoved Bobby, who had never heard of that local saying, and knew not that into the depths of Dozmary Pool the sword Excalibur had disappeared in the long, long ago. So all he said was 'Well, why not?' and hung up, and the superintendent was very cross indeed.

Then London had to be communicated with, and after that Bobby, the more immediate claims of duty satisfied, allowed himself a hot bath, made a supper of some bread and cheese he bribed the hotel porter to secure for him, sneezed once or twice, hoped gloomily that did not mean a cold was on the way, began to write a report of the day's happenings, went to sleep over it once or twice, finally towards the small hours got it completed and settled down in bed for what remained of the night.

It was late next morning when he awoke with happily no longer any perceptible sneezing tendencies. For a time he lay in bed, listening to wind and rain still busy without. It did not sound as if much could be done for a day or two towards the recovery of the crashed motor-car. None the less, things were certainly beginning to move at last, at long last. From out the baffling fog of doubt and speculation through which till now he had had to grope his way, facts were beginning to appear. Difficult to co-ordinate at present what were none the less assured facts. A wrecked car. Vea Burden seen again; and what was she after? A nocturnal sojourner at a derelict mine; and why? A pistol-shot; murderous? or warning? or something else? A light seen at that same mine on an earlier occasion, a light like a fire. Three girl hikers who gave false names and addresses, and why? Could he add to this list the vague and wandering talk of an old, old man?

Lying there warm in bed, thinking how nice it was to be there instead of being one of the unlucky juniors no doubt at that very moment busy in this abominable weather at the Round Table Mine, thinking also how lucky it was that a due regard for etiquette and the deference due to the local people allowed him to stay in bed, instead of having himself to be on the spot to look after things, as would have been the case in his own domain. He wondered lazily if the superintendent were there, and if so if he were getting very wet.

Turning from these pleasant speculations, he tried to assess in turn the value of each new item of fact and information.

The wrecked car he felt he could assume was that which Bella Winlock had hired from the London garage.

But what had it taken with it when it made that last dreadful plunge four hundred feet or more over the edge of the cliff into the depths of the sea? Anything? Nothing? At any rate, it had not taken with it a rug, a bloodstained cushion, some tools, and so on. Why? Bobby thought he might guess an answer to that question; but, then, what is the good of a guess?

The nocturnal visitor to the mine?

Vea Burden or another?

Not much use bothering to answer that, since probably expert examination would soon provide an answer. Fingerprints, perhaps. Or footmarks, if at least this wind and rain had not obliterated them. Almost certainly evidence to show whether it had been man or woman. If the first, signs of shaving. If the second, traces of powder or lipstick, perhaps, or a long hair or two. Something like that.

The pistol shot?

Over that Bobby wrinkled a puzzled brow.

Had it been a deliberate attempt at murder? Or a warning to keep out? Or even a hint that the mine premises were worth examination? Or the mere panic of a fugitive who feared pursuit? On the whole, he was inclined to think this last supposition the most likely.

Vea Burden, too, seen cycling away from the mine on a previous occasion. And actually seen in person, her presence not merely deduced or guessed at, as before. But on what errand was she bound that brought her thus from time to time into the ambit of events, seen for a moment only, and then vanishing again? Impossible, he felt, to guess the motives, to foresee the actions of this woman, who, it seemed, felt fiercely free to go her own way, choose her own path, under the protection of that death she knew so hard upon her heels, no matter how she flung at it her defiance. Bobby made a fresh note to impress upon all concerned the urgent necessity of making every possible effort to find her.

A light seen at the mine—a light like a fire. A tramp cooking his supper? Or something else? An effort must be made to make sure of the exact date. 'A few days ago' was the expression used, he remembered. Did that mean after or before the Bexley House happening? Or the same night, perhaps? One must try to be sure.

The girl hikers, the three Marys as he called them to himself; and why had they, apparently so innocently engaged, thought it necessary to give false names and addresses? They must be found and questioned, but not such an easy task to accomplish. Among the fifty or so odd million of us, easy for two or three to pass unperceived. Possibly, though, the always powerful help of the radio and the Press might be effective. Some one, reading or hearing, might easily say: "Girl hiking in Cornwall, first name Mary. Why, that girl in our office went hiking somewhere in her holiday. Can it be her? She's a Mary, too."

Finally, could any importance be attached to the wandering talk of that ancient man in the cottage near the Round Table Mine? Could he have seen or heard or somehow become aware of some activity that somehow had become associated in his mind with a tragedy of long ago?

So there, Bobby felt, were the elements of a solution at last beginning faintly to appear, if only he could put them together to form a coherent pattern.

He decided it was time to get up. Many possible theories, and now a start had been made; at any moment some new fact or another might well emerge to show in which one lay the truth.

"Oh, fact, how lovely thou art, and how much to be admired above all things," he murmured as he shaved, and added thoughtfully: "And how devilishly misleading, as often as not."

With that he went down to breakfast, and had scarcely finished when a car drove up and there appeared his friend the superintendent, clucking disapproval when he saw Bobby still dallying over a cup of tea and a fragment of toast and marmalade.

"I," he said, "I've been up and at work since a quarter past five."

"Me," said Bobby, finishing his tea, "since a quarter to."

"What you been doing?" asked the superintendent, rather more than doubtfully.

"Thinking," said Bobby.

"Huh," said the superintendent, who didn't think much of that. "In bed and asleep, if you ask me."

"My unconscious hard at it," explained Bobby. "Simply racing along."

"Huh," said the superintendent, who thought still less of that. "Hurry up. I'm going to take you to a pub."

"Good," said Bobby.

"Oh, not for a drink," said the superintendent.

"Not likely," said Bobby.

"Well, come along," said the superintendent.

"Man or woman?" asked Bobby.

"On it, are you?" said the superintendent, displeased. "Man. Or was once. They found the body immediately. The thing is, can you identify it? Not so easy. There's been a try at burning it. Petrol."

"A fire was seen," Bobby told him. "That could be it. Got to try to find out exactly when. I've an idea it will coincide with the Bexley House affair."

"Shouldn't wonder," agreed the superintendent. "We've the photo you people circulated. You've seen him, haven't you? I mean Monk. If it is Monk, that is."

"Who else?" asked Bobby sombrely. He went on: "I only saw him that once. At his trial. And that's a goodish bit ago. But now there's something definite to go on, it shouldn't be hard to make sure."

The superintendent agreed. London, he thought, ought to be able to dig up details. He had a slight air of suggesting that this would give London something to do, instead of leaving all the hard work to over-burdened Cornwall. He explained, too, the various steps that had already been taken. To try to find Vea Burden first of all. Unfortunate that the chief detail by which she could be recognized—those conspicuous and unusual earrings of hers—could not be mentioned publicly, since if they were she would, of course, at once remove them. The bullet fired at Bobby had been found in the wall in which it had embedded itself. It had been extracted, and would be sent to an expert for a report to be made. Finger-prints had also been found, and, with other evidence, showed that the nocturnal sojourner had been a man. Car-tracks, too, but these had been so affected by the heavy rain that not much could be made of them. A plain-clothes man had gone to the farm whence the light at the mine had been seen, to make further inquiries there. He was also to call at the neighbouring cottage in the hope of being able to get a little more from the old man who had talked to Bobby.

All this and more the superintendent explained as they drove along, and when he had finished he waited, slightly on the defensive, to hear if the Scotland Yard man had any criticism or comment to make. None came. It was all good routine, efficiently carried out. The police, Bobby reflected, whether London or provincial, seldom or never fell down on routine, and routine is the solid foundation of all good work. Imagination, intuition, that which is founded on reason, but goes beyond reason, was perhaps occasionally lacking. And not only in police work.

Presently they reached the small and lonely public house-cum tea garden-cum small holding, where an outbuilding had been turned into a temporary mortuary. It had served that purpose more than once before when fatal accidents had occurred at the Round Table Mine of unlucky reputation.

It was not a pleasant task Bobby had now to perform, though one every officer of police has to be prepared to face. All he could say, however, when he had seen that charred and burnt and melancholy relic, was that it might well be that of Mark Monk. Nothing at least plainly inconsistent. Objects the fire had not destroyed—a watch, two rings, keys, and so on—would almost certainly in time provide proof, one way or another. Not that there remained in Bobby's mind a vestige of doubt.

"Quite safe," he told his companion as they drove away, "to work on the assumption that it is Mark Monk."

"Well, then, who killed him?" the superintendent asked.

"Exactly," said Bobby.

"And why?" said the superintendent.

"If we knew the why," said Bobby, "we should know the who."

"That suit-case," the superintendent said, "at your hotel. Left before or after? Explains why it was never claimed?"

"Oh, after," Bobby answered. "I think the state of the body proves that. Left there to make us think he was still alive so we should spend our time trying to trace him instead of . . ."

He left the sentence unfinished, and the superintendent nodded.

"Trying to lead us up the garden path," he said. "Smart idea, but not smart enough. Though it might have worked," he admitted, "if you hadn't gone nosing round." He paused and then went on, remembering his own daughter: "It's the Winlock girl I'm thinking of. What's become of her? That's what's worrying me."

"Yes, I know," said Bobby.

"I'm not bothering my head so much about him," the superintendent went on, jerking a thumb over his shoulder in the direction, more or less, of the public-house they had just left. "I remember his trial for murder. I always thought Monk was guilty and ought to have swung. If he's got his now, I'm not worrying. It's the girl. Suppose she saw it happen? She was at Bexley House all right. We know that. Very well. If she did see anything, wouldn't they want to make sure she didn't tell?"

"There's that," agreed Bobby cautiously.

"And how could they?" asked the superintendent. "Except—well, you can't keep people shut up in England. Not for long. Can't be done. You can't smuggle them abroad. There's ways, of course. At least, there is with a girl."

"Yes," agreed Bobby.

"It's that car," the superintendent said. "That's what I'm thinking. No chance of salvaging it in this weather. And when it clears there may be no car left—or, if there is, nothing else."

"No," said Bobby this time.

"Well, then," said the superintendent, and lapsed into silence.

Nor did Bobby say anything. He was trying to decide the lines on which it would be best to work and finding it difficult when the theory that had been so long and so gradually framing itself in his mind might so soon be either confirmed or proved entirely wrong on the recovery of the wrecked car. After a time he remarked:

"What's worrying me as much as anything is the way Vea Burden keeps showing and then vanishing again. I feel she means something, and yet it's not so easy to fit her in."

"May be she doesn't fit and that's why," suggested the superintendent, who did not really suppose that this lady of the vanishing trick was likely to be a very important factor. "Now Jerry George and his cigarettes come into it all right. If you ask me, it's all a gang game, and none of that lovers' quarrelling you were talking about. Good thing, too. Gang work—that's just natural, honest-to-goodness, healthy crime. In a manner of speaking," he added, not quite sure now that he had chosen wholly appropriate epithets. When Bobby did not speak, he went on: "What I really hate is when a boy and a girl start popping each other off just because they haven't sense enough to realize that in ten years they wouldn't even remember what it was all about."

They had now reached the Round Table Mine, where many activities were still in progress. The plain-clothes man who had been sent to the adjacent farm and cottage returned soon with information that the fire at the mine had been seen very late at night, or rather very early in the morning following the Bexley House affair. A safe assumption that what had been seen had been the attempt to destroy and conceal the identity of the dead man by first pouring petrol on the body and setting it alight, and then by shovelling down rubble and other waste stuff from one of the great piles standing here and there. In the later stages of the working of the mine, with closure already in sight, no attempt had been made to clear these away. It had been easy to shovel down enough of the stuff, loosened by recent rain, to cover the body several feet deep.

"There must have been two or three of 'em at it, though," said the superintendent. "Half a ton or so or more to cover it, and most likely never would have been found but for looking."

"Probably," Bobby remarked, "the idea was that even if in the course of years a body was found, it would be taken to be the one that was never recovered after an accident here. By that time all the details would have got mixed up or forgotten, except the one fact that a body had never been found. So it would naturally be concluded that this was it."

"I was just thinking," the superintendent said. "Two or three of 'em working like hell in the night at a job like that. Trying to burn the body of the man they had murdered, and then hiding it under heaps of rubbish and running for it when the first light they had dreaded began to show. Wanted nerve all right."

"Yes, indeed," Bobby said gravely. "Wanted nerve. But I shouldn't say there must have been two or three of them. Wonderful what one person alone can do—in the shadow of the gallows. Afraid, afraid of everything, including themselves. And fear's a powerful incentive, as they say to-day." He turned to speak to the plain-clothes man. "Get anything from the old boy at the cottage?"

"Oh, him," came the answer. "Oh, yes, I meant to say. I forgot. Dead. Passed out in the night, cold and stiff they found him this morning. Fair cut up they seemed about it, too, and said I was to tell you not to heed what he said. He rambled at times, being so old, and so they never paid attention."

"No, I know," Bobby said.

Another of the superintendent's men came hurrying up.

"There's a lady," he reported. "Cycling down the road she was, and now she isn't any more."

"What's that?" snapped the superintendent.

"It's where the road dips," the man explained. "I saw her go behind the bank, and she never came out in the clear again, and she didn't turn back, neither."

"Well, what about it?" asked the superintendent. "Having a sit down for a time, most likely."

"Yes, sir," said the other. "Only there's a man none of us has seen before, and he's gone off the other way, riding a lady's cycle hard as he can go."

CHAPTER XXIV
"HE DIDN'T COME BACK"

"Well, get after him," snapped the superintendent. "Bring him back. If he makes trouble, charge him with stealing the bike. Sharp's the word."

The other turned and fled. Bobby said:

"What about going to have a look? It may be Vea Burden again."

"What's her game?" the superintendent asked.

"I wish I knew," Bobby answered; "but I'm sure it's mischief of one sort or another."

"I was wondering if it could be Miss Winlock," the superintendent said.

Bobby did not think that likely, but said nothing. They hurried away together. On the farther side of the road, where it dipped under the slope of the hill, was a small spinney, overgrown by a tangle of bramble and brushwood, and looking at the moment very damp and dismal in the still steadily falling rain. Into its soaking recesses they plunged, and saw limping towards them a flushed, dishevelled, exceedingly wet young woman with a badly scratched face.

"Dear me, Miss Kerr," Bobby said amiably. "I didn't expect to meet you here. What's been happening?"

Maggie favoured him with a glare of extreme dislike, though this seemed not so much personal as aimed at all the world and all therein.

"A man," she said in a voice hovering between indignation and tears, "pushed me over into the ditch right on top of an awful great blackberry bush. Just look at the state I'm in. And now he's stolen my bicycle."

"Who was it?" the superintendent asked.

"I don't know," Maggie answered. "I couldn't see. He came up behind and gave me a great push. Please, I want my bicycle back."

"There's a car gone after him," Bobby said. "Will you please tell us what you are doing here?"

"I wanted to see if I could find Mr Pope," she explained—reluctantly. "He didn't come back."

"Come back where? When?"

"Last night. To the hotel. He was going to call for me this morning, and he never did. So I rang up to ask, and the hotel said he hadn't been back all night and he hadn't been in to dinner either."

"Another gone missing," grunted the superintendent with great annoyance.

"Did you expect to find him here?" Bobby asked.

"I didn't know," Maggie answered. "It belongs to him, doesn't it? Or his father or some one, and he said he had been, and some one was trespassing. I thought he might have been again, and something had happened."

"What were you doing in here, in this spinney?" Bobby asked next.

"Well, I saw there were people there," she explained. "I thought I had better try to see who they were and what they were doing."

"Apparently some one else had the same idea," Bobby remarked. "You know Miss Winlock hasn't been heard of yet?"

"Yes," she said, and looked frightened.

"Do you think Mr Pope had anything to do with her disappearance?"

"Oh, no, no," she protested, and looked more frightened still. Then she added: "I've asked him, and he said he hadn't. Only he knew you thought he had, and so he wanted to find her. Because he's so upset about it. That's all."

"There's more than him upset about it," growled the superintendent. He looked at Bobby. He said: "I think we shall have to ask this young lady a few more questions, don't you? Wet here, though, so perhaps she won't mind coming back to Redruth with us." To Maggie he said: "There was a dead man here."

"Oh, not . . . not . . ." she cried.

"Not Mr Pope," Bobby told her quickly. "Identity has not been completely established, but it seems probable it is Mark Monk. That makes even more puzzling what happened at Bexley House and why Miss Winlock has disappeared. It also makes it necessary that Mr Pope should be found. It would be best for him to come forward at once of his own accord. It is certain the body was hidden here by some one who knew the mine and where it was and all about it."

"Lots of people do," Maggie said in a voice that was barely audible.

"But not so many who also knew Bexley House," Bobby said gravely. "I believe you visited the Round Table Mine with Mr Pope, didn't you?"

She did not answer that, and Bobby did not press her. Instead he said to the superintendent:

"What about going back to see if the chap with Miss Kerr's cycle has been caught?"

"If he hasn't been, I shall want to know why," said the superintendent severely. "A car ought to catch up with a cycle soon enough."

Accompanied by a thoroughly frightened, even more thoroughly wet, and rather sulky Maggie, the two men made their way back to the mine premises. There Maggie was deposited in the shelter of an outbuilding, out of the still-falling rain, and one of the police was told to make sure that she didn't slip away unseen. She wasn't under arrest, he was instructed; it was just a case of asking her a few questions. It is a distinction that sometimes seems a bit fine-drawn, but it is one the police understand well, as did the man to whom the superintendent spoke. Returning to Bobby, the superintendent said:

"What do you make of her? Fishy, in my view."

"All sorts of possibilities," Bobby said. "A lot to take into consideration, though. She may be in it up to the neck."

"Looks to me as if she and Pope knew Monk's body was here and were planning to move it somewhere safer."

"What about Miss Winlock?" asked Bobby.

"There's always her," agreed the superintendent. "If Pope did in Monk in a quarrel over a girl, did Miss Winlock know and so has she got to be kept quiet? How? Marrying her? Or—well, another way? There's that car went over the cliff. What about that?"

"Yes, I know," Bobby agreed. "And the cushion and the rug that didn't go over the cliff with the car but stayed on the cliff edge. What about that?"

"Well, what?" asked the superintendent, puzzled.

"Anyhow," Bobby went on, "there's clearly enough for a general call to go out to pull in young Pope. If he doesn't come forward, there'll have to be a good reason. As there may be," he added heavily. "I told you Vea Burden had been seen hereabouts."

"Well," the superintendent pointed out, "if it's right she's really Mrs Mark Monk, natural enough for her to want to find him."

"I hope that's all there's to it," Bobby answered. "But I would like to have a chance to talk to her—and like it still better if we could think up some excuse to hold her for questioning."

"Why?" asked the superintendent. "Got her on your nerves all right, haven't you?"

"I have," agreed Bobby, grimly enough.

"I don't see why. Is there any chance there was a put-up job between Miss Kerr and the chap who scooted off, whoever he was? Pope, as likely as not, or some one else she had arranged to meet; only when they saw us, the chap got the wind up and thought it was time to bunk and better to leave the girl to face the music, if any."

"She's got a pretty badly scratched face to show," Bobby remarked. "Kind of guarantee of good faith."

"There's that," admitted the superintendent; "but when a girl is really dotty on a man, there's practically nothing she'll stick at."

"Not even at a scratched face?" Bobby asked.

"Oh, well," said the superintendent, slightly shaken.

"Anyhow, your chaps have got their man all right," said Bobby, who had been watching the entrance to the mine premises. "Here they are back again, and bringing some one with them." A moment later, he added: "Not young Pope, though. It's Jerry George."

"Now," said the superintendent, with much satisfaction, "now we really are getting somewhere. I always thought those cigarettes were at the bottom of the whole thing, and not so much the love-a-duck business you've talked about all the time. We can hold Jerry on a charge of stealing the lady's bike, and that'll give us a good chance to put him through it."

He looked very confident indeed, as though he felt that now at last the trump card was in their hands. Bobby felt less assured. He knew his Jerry George better than did the superintendent, and held him for one of the cleverest rogues of his acquaintance—and one of the deadliest: all the deadlier in that he never risked his own skin if he could help it. Now Jerry and his escort were near, and Bobby could see that neither of the two constables looked particularly confident. As soon as they were within earshot, Jerry stepped forward briskly, bestowed upon Bobby a friendly smile and nod of recognition and called out loudly:

"If you're in charge here, I want a summons against these men for dangerous driving. Most disgraceful thing I ever saw. Pelting round a blind corner on the wrong side full tilt. It's a wonder I'm alive."

"We weren't," said the constable who had been driving. "I was driving careful, though maybe a bit to the centre on account of the state of the road, and you were a lot more wrong side than we were."

"Now, now, aren't there the tracks to show?" demanded Jerry reproachfully.

"Not so much now you've done your best to mess 'em up," retorted the other. "Drove sideways you did—and backed and did a skid and all on purpose, so as the tracks wouldn't make sense in all the mud there was."

"What's all this?" demanded the superintendent.

"That's what I want to know," declared Jerry volubly. "There I was driving quietly along, eyes on the road, and first comes a lunatic tearing away on a push-bike. He sees me, lets out a yell, jumps off his bike, throws it into the ditch, and bunks off cross country as fast as he can on his own flat feet. Trying to beat the Olympic record, it looked like. Well, no business of mine, so I started up again, and then these fellows of yours came pelting hell for leather round that blind corner. On the wrong side of the road, too. If I hadn't been mighty smart there'd have been a crash all right. As good a bit of driving," declared Jerry George complacently, "as ever was, though I say it myself. As near as nothing you had one dead, me, and two deaders of your own chaps all set for an inquest."

"It was him on the bike all right," said one of the constables. "We saw him. It wasn't too good driving on that road—all mud and rain—so we didn't put on speed, being sure of him, us doing forty to his twenty, and able to keep it up as he couldn't. And a clear road and open country both sides. But he slipped round a corner where the road turned. Wasn't out of sight more than two minutes. We nearly did a skid, and that held us a minute or so, and when we rounded the corner there was him in a car driving straight at us and the bike in the ditch, and no sign anywhere of any one but him sitting there in his car grinning at us."

"Not grinning," protested Jerry in a very hurt voice. "You don't grin when you've just missed being killed by inches. And the bloke was there to see all right if you had looked, which you never did. Scooting away he was for all he was worth. I could have shown you, only I didn't know what it was all about, besides being busy thanking my stars I was still alive. I ought to take the case into court, and so I would, only for it's being police. Because I do know you do your best, and when you make bloomers like this, it's generally only excess of zeal, and not meant. So," said Jerry generously, "we'll say no more about it. After all, no harm done, and if it wasn't for the police where would we all be? Gangsters and black market getting a free run, and decent respectable people like me unable to sleep in our beds in peace."

Bobby said admiringly:

"A most handsome tribute to our work. I'm sure we all appreciate it."

The superintendent said nothing, for the very good reason that he was speechless.

"It's why he pinched the lady's bike," said the constable. "There was his car parked where he had left it, engine running and all, and he knew he had to get to it in a hurry. As he did, and pitched the bike into the ditch and drove his car straight back at us, making up his fairy story at the same time."

"Oh, come, come," said Jerry reproachfully. "But there," he added, tolerant now, "I suppose you have to put up some sort of story as an excuse."

"Finger-prints?" asked the superintendent, recovering slightly.

"Mine," said Mr George. "All over. Had to pick the bike up to show your chaps where it was. Or I do believe it would be there still."

"Backed twenty yards he did," said the constable, "shouting at us all the time, and then jumped out and grabbed the bike so as to explain his dabs."

"What are dabs?" asked Jerry George, all puzzled innocence.

"Quite a good story you've managed to put up," Bobby told him. "Jolly clever. By the way, can you tell us what this man you say you saw was like?"

"Oh, didn't I say?" asked Jerry. "Sorry. Stupid of me, but I really was a bit upset. It was a young chap of the name of Pope, David Pope, I think. I've seen him at Bexley House."

CHAPTER XXV
"STIR THE BROTH"

NEITHER BOBBY nor the superintendent quite knew what to make of this; or, for that matter, whether to believe a word of it. But at least, if not true, it was well invented. Bobby had an idea that Jerry was slyly pleased with himself and what he had just said. He was the first to break the silence. He said:

"Well, if that's all I suppose I can get on, can I? And I warn you, if I catch cold, standing out in the rain like this, I'll expect you to pay the doctor's bill."

"Awfully sorry," Bobby apologized. "We are so wet ourselves we never thought of that."

"Soaked through and through already he was," interposed one of the constables. "Soaked as he wouldn't if he had been in his car driving all the time, as he let on he was. Dry as a bone he would have been, and he wasn't, not him. Dripping."

"That was because of having to hop out in the wet to show you where the bike was in the ditch," explained Jerry smoothly.

"An answer for everything, Mr George, haven't you?" observed Bobby, with real admiration.

"Along," said Jerry, turning his eyes up, "—along of always speaking the truth, as I was taught at my mother's knee. 'Speak the truth, my child, and shame the devil,' was what she always said. And I've never forgotten."

He looked round, as if seeking approbation. He observed instead only signs of gloom and great annoyance. This pleased him enormously. He could not resist giving an almost imperceptible wink, a faint flutter of an eyelid rather, in the direction of Bobby, who alone he felt really appreciated him. The superintendent exchanged a whisper or two with Bobby. Then he said:

"We've found a dead man's body here."

Jerry stared. He was clearly not quite sure whether this was meant seriously.

"A dead man's body?" he repeated. "Having me on, aren't you?"

"We want you to see if you can identify it," the superintendent continued, ignoring this.

"A dead man," Jerry repeated once again. He looked scared now and doubtful. He uttered a resounding—and irrelevant— blasphemy. He said: "A deader? You mean it? Honest? It's not one of your tricks?"

"We don't play tricks," said the superintendent with dignity.

"If you don't mind coming with us," suggested Bobby, "you can see for yourself."

"Who is it?" Jerry asked, still very pale and disturbed.

"That's where we want your help," Bobby told him. "We think it may possibly be some one you know."

"Not young Pope?" Jerry asked, almost in a whisper.

"Wouldn't it be better if we waited to see what you thought, without our naming any one first?" Bobby suggested.

"I never did care for seeing stiffs," Jerry muttered, and certainly his looks confirmed his words. "Is . . . is it all knocked about?"

The superintendent came back. He had been to give directions for his car to be brought round. He had also, as Bobby had suggested, sent one of his men off with instructions to have a look-out kept for Pope, or any other stray pedestrian or stranger in the neighbourhood. This was on the off-chance that Jerry had been speaking something even remotely resembling the truth. Not that this appeared to either of them a very likely contingency; but, then, one never knows. Jerry now expressed a preference for driving his own car rather than accompanying them in theirs, and to this there was no objection.

They started off accordingly, and the superintendent observed as they drove away:

"You heard at first he thought it might be Pope's body was found. Shows him up for the liar he is, saying it was Pope he saw on the bike."

"He would say," Bobby pointed out, "that he thought it was Pope he saw, and then thought he might have been mistaken. He could get away with it like that."

"He could get away with anything," grumbled the superintendent; and Bobby was almost inclined to agree, even though long experience had taught him that in the end that axiom always failed—once, and once was generally enough. "'Never forgot what he learned at his mother's knee,'" quoted the superintendent bitterly.

"He is plainly both upset and frightened," Bobby went on. "The thing is, how deep in is he? He is fully capable of murder, but only, I think, as the back-room boy; pulling the strings, but never showing in person. You noticed he didn't ask what we were doing at the mine, though he was certainly in the spinney, like the Maggie Kerr girl, trying to find out. You can get a good view from the farther end where the ground rises. I take that to mean he took it for granted we were after the missing lorry load of cigarettes he seems to think Monk double-crossed him over. What he wanted was to see if we had found it."

"Wheels within wheels," said the superintendent, with some show of temper. "And then some."

"And then some," repeated Bobby. "Still, things are moving."

"Where?" asked the superintendent; and Bobby did not answer a question that only reflected his own uneasiness. "Give me," said the superintendent, with passionate intensity, "a nice, clean, uncomplicated murder, not one all mixed up with loving and kissing and black-market cigarettes, and girls pinching each other's boys, and missing lorries, and women not caring because they know they're going to die anyhow, and a heap of suspects popping in and out one after the other like—like peas in a pod," concluded the superintendent, because he couldn't think of any other simile.

Bobby sympathized. They reached the little lonely public-house where lay the dead man in the silence of all-equalizing death. The innkeeper left his work in his garden, where he had been busy, and came across to them, bringing with him the key of the temporary mortuary.

"A lady's been," he said. "Said she had heard and there was a friend of hers hadn't been home. I told her it wasn't no sight for a woman, but she didn't take notice."

"Did you let her go in?" the superintendent asked.

"There wasn't no harm in that, was there?" the innkeeper asked in return. "There was something about her," he added.

"Did she say anything?" Bobby asked.

"No, not a word, and I didn't ask. She stood and looked, and that was all, and then she went away. Queer she looked. Like death, like it was death itself come to make sure of death."

"Can you describe her?" Bobby asked.

"More like a corpse than a living woman," the innkeeper said again. "And when she coughed, then it was like that would kill her all over again."

"Vea Burden," interposed Jerry, who had been listening to all this. "Was she wearing long earrings?"

"That's right," the other answered. "To and fro they went, so you had to watch. I wasn't sorry when she went. I asked who I was to say had been, but she didn't take notice. Only stared at you and went away."

"Vea Burden?" repeated Jerry uneasily. "What's she want?"

No one attempted to answer him. They entered the shed, and the superintendent turned down the sheet with which those sad remains had been covered. Jerry gave one glance and turned away. From the door of the shed, his back to them, he said:

"It's him all right—Mark Monk. Not much to go on, but it's him. His wrist watch. He tried to sell it me once. Got his initials inside. M. M. Looks like there had been a try to burn it up."

"Petrol," said the superintendent. "To destroy identity. You never can."

He and Bobby followed Jerry outside, relieved, both of them, to get away from the heavy odour of death that filled the little shed. Bobby said:

"I think we may take it for certain Vea Burden knew. So I think we may take it, too, that she's got half of what she wanted."

"To know what had happened to Monk?" said the superintendent.

"Yes," said Bobby.

"Think she'll clear off home again now?" asked Jerry hopefully.

"No," said Bobby.

"You mean," said the superintendent, "the other half she wants is to know who did it?"

"Well, what for? What's the good?" muttered Jerry. "Can't bring him back to life, can she? and her with one foot in the grave herself."

"That's always in her mind," Bobby told them. "Not much time."

"Ought to make her settle down quiet and peaceful," declared Jerry.

"It's what we've got to know, too," observed the superintendent, but not hopefully. "This Vea Burden you all keep talking about and I've never seen, will have to be told to keep out."

"Yes, of course," agreed Jerry eagerly.

"The difficulty," Bobby explained, "is that we can't act without given cause. Evidence. But she may. Act, I mean. And I don't know what we can do about it."

"It's your job, up to you," declared Jerry, indignant now. "Your duty. What's police for?"

"Oh, yes, up to us all right," Bobby agreed. "But nothing we can do. There's no charge we can make. Unless, of course," he added, "some one provides us with evidence that she was mixed up in something illegal. Like the theft of that lorry-load of cigarettes. If we had proof of that, we could get her put out of the way of doing mischief for a few months, and by that time she might see things differently, have second thoughts."

Jerry was looking about as scared and dismayed as any man well could, his fat white face all a-quiver with fear and doubt and hesitation.

"Suppose," he quavered presently, "you got a letter to-night—it mightn't be signed."

"Anonymous letters are no good to us," Bobby said. He yawned. "Unless, of course," he added, "it gives concrete evidence. By the way, Mr George, you and Monk had some sort of disagreement that same night at Bexley House, hadn't you? I wonder if Vea Burden knows? Oh, well, I daresay we shall know all about it if she does bring it off."

"Bring what off?" demanded Jerry angrily; but did not wait for, or expect, or even desire, an answer. "Nice way to talk," he complained. "Police all over. Don't care two curls of a pig's tail what happens to any one if only they can make a splash about it for themselves."

Bobby suppressed another yawn.

"Well, Mr George," he said sweetly, "if a rogue gets his throat cut, what can we do but come together and thank Heaven we are quit of him?"

Under his breath Jerry said something. Just as well it was inaudible. Then he went off to his car. They watched him drive away. The superintendent said:

"You've put the wind up him all right."

"Help to push things along," Bobby said. "Nothing like greasing the wheels. When things do move, you have a chance. You haven't any chance at all if everything stops just as it was. Stir the broth. That's what I always tell our chaps."

"Does that mean you think he is our man?"

"Might be," Bobby answered cautiously. "We've got to consider it as a possibility. But we'll have to be a lot more clear about how all these people stand to each other."

"Suppose," said the superintendent, "he does get bumped off by this Vea Burden girl, which is what I suppose you have in mind . . .?"

"At any rate," retorted Bobby grimly, "Jerry has it in his, and he knows her pretty well—better than I do."

"Gives us," complained the superintendent, "no chance to get on with our proper work, all these murders and things."

"I shouldn't much care," Bobby went on, pursuing his own line of thought, "to be in the shoes of any one—any one at all, man or woman—Vea Burden chooses to believe did—that." He glanced over his shoulder at the closed door of the shed behind them. He gave a faint smile. He said: "Jerry's up against it, and knows it. He'll get no sympathy from me—as big a scoundrel as any I know. He is quite well aware Vea may think he is the man, even if he isn't."

"He can't very well help knowing that, the way you rubbed it in," observed the superintendent. "And I shouldn't wonder if he isn't more than half afraid you may tell her as much and set her on him with the idea of making it easy for us to pull her in afterwards. What he meant about making a splash."

"I hadn't thought of it like that," Bobby admitted. "Anyhow, if he does think so, it'll all help. Get it moving. That's what I want. I was beginning to be afraid we were up against a dead end."

"Does all that," asked the superintendent, "come under the Home Office regulations?"

"I'll look 'em up and see," Bobby promised. "But regulations are only the hurdles you've got to clear if you mean to get there first. Jerry's got to weigh it all up, and it'll be quite interesting to see what he does, and probably useful as well. Vea may very well get after him, or he's scared she may, which comes to the same thing. Yet he can't do much about it or ask our help without losing all chance of getting his cigarettes back—and that might mean a loss of four thousand pounds—enough to sink him, he said. His money or his life, in fact, and he's got to choose which to risk."

CHAPTER XXVI
"WHAT'S SHE DONE?"

ALL THIS had taken so much time that Bobby, at least, was glad to return to his hotel to relax into a bath with dinner to follow and the prospect of an early bed. So probably were most of the others concerned in the investigation, though officers of the police, when engaged on an important case, know nothing of five-day weeks or double pay for overtime.

The rain stopped during the night and the wind fell. But when Bobby inquired he was told that the sea would be still far too rough for any attempt to be made as yet to recover the crashed motor-car.

"Even if there's anything of it left," the pessimistic comment was added.

There was, too, a message from London. It was to the effect that one of the 'three Marys' had been traced. She was a Miss Martin—that was her real name—and she was employed as a receptionist at a Bodmin hotel. 'Very handy and convenient, too,' said the message, hinting subtly that Bobby was just being too lucky—as always. So Bobby rang up the superintendent and suggested they should go to Bodmin together and see if Miss Martin had anything of interest to say. The superintendent pleaded pressure of work.

"Got my hands full," said the superintendent. "This Round Table business. Not a man or a minute to spare. There were seven reporters on my doorstep this morning, and I've got to see the Guv. as well and tell him all about it. He's only just got back from abroad, you know. If you must have murders in London," he added plaintively, "I do wish you would keep them there. They don't go with Cornish air."

The 'Guv.' was, of course, the Chief Constable, who would naturally wish to be informed in full detail of all these sensational events occurring during his absence. The superintendent added that he didn't suppose Miss Martin would have anything much to say. How could she? For his part, he didn't know why Bobby had been making such a fuss about finding her and the other two Marys. Did he, asked the superintendent, with a touch of irony, expect Miss Martin to turn out to be the missing Bella Winlock? Bobby said very seriously that one never knew. In his experience anything was always liable to turn out to be something else. So the superintendent said anyhow it was a nice morning after the storm, and no doubt Bobby would enjoy the drive to Bodmin. 'Into Bodmin and out of the world', the superintendent quoted the old Cornish saying, and then hung up, and Bobby went to get the small car he was now provided with.

It was, in fact, a very pleasant morning, and Bobby would no doubt have found it a pleasant drive had not his mind been so much preoccupied with so many and such varying thoughts, and had he not also managed to miss his way, so that it was lunchtime before he reached the ancient 'city of the monks,' and the hotel where Miss Martin's presence had been reported.

However, he had no objection to giving lunch what the officials call 'first priority', especially as the glance he had of a big, handsome, rather showy girl at the receptionist's desk assured him that she was certainly not Bella.

Not, then, till after lunch did he explain his identity and ask for the privilege of a quiet chat with Miss Martin. Not, he explained, as he was always careful to do in such cases, anything that concerned her personally, but it was possible she might be able to give some useful information.

All the same, it was a very nervous Miss Martin who came to share coffee with him in a quiet corner of the lounge.

"It's about our not giving our own names, isn't it?" she asked, with mingled resentment and trepidation. "We didn't want to be mixed up with police. It doesn't do you any good, especially in our line."

"Oh, come, not so bad as all that," Bobby protested. "Why, the most blameless bishop on the bench might know something to help us, and then we should have to ask him."

"I'm not a bishop," Miss Martin pointed out with simple finality.

Bobby admitted the fact, and produced a photograph of Bella Winlock.

"Recognize it?" he asked.

"It's her all right," Miss Martin said at once. "I thought it was her was the trouble. Coo! You would never have expected it and her such a nice, quiet, shy sort of kid. Couldn't say 'Boo' to a goose, you'd have thought. What's she done?"

"Run away from home," Bobby said carelessly. "There's some missing jewellery, too. But I mustn't say more. There may be some explanation. Whose idea was it to give false names and addresses?"

"Oh, it was hers all right," Miss Martin declared. "She seemed pretty well frightened out of her skin when she knew we were being asked for. She told us it was about drugs. Going to be a big sensation. She said a man named Bobby Owen she knew had told her all about it. He was a sort of disreputable hanger-on of the police, she said."

"Oh, she did, did she?" asked Bobby, slightly taken aback.

"It was all mixed up with that car that nearly knocked us down," Miss Martin went on. "It nearly knocked her down, too, almost at the same time."

"Oh, it did, did it?" asked Bobby, which was at any rate a slight change from his previous remark, and all for the moment he felt capable of.

"Drugs," said Miss Martin, who was beginning to feel more at her ease, and therefore more chatty. "Packed with 'em, that car, and why they were speeding the way they were. Simply had to."

"No doubt," agreed Bobby.

"In a way it's how we came to pal up," Miss Martin continued. "She had heard of us being nearly run down and killed, and she had, too. And then it turned out her name was the same as mine—Mary Martin. It was rather funny, wasn't it?"

"It was very funny," agreed Bobby once again.

"She seemed awfully nice," Miss Martin went on, "and rather jolly in a quiet way though awfully shy, especially of boys. We used to have her on about that—turn pale she would if anything like a man came near. Lots of money, too, and free with it. Always wanted to pay for everything. Of course, we wouldn't let her. She said it was so nice of us to let her join on. She had been going hiking with a girl friend, you see, and she had never turned up. She didn't know why, and she had been feeling all lost and lonely on her own."

"I suppose she would," agreed Bobby. "But why did she suggest your giving wrong names?"

"Well, none of us wanted to get mixed up with talk about drugs—especially me. You do hear of it sometimes in our line. You have to keep your eyes open in the hotel business. Never know what guests are up to, you don't. You've got to watch 'em. I could tell you things about guests you would never believe," she added, regarding him with wide eyes.

Bobby said he was sure she could, and gently brought her back to the point.

"It wasn't only that," she admitted. "She let on, too, she didn't want it to come out she was hiking in Cornwall when her people thought she was visiting an aunt in Aberdeen. Only she had cut it, because of her aunt being such a pious old cat, and if it came out there would be an awful scene. It was a little like that with me, too."

"Dear me," said Bobby. "I hope you haven't an aunt in Aberdeen, too, or, if you have, that she isn't a pious old cat."

"It wasn't that," Miss Martin explained and added, a little proudly, that her aunt was a chorus-girl. "Only where I was before," she went on, "they asked me to stay another week till the new receptionist came, and I didn't want, because I thought I would like a holiday before coming here. So I said I had to start here at once, or I would lose the job. But if they got to know I had had them on a bit they wouldn't like it, and I might want to go back. You never know in our line where you may be next."

"I see," said Bobby. "And the other young lady?"

"Oh, she just joined in with us; she thought it was fun. Of course, she didn't like the idea of being mixed up in anything to do with opium and things. No one would. People talk so."

"They do," admitted Bobby. "Did your namesake ever talk about herself?"

"Oh, no, hardly ever. She was very quiet always, so you hardly knew she was there, and always grateful if you spoke to her or took any notice. She did say she was looking for a new job because her boss had been cheeky one day and so she never went back, and she thought she would have a holiday before trying anywhere else. If you ask me," Miss Martin went on, "I think she had had an upset with her boy. We teased her sometimes, me and my friend, about her being so frightened of men and hadn't she ever had a boy? She looked ever so queer, you can't think, and she said she had lost him."

"Did she say how?"

"Oh, no. We didn't ask. She seemed real upset. I think that was why she always kept out of the way of men much as she could. I told her she wouldn't do for the hotel business."

"Was she thinking of it?"

"She asked a lot of questions. People often do. Everyone seems to think it's just lovely, working in an hotel. They soon know better if they do—jolly soon. One place I had the job of arranging flowers for the banquets. Every one thought it was ever so nice, just arranging flowers. They ought to try it on a cold morning with your fingers in cold water for hours and thorns and all."

"You rather put her off, I suppose," Bobby suggested.

"She wouldn't ever have done," declared Miss Martin with emphasis. "And her that shy with men. In our job you have to know how to give the men as good as you get—and then some. Only not being sniffy about it, so as they'll go sulky and perhaps leave, or else complain about you being stuck up. Take a box of chocolates if it comes your way—which isn't ever now, with points and all—but watch your step—and him. Keep 'em where they belong."

"Moral maxims for a receptionist," smiled Bobby. "I hope the young lady understood."

"She was that soft she wanted to know if there wasn't any hotel job where you could keep away from men. As if you ever could—or wanted to," added Miss Martin in a burst of candour. "I said, well, she might try the kitchen, if she knew how to cook, and she said she didn't but she could wash up. I had to laugh."

"I shouldn't think washing up would appeal to her," Bobby said.

"She was that soft," repeated Miss Martin. "Like a baby. Innocent she was, as if she hadn't been born more than a week or two. She'll learn. I said if she wanted to try, there wasn't an hotel in the country from the Ritz down to any village pub that didn't want help with the washing up. All she had to do was to ask, and they would have her on the job before she knew where she was—and before she had time to wish she wasn't."

Bobby thanked her warmly for a most interesting and instructive talk. It had given him a lot to think over, especially in what she had said about the drug smuggling. He would, he said, frowning portentously, have to keep an eye on that police hanger-on—what was his name?—oh, yes, Bobby Owen—who seemed to know so much about what was going on. Less than he thought though, perhaps. Could Miss Martin tell him, finally, what was her general impression of her namesake? And, by the way, was she in hiking outfit when she joined them?

"Oh, yes, very posh," declared Miss Martin. "More like a 'Vogue' outfit, though, than what you really want for a proper hike. Like the little innocent she was, to go in for that sort of outfit. She was awfully sweet, all the same. Always ready to do anything you asked." Miss Martin paused and seemed to hesitate for a moment. "All the same, she had a little temper of her own," she went on. "I saw her once—it gave me quite a turn. Something had upset her, I don't know what. All over at once." Miss Martin paused again and this time looked a trifle puzzled, a little worried. "It was funny," she said. "The kid never wanted her own way, and yet it was always what she said that we did."

"Force of personality," Bobby suggested.

But Miss Martin, surprised, said: "Oh, no, it wasn't that, because she hadn't any." Bobby didn't pursue the point, but once again expressed his gratitude for a most interesting talk. He couldn't, he said, offer her a box of chocolates, because he hadn't any points, but he would venture to send her a few flowers, if she would accept them, and she could depend on his always staying where he belonged. Highly delighted, Miss Martin told him to get away with him. So they parted on the best of terms, Bobby extracting a final promise that she wouldn't say anything for the time about their pleasant little chat. It was a promise he had not much hope she would be able to keep for long, though he hoped the flowers might help.

It was to the local police station that he went next. There after a time he got in touch with his superintendent friend.

"I've had my talk with the Martin girl," he reported, "and she's told me a lot. What she says seems to fit in with my own theory of what happened, and I think I know now where Miss Winlock may be."

To Bobby's surprise, he could hear the superintendent chuckling, a warm, rich, well-satisfied chuckle.

"You're just a day behind the fair, old man," said the superintendent. "We've got full information now. A complete confession. And we know where to pick up our little lost Bella. A nice chase that young woman has led us, too. I'll talk to her like a Dutch uncle. When I've done with her she won't want to play any more tricks for a bit. I'm coming right along. Tell you all about it as soon as I can get there. Just you stay where you are for the time."

The superintendent hung up then, and Bobby sat back, looking more surprised than perhaps he had ever done before.

CHAPTER XXVII
"THE POOR KID"

SINCE THERE was, till the superintendent arrived, nothing to be done, Bobby went back to the hotel. There he sat and wondered at this new development till presently the superintendent came bustling in, all smiles and hearty confidence.

"Got it all clear at last," he announced. "Full statement. Seems you weren't quite on the right track."

"I was never quite sure," Bobby protested, "which was the right track. So many of them, all different, all had to be followed up."

"Well, you did rather fancy one, didn't you?" the superintendent pointed out, "and that's the one that's gone west now."

"Oh, I had my favourite," Bobby admitted, and didn't say, but thought, that he was sticking to it till he knew more.

"Not that in my view," said the superintendent generously, "you ever had a chance. Too many dashed clever false clues laid on."

"Like the car driven over the cliffs into the sea?" Bobby remarked.

"You spotted that all right," the superintendent admitted, still being generous. "Smelt a rat, didn't you? Well, you were right. A plant to put us off, it's turned out, because if we thought it was the murderer done a suicide jump—well, no good looking any more. Always a mistake to take things at face value, and I give you full marks there."

"Thank you," said Bobby, more meekly still.

"Though it was fairly plain, too," the superintendent added, fearing that so much praise might go to Bobby's head. "Once you took it in that the rug and cushion and so on had been deliberately left to call attention. Only necessary to stop and think a bit. Because no one going to do a suicide jump like that was likely to go throwing out rugs and cushions to show what had happened."

"True," said Bobby. "Only so few do."

"So few do?" repeated the superintendent, puzzled. "Oh, stop to think, you mean." He looked a little doubtful, as if vaguely aware of undertones, and then decided that, having kept Bobby on tenterhooks long enough, he would get on with his story. "Know all about it now," he repeated, and went to the door. "Ask the gentleman to come in, will you?" he called to the constable outside.

"Gentleman?" Bobby asked questioningly.

"Oh, it's not the lady of the earrings," the superintendent told him smilingly. "Thinking of her, were you?"

"I'm thinking of her all the time," Bobby answered, with a certain grimness the superintendent failed to notice. "I'm a long way from feeling happy about her."

"We're keeping a look-out for her," the superintendent said, "but nothing much we can do. No possible charge. No evidence. We could warn her we were watching her."

"She knows that Death is watching her," Bobby said. "It makes her unpredictable," and before he could say more the door opened to admit a somewhat uncomfortable-looking David Pope.

Bobby greeted him. David nodded a sulky acknowledgment. The superintendent said to him:

"Mr Owen had a talk with you in town, hadn't he?" and again Pope nodded a sulky assent.

"Came to my office," he said, "and asked a lot of questions about things I didn't know anything about."

"And one or two you did," Bobby remarked. "A snuff-box, for instance."

"Well, never mind that now," the superintendent interposed. "Just tell Mr Owen what you've told me. Right from the start."

"Well, it's this way," David obeyed. "I felt jolly uncomfortable after all that talk about the snuff-box and the rest of it. I went to see Maggie—Miss Kerr, I mean—and she told me about you knocking her up in the middle of the night and something having happened at Bexley House and bloodstains on her handbag. And then no one seemed to know what had become of Bella Winlock, and you had talked as if you thought she had something to do with it. Dropping on me, too, as if I had murdered Bella and stolen that beastly snuff-box of hers. Maggie said it sounded as if you thought we had done it together. It was awfully upsetting for both of us. So I made up my mind I had better try to find out what had really happened and see if I could get hold of Bella and ask her."

"Quite the little detective," remarked the superintendent tolerantly.

"It wasn't that," protested David. "Hang it all, with you chaps after me and Maggie as well, I had to do something, hadn't I?"

"What made you think of Cornwall?" Bobby asked.

"It was something Bella said when she was asking me about the snuff-box. I forget exactly, but it made me think she might be there. Anyhow, it seemed clear something was jolly wrong, and I didn't want any more police turning up at the office. After what Maggie told me, it did look as if there had been bad trouble at Bexley House and Bella was trying to keep out of the way for a time. It struck me if she had gone into hiding she might have remembered the Round Table Mine. If you took some tinned stuff with you, you could hang out there as long as you liked. You could light a fire at night in any of the outbuildings and do a little cooking or boil some water. No one would dream of looking there. Only now you've found Mark Monk's body, haven't you? I suppose next thing you'll be thinking that was me." He had an uneasy air when he said this, and paused, evidently hoping for the reassurance he did not receive. He went on: "You can be jolly sure if I had known I shouldn't have slept quite as well as I did. You see, there was a suit-case there, with Bella's initials, in one of the outbuildings. I thought she was sure to come for it, and I waited to see."

"She did come?"

"Oh yes. It was a bit of a shock when she saw me. I thought she would faint, or run away, or something. I told her the fix I was in with you after Maggie and me. She was awfully sorry about that, only the poor kid was in a jolly sight worse fix herself. She told me all about it."

"About what happened at Bexley House?" Bobby asked.

"That's right. She was arranging to go off with Mark Monk. They had been married privately."

"Married?" repeated Bobby, surprised, for this was something that had not occurred to him.

"It's really how the whole thing started," David explained. "She said she was of age and she wasn't, she was under twenty-one at the time of the marriage. I suppose that could be called perjury?"

"It could," agreed Bobby.

"Monk ought to have had more sense than to let her," declared David severely. "She didn't understand how serious it was. She wouldn't, would she?"

"Wouldn't she?" said Bobby.

"Well, I mean, women always are a bit funny about their age, aren't they? They don't think of it as telling lies. But a chap called Harper got to know."

"He comes into it, does he?" Bobby exclaimed, but less surprised this time.

"I should say he did," declared David. "Why, he's the whole thing. First of all he tried to blackmail Bella. Told her she would be sent to prison for perjury if it was found out. The poor kid. She was frightened out of her life. That was one reason why she agreed to run away with Monk. Harper got to know about that, too, and how she and Monk had arranged to meet at Bexley House. But when she got there, it was Harper waiting. He told her a policeman had come to arrest her. He said Monk had tried to get rid of the policeman and there had been a fight and the policeman had been knocked out, but so had Monk. It would be penal servitude for Monk, Harper told her, if the police got hold of him. The only thing for them to do, Harper said, was to get him as far away as possible at once, and for them both—Bella and Mark Monk—to go into hiding for a time till it blew over. He said if she would drive the car, he would put Monk, who was still unconscious, he said, in the back of the car. She must drive off as fast as she could till he recovered. It was his only chance, Harper said. Harper carried Monk out of the house and put him in the back of the car, and he said he had made Monk comfortable, and he mustn't be disturbed. Can you imagine any man playing such a ghastly farce?"

"Go on," Bobby said.

"You see the idea?" David asked. "I never knew any man could be such an awful villain. He was pushing it all off on her. Because of course the poor devil was dead, and Harper himself had done it. Of course, there hadn't been any policeman at all!"

"Of course not," Bobby agreed.

"A hellish trick," said the superintendent, and David gave him a grateful look.

"He was calculating that if she was found with the dead man in the car, then every one would think she had done it. You would, wouldn't you?"

"Pretty good circumstantial evidence," said the superintendent.

"We should have looked for confirmation, I hope," Bobby said. "Our job to check up on everything."

"Even after finding a girl driving away with a dead man in the back of her car?" asked David. "You would never have believed she didn't know. Well, anyhow, you can imagine how she felt. Or can you? Can any one? I mean, when she stopped after a time to see how he was getting on and found he was dead. It's a wonder she didn't go mad. She says she thinks she did. Go mad,

I mean. She just jumped back into the driving-seat and drove off as hard as she could. She says she thinks she was trying to get away from it. Poor kid! Of course, it didn't matter how fast she drove, she was taking it with her. Did you ever hear of anything more terrible? That poor child driving like mad through the night, knowing the murdered body of her dead husband was in the back of her car."

"I have not often heard of anything worse," Bobby admitted.

"It sounds like some of the horror stories you got from Germany," the superintendent said, and indeed he was looking pale.

"What happened next?" Bobby asked.

"She doesn't remember very clearly," David answered. "The next thing she is clear about she was at the Round Table Mine and she was screaming. She remembers that quite clearly. Only Harper was there before her, and he hit her to make her shut up, and then she saw he had got Monk's body out of the car and was carrying it away. So she ran for it as hard as she could. Luckily it was dark. She heard Harper shouting to her to come back, but she didn't, and a good thing, too, or he would have murdered her most likely, and now I'm afraid that that's what has happened."

"Why?" asked Bobby.

"She asked me to meet her again. She never came," David answered. "I'm sure she would have if she could. After she ran away from Harper she had only a little money, and no clothes or anything. So she went back and waited and made sure Harper had gone. But the car was there, so she got her suitcase from it and her money and changed into hiking things she had with her in her suit-case. Then, when she was leaving, she ran bang into Harper. You can imagine how she felt. Luckily there were some men working on the road near, so it was all right. He couldn't do anything to her while they were watching. Harper said he had got rid of Monk's body where no one would ever find it, and no one would ever know anything about it, and the best thing she could do was to let him drive her back to her father and mother so they could look after her. Luckily she had more sense than to trust him. Then he said they couldn't leave the car there for any one to find and he would drive it over the cliffs into the sea.

If she had gone with him, he would have sent her over the cliffs with it, ten to one."

"Probably," agreed the superintendent. "And then we should have found her body in the car. Verdict: Murder and suicide. And every one satisfied. Eh?"

He looked at Bobby for approval. Bobby said:

"I take it, Mr Pope, Miss Winlock told you all this when she found you at the Round Table Mine? How did she get in touch with you again?"

"I told her where I was staying. She rang me up. She asked me to meet her again, and I did. She was awfully nervy. She said she was still being followed. Harper. She was sure he meant to kill her. The poor kid! I was in the war, and I've seen how chaps look when the German Tiger tanks were on top of them and they in the open. I expect I looked that way myself. You don't forget. You haven't an earthly when the tanks catch you like that. Unless help comes, you know it's the end. Well, that's the way she looked, and if you've seen it once, you know it again all right. She knew she hadn't an earthly unless help came."

"I think she knew," Bobby agreed slowly. "I think she knew it was the end unless she got help. What makes you say you believe Harper has got hold of her?"

"Well, we had it all fixed up," David explained. "Maggie was going to help. We felt what we had to do was to get her safe from Harper and back with her people for them to look after her."

"Why didn't you come to us if you thought she was in danger?" demanded the superintendent, now official and severe again. "We would have seen nothing happened to her."

"She was sure you would just send her off to prison at once," David explained, "and both Miss Kerr and I thought the best thing was to get her back home first of all. Then they could decide what to do. Both Maggie and I were afraid she might kill herself unless we promised to do what she asked. She hinted at it once or twice, hinted she had some poison ready. When she didn't come, that's what I thought first. But where she was staying they said she had had a message from a Mr Pope asking her to go and meet him. It wasn't from me. I hadn't sent any message or anything. It must have been Harper using my name to get hold of her. If he has . . ."

"Sounds as if it might be him," agreed the superintendent. "Bad look-out if it was." He went on: "Well, Mr Pope, we'll have to ask you to put all this in writing. I'll get the inspector in charge here to take it. It'll take some time, because we shall want full details, commencing from the very first. Mr Owen and I will have to get busy. We don't want another murder on our hands, and in my view what you've told us justifies us in pulling in Mr Harper and hearing what he has to say. No time to lose, either."

CHAPTER XXVIII
"A LONE SHE-WOLF"

POPE WAS therefore sent off in the company of an inspector to have his statement taken down in full—a lengthy process, since every detail and phrase had to be carefully weighed and considered.

This settled, the superintendent came back to where Bobby was waiting, doodling idly on a scrap of paper in front of him.

"Good clear statement," the superintendent said. "In my view, what we've to do first and foremost is bring in this Harper bird. In my view, we might ask the Press to help. As much publicity as possible at this stage. If it does nothing else, it'll let Harper know he's wanted. Frighten him off the Winlock girl. She's had a narrow escape. Her own fault in a way, of course. In my view, if she had been stopped with that poor devil of a Monk's dead body in her car—well, who would have believed she didn't know all about it?"

"No one," said Bobby. "I wouldn't, for one."

"Well, there you are," said the superintendent, pleased. "Circumstantial evidence may be tricky, but when it's as strong as that it takes some getting round. At least, that's my view. And if we had found the poor child's body in the wrecked car when we recover it—well, there again. Closed the case for certain. Cunning. Murder and suicide would have been the verdict. And in my view Bella Winlock is in deadly danger still. While Harper's loose."

"In my view, too," said Bobby. "But not so much perhaps from Harper. Remember the dabs that weren't there?"

"Dabs? Finger-prints? Why? Where weren't they?"

"Not on the knife found at Bexley House?" Bobby reminded him.

"Gloves," the superintendent reminded Bobby. "Your own man said so. In his report."

"Would Harper be likely to be wearing gloves?" Bobby asked. "What is suggested is that there was a quarrel over Harper's attempt either at blackmail or possibly to stop Miss Winlock's running off with Mark Monk, because he was in love with her himself. Is he likely to have put on his gloves first? He is not a man likely to wear gloves habitually. The knife used was snatched up from a table already laid for a dance supper. That is consistent with the blazing up of a sudden passionate quarrel, not with premeditation. Also Harper was a trained commando. I don't see Harper picking up a knife if a row broke out. Not the instinct of a man trained in unarmed combat."

"Well, but—" said the superintendent.

"Women wear gloves," said Bobby.

"Well, but—" said the superintendent again and paused, and then there appeared a constable.

"Beg pardon, sir," he said. "A lady's here. Says she wants to see Mr Owen. Says it's important."

"A lady?" Bobby said. "Any earrings?"

"Earrings?" repeated the constable, taken aback by the question, suddenly afraid his powers of observation were being tested. "I . . . I didn't notice, sir," he confessed, and braced himself for the rebuke he expected.

"Good," said Bobby. "You would have noticed all right if she had them."

"Yes, sir," agreed the constable, whatever his inward doubts.

"You mean you thought it might be Vea Burden?" asked the superintendent. "Well, fetch her in, whoever it is," he said to the constable. He added: "The way that Vea Burden woman pops in and out! Gets on your nerves, doesn't it?"

"It does on mine," said Bobby grimly. "I hoped it might be her, though I suppose it wasn't likely. She plays a lone hand—a lone she-wolf. If it had been Vea, I was going to ask you to detain her for inquiries. We can always do that, can't we?"

"Well, but . . ." said the superintendent; and the constable reappeared, ushering in Grace Williams.

Bobby greeted her pleasantly, and explained to the superintendent that she had been at Bexley House and knew both Vea Burden and Harper.

"It's about Mr Harper," she explained. "He was to have met me, and he's never come."

"Another appointment not kept," Bobby remarked. "That's the second."

"Where were you to meet?" the superintendent asked.

"At the railway station—the bookstall," Grace answered. "He said he thought he had better go by himself first of all just to see, and when he didn't come I went to look. But I can't get any answer, and there's a boy says he saw a lorry drive away, and then a lady came and went away again."

"Done a bunk," exclaimed the superintendent. "Well, he won't get far."

"Not Alf Harper, he wouldn't, not on me. Why should he?" demanded Grace angrily.

"Where do you mean you went to look?" Bobby interposed. "Tell us all about it from the start, won't you?"

"It was Alf Harper came and told me," Grace explained. "That little devil of a Bella Winlock—as bad a piece of goods as ever was and couldn't leave a boy alone not to save her life— what had been ringing him up. What went on at Bexley House the night Mr Owen was there I never knew, and never asked, knowing enough to keep out of what wasn't my business. Something pretty bad, though, and if you ask me it was Jerry George, over the stuff him and Mark Monk had lifted."

"'"Convey," the wise it call',' Bobby murmured, but neither of the other two noticed. "Go on," he said to Grace.

"Whatever it was, Bella was mixed up in it. If you ask me, she was at the bottom of the whole thing. And it was her dragged in Alf. She would. Doing her poor-little-me stunt and getting her claws into Alf, same as with every fool of a man who came near her. She was that sort—a man-eater if ever there was. Things being a bit warm at Bexley House, and Mr Owen poking round and likely to go on poking away till he had it all out, she got Alf to help her clear out. And what he or any one else sees in that pale-faced, insignificant, little bit of nothingness beats me."

"Never mind that," Bobby said. "Go on with what you have to tell us."

"What Alf says is that he was in the cart, too, as well as her, and he had to see it through," Grace continued. "That's why he came chasing after her. But you could see he didn't feel the same way he did before. You can always tell. Whatever it was at Bexley House, it had turned him right round, and he hadn't any use for her any more. If you ask me, I think he was a bit scared. Of her, I mean."

"Quite likely," Bobby agreed. "You followed them both here, then. Was that it?"

"Well, I wasn't going to see her get off with Alf if I could help it," Grace explained. "Not me, not after all he had said. I went to a place where him and me had been once before. He wasn't there, but he heard about me asking. He came along, and wanted me to go back to town, and I said O.K., if he would come, too. He said he couldn't, him being in the jam he was, and getting worse, because Vea Burden was knocking around, and he said wherever she went there was a smell of death went with her."

"I know," Bobby said. "Yes. Go on."

"Alf said there had been enough of that sort of thing," Grace went on. "Next time I saw him he said he had seen Bella and she was panicking. She said Alf must help her or she would go straight to Mr Owen and tell him it was Alf done it all."

"Used young Pope," Bobby remarked, "as her messenger instead. Equally effective, and kept her out of my way."

"She said Alf was to meet her at a place in Upper Low Street here," Grace continued. "She said it was where Jerry George had the stuff hidden—I mean to say the stuff he and Mark Monk had got hold of."

"Jerry George?" repeated Bobby thoughtfully. "I don't think so. No. He was hunting for it all right. Probably where Mark Monk had it tucked away. Double crossing each other after the way of crooks all the world over. Probably Monk told Bella Winlock, and that's how she knew. Is Upper Low Street where you couldn't get an answer?"

"That's right," Grace answered. "I wanted to go along with Alf, but Alf said he had better be by himself first and then he would come back. He never did. So I went to see. There's an old place there of some sort all locked up, and I couldn't get any answer or anything. I asked some boys, and one of them said there had been a lorry drive away, and afterwards a lady had come and gone in, and then she had come out again and gone away, too."

"Could they say who was driving the lorry? Or what the lady was like?"

"No, they hadn't noticed. But one of them had a note of the number of the lorry. It's a game boys play."

She gave it, and the superintendent said with satisfaction:

"Well, he won't get far—whether it's Jerry George or Alf Harper or both of them—or any one else."

He hurried away to give the necessary instructions for the interception of the lorry, and Bobby asked Grace if the boys had said if the lady had stayed inside the building for any length of time.

"They didn't seem to know," Grace answered. "But they all said she didn't come out at once."

"I wonder what she was doing," Bobby said. "I think we had better push along at once and see if we can find out."

"That's what I want," Grace said.

The superintendent came back.

"That lorry won't get far," he repeated. "Thank the Lord for all small boys." Much surprised at himself for having said this, and remembering past and bitter experience, he added: "Little pests, want a good spanking, all of them."

"Don't be ungrateful," Bobby said. "What about paying a visit to Upper Low Street?"

CHAPTER XXIX
"ONLY ONE WENT AWAY"

UPPER LOW STREET proved to be a quiet little backwater of a place tucked away behind the ancient guildhall. At one end were a few of the typical Bodmin houses, small and squat, built of the local 'killas stone'. At the farther end was an old, long-deserted garage, whose struggling life had been snuffed out by the outbreak of the Second World War.

The high, heavy doors were locked, and the superintendent hesitated about forcing an entry. He asked: Were they justified in breaking in? Bobby said he didn't know, but he hadn't much liked that story told by the small boys of the lady who had entered and stayed a while and then gone away again. He would like to find out, if possible, what she had been up to. So, unless the superintendent absolutely forbade it, he would go ahead himself and take full responsibility.

The superintendent said nothing, which is always wise. The lock was of simple construction, it had recently been oiled, and in a very few minutes Bobby had the doors open.

Within was a vast, barn-like place, 'full of emptiness', as the Irishman said. Not swept and garnished, indeed, but void. Dirt, dust, cobwebs, certainly, and that was all. Sufficient traces, no doubt, in the shape of wheel-tracks and other confused markings, to show there had been recent visitors. A patch of oil, for example, on the floor, and other evident disturbances of the dust accumulated throughout long years of neglect. Nothing else. Only the unaccustomed light entering by the open doors, and, in the corners, shadows that by contrast seemed to lie there all the deeper.

"Nothing doing," said the superintendent. "A clean getaway. Not even anything where there would be a chance to find a dab or two."

"Nothing," agreed Bobby. "Wants explaining."

"Can't explain nothing, can you?" asked the superintendent. "Nothing comes of nothing," and this he said without any idea that he had enunciated a profound metaphysical truth or quoted a great Roman thinker.

"If there's nothing," Bobby said again, as he stood and stared around with that slow and careful gaze of his that asked of everything it rested on what secret was therein concealed, "if there's nothing, why did our girl friend those boys told about stay as long as she did?"

"Oh, well," the superintendent answered, "wanted a rest, perhaps, or powder her nose or something."

"Might be that," agreed Bobby.

He walked slowly up and down the empty building. Then he went into the yard at the back. This also was completely empty, and it was overlooked on both sides, so that clearly nothing much could have taken place here without its being noticed. There was no back entrance, and no sign that the yard had recently been used. He went back into the garage. The superintendent said:

"Aren't we rather losing time? Didn't you say you thought you knew now where Miss Winlock was? Hadn't we better get after her? No time to waste."

"No, indeed," Bobby agreed. "No. But all the same . . . all the same," he repeated vaguely.

"Any idea Harper might be hiding here? Is that it?" the superintendent asked. "I don't see where."

"I don't know that 'hiding' is the word I was thinking of," Bobby answered. "Miss Martin, without knowing it, dropped a hint when I was talking to her that made me think I could guess where Miss Winlock might be. But if it was our lost Bella those boys saw, then she may have departed elsewhere by now."

"In my view," declared the superintendent, "just as likely or more that it was Vea Burden they saw. She has a way of popping up."

"She has," agreed Bobby wholeheartedly. "What I'm afraid of is that she may pop out for a change. But the story young David Pope told us did suggest it was the Winlock girl knew about this place, not Vea. And not likely they both knew. Though, of course, that's possible. But not likely. What I think is that Bella came along to see how things had worked out."

"Wouldn't take her long," grunted the superintendent, who was growing impatient.

"Something did apparently," Bobby pointed out.

"Could she have met Vea Burden here?" the superintendent suggested.

"I hadn't thought of that," Bobby admitted, uneasily—so uneasily, indeed, that the superintendent grew uneasy, too.

"Only one went away," he said.

While the others watched, Bobby went again in turn into each of those dark corners of the garage, where already he had assured himself that nothing lay unperceived. But now he used his electric torch, bending down and examining carefully the flooring in each corner in turn. From that farther from the door, where the shadows lay the deepest, he called:

"There is a trap-door here. A cellar."

The superintendent and his men came over and joined him. They lifted the trap-door, and Bobby shone the light of his torch down the steep, wooden, ladder-like steps now disclosed.

"There's something there," the superintendent said. "It's a dead body. Have we found Bella Winlock at last? Was Vea Burden or some one waiting for her here?"

Two of his men were already clambering down the wooden steps, or ladder, rather. One of them called:

"It's a man. He's tied up. He's still alive. Not much more, though."

"A man?" the superintendent repeated. "If it's Jerry George, bit of a pity we did find him."

"More likely Harper," Bobby said. "The pieces are beginning to fit."

"Are they?" said the superintendent. "Blessed if I see it. The whole lot of 'em at cross purposes."

"Our Bella pulling the strings," Bobby said. "Bella, not Bunty this time."

"Who is Bunty?" asked the superintendent, no student of the drama.

Bobby went to help the two men who were bringing that inert, corpse-like, parcelled figure to the surface. The superintendent sent one of his other men to summon an ambulance. Bobby recognized Harper. He had been swathed in rope till he looked like a mummy. His mouth had been secured by surgical plaster. The ropes securing him were cut loose. His cramped and swollen limbs were massaged to restore circulation. Water was brought from a neighbouring house where-with to remove the surgical plaster. It was probably the pain caused by the renewed flow of blood through veins and arteries that did as much to restore consciousness as did the brandy given him at the first sign of returning life. He seemed to recognize Bobby, and muttered something inaudible.

Bobby knelt by his side.

"Can you tell us what happened?" he asked.

"Bella, it was Bella," Harper muttered. "It's hurting—hurting like hell," he complained.

"We're trying to get the circulation going again," Bobby explained. "What about Bella?"

Harper began to tell his story, interspersing it with many groans, and once with a sudden relapse into unconsciousness.

"Bella asked me to meet her here," he said, or rather gasped in detached and repetitive sentences. "She said she had made up her mind to tell the whole story. Only she wanted to see me first. She said she couldn't stand it any longer, not now she knew Bobby Owen was after her." Harper managed to produce something remotely resembling a smile. "She said you always got there in the end because you were too thick-headed to give up when you knew it was no good going on."

"Well, of all the cheek," commented Bobby, annoyed.

"She said most likely you would this time, too," Harper went on, "and she thought you must have guessed some of it already, so she might as well own up. Only what did I think? Because I knew."

"Knew what?" interposed the superintendent.

"I saw her," Harper said. "She didn't mean. She went wild when she knew. She grabbed a knife and jabbed it at him, and it was sharp, and it went in at the neck. All over in a minute. She said to meet her here. She never let on it was where Monk had stored that lorry-load of stuff because of Jerry George trying to do him down over his share. I didn't altogether trust her. I brought Grace along. We had sort of made it up, see? I didn't feel the same about Bella after what I saw, and Grace had come on her own because she knew things were all balled up, and she wanted to do something. So I asked her to come along, but to wait for me at the railway station."

"Good thing you did," Bobby remarked. "Or we might not have found you till too late. And that wouldn't have been so long. Go on."

"Soon as I got here I copped it," Harper said. "From behind. K.O. When I came to myself I was lying all tied up, and Jerry was fixing up a lorry ready for his getaway. I yelled to him to let me loose. He came over and kicked me in the ribs. He said that would teach me to come trying to sneak off with his stuff. He said I was a dirty thief, and I could lie there and rot. When I tried to speak he kicked me again, and then he shoved some rags in my mouth, so I couldn't talk, and went on with the lorry. When he was ready he came back and put a blunt sort of dinner-knife in my hands where he had them tied to my side, and said I could get myself free with that if I worked hard. He gave me a few more kicks and went off. He said I ought to be grateful to him for not doing me in. Then Bella came. God, I was glad to see her. God, I never dreamed, never."

"What happened?"

"She never spoke a word," Harper said; and as he lay he began to tremble. As he lay he trembled till he could no longer speak, and on his pale and pain-contorted features there showed a thin veil of sweat.

"Take it easy," said the superintendent; "take it easy, boy."

Harper tried again to speak, but could not. He began to cry. They waited a little, and Bobby gave him a drop more brandy.

"God in heaven!" Harper said. "I couldn't believe it. I thought she must be mad. I thought it might be all a dream. After I had helped her. After what I had done. She never spoke. Not one word. Not all the time. At first I thought she was trying to undo the knots. I managed to spit out the rags Jerry had pushed in my mouth. I said to her to mind. I said she was only tightening the knots. I said to take the knife Jerry had left and cut the rope. I said she was only making it tighter. She never spoke. She just went on tying and tying, and never said a word. I told her not to. I asked her what she was doing. I couldn't make it out.

She got some more cord—long, thin cord—and she tied it round and round me, and sometimes she pushed me over and then back again, and all the time she went on tying and never spoke a word. I kept asking her what she was doing. I said for God's sake to stop fooling. I said if it was a joke she had me scared all right. I said didn't she remember how I had helped her? I said wasn't it me planted his suitcase at the hotel for her, so as the cops would think he was still alive and let up. I promised to do anything she liked if only she would cut me loose instead of tying me up tighter than before. She never took notice. She mightn't have heard. She never said a word. I thought that I was going mad, or else that she was. I began to scream then. There wasn't any one to hear, and she had some surgical plaster she fastened over my mouth. Then she began to drag me along the floor. A long way. I didn't understand that either. I'm heavy, and sometimes she had to stop. She got me to the edge of a hole, and she pushed me over. Next thing I remember I was lying there in the dark and I couldn't move or anything. She had made a good job of it all right. Then it was you. What day is it? I must have been there days."

"About two hours," Bobby said, "and long enough. You're all right now, though, and here's the ambulance. They'll soon have you on your legs again in hospital."

"I'll never be the same again," Harper muttered. "Tell Grace, will you?"

CHAPTER XXX
"DRIVEN BY THE FURIES"

The ambulance departed. More help arrived. The superintendent began to waken from the sort of dazed trance into which these developments had plunged him. Not that that had prevented him from going very efficiently through the motions required to ensure that all necessary action was taken. But now that the unlucky Harper had been dispatched to hospital, and the ordinary routine was in full swing—sketching, photographing, measuring, all the rest of it—the superintendent found himself able to give his bewilderment and surprise full expression.

He caught hold of Bobby's arm as Bobby was trying to explain to the police photographers exactly what pictures he wanted taken and from what angle.

"Mr Owen," said the superintendent. He paused to gather his thoughts. He drew a deep breath. "Mr Owen," he said. "Well, now. Now then," and he looked anxiously for a response.

"Yes, indeed," Bobby answered sympathetically, knowing well how the superintendent felt, since in other cases he had felt much the same when elaborately constructed theories based on what had seemed firm premises collapsed beneath the destroying finger of fact.

"A young girl," said the superintendent. "A young girl like her. Pretty, too. A good looker. And then—this. Can you trust Harper's story?"

"Well, there's a certain amount of circumstantial evidence," suggested Bobby mildly. "Harper certainly didn't tie himself up like that or roll himself down those rather steep cellar steps."

"I wasn't meaning that," the superintendent said. "Couldn't it have been some one else? The Vea Burden woman or some one? Only he didn't want to say?"

"I don't think Harper could have been lying," Bobby answered. "I don't see why he should, and I don't think he was in any condition to invent fairy tales. The truth very literally squeezed out of him, I should say."

"Well, then," said the superintendent, facing it bravely, "that means Bella Winlock killed Monk. And hid his body."

"It does," agreed Bobby. "Always clear that some one killed some one that night at Bexley House. No direct evidence who was killed till we found Monk's dead body at the Round Table Mine. No direct evidence who did the killing till we got Harper's statement."

"But why—why should she? Why at the very start of their going off together? Afterwards, yes. If she found out he was going to dish her, as chaps like him mostly do. But at the very first. It doesn't—gell," said the superintendent with emphasis.

"At a guess," Bobby said, "Vea Burden told her that night that she herself was married to Mark. There's evidence Bella had a pretty fierce temper under that 'poor-little-me' pose of hers; and when a fierce temper generally kept under does break out, it is all the more uncontrollable and unpredictable. She had played fast and loose with so many men herself probably it was a bad shock to her to find one of them had been treating her the same way. Most likely he tried to get back the money—the five hundred pounds—he had allowed her to win gambling at Bexley House. And laughed at her for a little fool. I expect, too, what made it worse for her was that she was, for the time, genuinely in love with Monk. One of those men for whom women seem to fall instinctively—God knows why. Or perhaps He doesn't, either. Remember the whole set-up suggested a sudden violent flare-up of passion out of control. Just as the absence of dabs on the knife suggested gloves, and gloves suggested a woman. But no proof."

"That's all very well," grumbled the superintendent. "But why Harper? He said he helped her. We can hold him for that," he added, with a passing glint of satisfaction. "Accessory."

"Oh, yes, he was that all right," Bobby agreed. "And it was precisely because of that—because he knew the truth—that he had to be got rid of. A witness who might tell. Not only that. We had to be provided with a fresh wild goose to hunt—poor Harper! he was a bit of a goose, too. She tried it before. Drove her car over the cliffs into the sea, taking care to leave things lying about so as to make sure of attracting attention. She got rid of Monk's body at the Round Table Mine after that night-mare drive of hers. Probably her first plan had been to leave the body in the car when she crashed it and hope it would never be recovered. But there was a good chance it would be. Often the sea gives up its dead. The last thing she wanted. So she changed her plan. Her best hope was to keep us guessing, wondering what had really happened—and to whom. Keep us guessing. That was her trump card. Probably she even hoped we might decide there wasn't enough evidence to justify us in continuing the investigation."

"What I thought often enough," admitted the superintendent. "What I got a hint some of them in London thought. If it hadn't been for you sticking to it the way you did, it might have been that way."

"Even if the car were recovered," Bobby went on, "she hoped we might still keep on looking for a body that might have been washed out to sea. So long as we were busy doing that—wild-goose chasing—no doubt she felt fairly safe. Meanwhile she went into hiding. Couldn't afford to be found and questioned; and hoped she wouldn't be looked for, if she could get it believed that she was the victim and her body in the sea."

"If you're right," grumbled the superintendent, "she had it all nicely thought out."

"A young lady of infinite resource," Bobby agreed. "Admirable in improvisation. Most—man or woman—would have wanted to get as far away as possible. She was different. She joined up with two girl hikers. That explained her. Gave her a background—and an alibi. She chose them because she had heard of their complaint that her car in that wild midnight race had nearly knocked them down. Well, then, if she could get herself identified with them, then clearly she wasn't the driver. Though I don't expect she had all that carefully thought out. I think she acted on instinct, just as she did when she snatched up a knife from the supper-table and jabbed it at Monk, and it happened to go in and cut what the doctor called the interior jugular, I think. Quite promising so far, with Monk's body safely hidden; with us, she hoped, busy chasing the wild goose she had provided; and with her getting accepted as a nearly run over victim of the very car she was herself driving. But it all went wrong when Monk's body was found and when the two girl hikers had to go back to work. Though her last exploit was to persuade them to give wrong names and addresses."

"I suppose that's why you were so keen on tracing them," the superintendent remarked. "But I still don't see what put you on to them at first."

"I happened to remember," Bobby explained, much as he hated explaining because he knew the moment an explanation was given, every one immediately saw how simple it had all been and nothing deserving any credit. Much better to leave your methods wrapped in mystery—if you were allowed to: "I happened to remember that originally two girls had been spoken of, and then it seemed there were three. I began to wonder where the third had come from, and if—of course, it was very much a shot in the dark at the time—if this third girl who seemed to have turned up all of a sudden was also the one who had vanished. Also all of a sudden. Then I noticed that all three girls had the same first name—Mary. Nothing much in that—Mary's a common enough name. But a bit of a coincidence for all three to be Mary. And it might have been a way of starting a chat and paling up. 'How funny, we are all three Marys, isn't it odd?' That sort of thing. To break the ice. I thought it was worth following up. And there was an old ballad came into my head.

'There was Mary Beaton and Mary Seaton,
And Mary Carmichael and me.'"

"Yes, but what had that to do with it?" asked the superintendent.

"Oh, nothing," Bobby admitted. "Except that the 'me' in that old ballad was a murderess, and I wondered if perhaps this new third Mary wasn't also a 'me' and a murderess."

"Good guessing," approved the superintendent.

"I call it deduction," protested Bobby, in a slightly injured voice. "Anyhow, all her hopes and plans collapsed when Monk's body was found. She had hoped it would remain hidden for years while we worked on in a blind alley—on the assumption that she was the victim and Monk the murderer we had to find. Or, alternatively, in another blind alley—that nothing very serious had really happened, that she and Monk were enjoying themselves somewhere abroad, and nothing for us to worry about. As soon as she heard Monk's body had been found she must have realized she had to think up something fresh. That's where Harper came in. He had to disappear, both because he knew the truth and because we had to be provided with a new wild goose to chase. That was the aim of the yarn she told David Pope and hoped we would accept. Then we could get busy searching for him who all the time was dead in the cellar in this old building where no one ever came."

The superintendent was mopping his brow, and he had become a little pale.

"A devil incarnate," he said. "That's her."

"Yes," agreed Bobby. He added thoughtfully, speaking more to himself than to his companion: "Yes—or else driven by the Furies, by her own fears, her own terror of what she herself had done in one moment of uncontrolled passion so that in very truth she knew not what she did."

CHAPTER XXXI
"THEY WENT OFF TOGETHER"

By this time the routine work was nearly over, or at any rate had reached the stage at which supervision was no longer necessary. To Bobby, the superintendent said now, and with great decision:

"Next thing, that girl's got to be found, and the sooner the quicker."

"If it's not sooner, it may be never," Bobby told him.

"Eh? what's that?" asked the superintendent, struck by something in Bobby's tone. "Suicide? That what you're thinking?"

"No," Bobby answered. "She's not the suicide type. She's fighting too desperately to save herself to have any thought of suicide. But I'm inclined to think there's a factor she doesn't know or hasn't taken into account."

"Oh, yes," the superintendent agreed. "I remember. You said you thought you knew where she had got herself tucked away. Something Miss Martin told you just now, wasn't it?"

"Yes," Bobby answered. "But after what's happened, it's hard to say what may be her next move. I've been trying to think. Is there a 'phone box near?"

"Round the corner," the superintendent answered. "Why?"

"I want to ring up my Redruth hotel," Bobby explained.

"Don't think she's been staying there, do you?" asked the superintendent, smiling.

"You never know," Bobby answered, giving smile for smile. "Come along."

He hurried away, the superintendent by his side. Bobby borrowed coppers from him and put a call through. Connection made, he said:

"Mr Owen speaking. I want the manager. The manager himself. It's important. Oh, that you? Tell me, have you a Miss Mary Martin on your kitchen staff? You have? Good! Been with you long? Only a day or two? Is she there now? Oh, had the day off but due on duty this evening. Not there yet? Good! Thank you. On no account let any one—any one at all, you understand?—no one—neither Miss Martin herself nor any one, know I've been asking. Not a soul. I shall raise merry hell if she gets to know. Oppose the renewal of your licence very likely. Yes, yes. I know it'll be all right. I only want to rub it in how important it is. I want to talk to the young woman very specially indeed, and she has a gift for disappearing. The pea under the thimble has nothing on her. Good! All right."

Bobby turned to the superintendent then, but before he could speak the other broke out:

"But, hang it all, Mary Martin, she's here . . . I mean to say . . . at the hotel here . . . she can't be in two hotels at once."

"Why, no," Bobby agreed. "But a name's easily taken. Never mind that now. Will you get through to your people at Redruth, and tell them to put a man on to watch, back and front, to see if she arrives, and to make sure she doesn't leave again? Not to interfere with her unless she tries to leave. Only to make sure she doesn't go off again. I should rub that in."

The slightly dazed superintendent did as requested. Bobby bustled him off to their car, and in a very few minutes they were speeding Redruth way on a road Bobby was beginning to know well. He drove furiously, as opportunity permitted, and the superintendent, slightly recovered now, protested again:

"But Mary Martin . . . are there two of 'em?"

"Bella Winlock had to have a new name," Bobby explained. "If she was going to try to get a job, she would want a new identity card. And I remembered the first report said two of the girls hadn't their identity cards and the third had had it but had mislaid it. Or had she or had our Bella annexed it? A job gives the background, which is what matters if you're in hiding. She had it at first as being one of a party of girls on a hiking holiday. But that didn't last, and didn't look promising, either, when questions began to be asked. No questions likely about a girl working in an hotel kitchen. Nothing to make any one talk there.”

“But why this one hotel in especial?” the superintendent asked. “Out of all the dozens and dozens we have down here.”

“Well,” Bobby answered. “I knew Monk had stayed at this Redruth hotel, and I thought it likely he told Bella it was a quiet sort of place where no one was likely to take any notice of you. Commercial travellers mostly, all coming and going, and all busy with their own affairs. Not tourists with nothing to do but gossip about each other. So, as she knew of its name and where it was, and knew it was a quiet sort of place, clearly possible she might choose it. Besides, there had been one or two little incidents. Nothing much. Quite insignificant. A certain tendency to hover near when I was ’phoning that might have been entirely accidental or even some one waiting their turn. Trifles light as air, but I remembered them.”

“But why an hotel? Why not a shop or lodgings or anything?”

“That,” Bobby explained, “was the hint Miss Martin gave me—the real Miss Martin. She told me Bella had asked her a lot of questions about work in an hotel, and she had told her she could get a job helping in the kitchen anywhere, any time, even if she had never seen an hotel before. It seemed a hint of what was running in Bella’s mind and, as it turned out, a sound one.”

“I suppose,” said the superintendent, rather crossly, because it all sounded so simple now and he felt he ought to have known it all all along, only he hadn’t—“I suppose you call that deduction, too?”

“Well, shall we say putting two and two together and making four?” Bobby asked.

The superintendent approved. He didn’t say anything, but he was confirmed in his opinion that it had all been quite simple. No sensational pulling rabbits out of hats. You just put two and two together, and there was your answer. As simple as that. Yet here at his side was a man who did no more, and yet who, starting as a constable on a beat, was now a big noise at Scotland Yard. It didn’t seem quite fair; but there—some people had all the luck.

Occupied in these sage but somewhat melancholy reflections, the superintendent subsided into silence, and did not feel too sympathetic towards a certain haste, even a tendency to take risks at corners, or, still more reprehensible, an appearance once or twice of an attempt to rush traffic lights on the point of changing—one of the worst faults a motorist can commit. He was moved to remonstrate.

"I say," he said, "wasn't that running it a bit fine? No hurry, is there? I mean, whether you get there five minutes sooner or later."

"I don't know," Bobby answered, and muttered angrily when a lumbering, horse-drawn wagon forced him to slow down for a moment.

"Speaking for myself," said the superintendent, "it's not a job I'm looking forward to. I know it's got to be done. You can't let a young woman like her run about loose. No telling what she wouldn't be up to next. But, all the same, a young girl and all of us hunting her down to put a rope round that pretty neck of hers. I can't help wishing . . ." He paused, and then added apologetically: "I've got a girl of my own, and I wish to God some one else had this bit of work."

Bobby gave him a friendly glance.

"I know," he said, "but it has to be. And if we are hunting her down, perhaps others are, too, and it may be one half of our duty is to help her, to save her."

"What do you mean by that?" the superintendent asked, startled.

But Bobby did not attempt to answer. He rounded a corner, then another, and halted the car before his hotel. He jumped out, followed by the superintendent. A plain-clothes man came forward.

"Nothing doing, sir," he reported. "No one answering the description been here. Only one woman all the time, and she only stayed a minute."

"What was she like?" Bobby asked.

"Oh, quite different," the man answered confidently. "Tall and thin. Had a bad cough. Seemed to shake her all to bits and set her long earrings swinging so you thought they would swing themselves clean off."

Bobby went into the hotel. He said to the receptionist:

"A lady has been here. Did she ask to see one of your staff, Miss Martin?"

"That's right," the receptionist agreed. "Her mother's been knocked down by a car. The lady said it was bad, and Miss Martin was to go to the hospital at once. They went off together."

Bobby went back to the superintendent.

"Vea's got in first," he said. "She's warned Bella. They went away together."

"Warned her?" repeated the superintendent. "Warned her we wanted her?" He turned wrathfully on the plain-clothes man. "Perkins," he demanded, "didn't you see them go?"

"Easy to see how it happened," Bobby interposed. "First, Vea. Perkins wasn't interested. That was all right. Why should he be? Then Vea appears again. Probably she stood for a moment in the door, looking round—for a taxi or something. Perkins still not interested. Not the woman he was told to look out for. He's been told to be careful to avoid being noticed. So he turns his back and walks away. Vea's on the watch. She may have played the same trick before, she knows them all from the word 'go'. She makes Bella a sign, and Bella slips out, taking care to keep on the far side, and they walk away together. Perkins will be on the look out for that dodge another time."

Perkins gave Bobby a look of deep gratitude. He might still get a wigging, but the full force of it had been broken, and indeed Bobby was never severe, except in cases of wilful neglect or indolence. He knew so well that the best slip up at times. Luckily for Perkins, too, the superintendent was too puzzled by this new development to have much time or thought to spare for rebuking subordinates. He said:

"Well, if they've gone away together, where to?"

"Yes, I know," Bobby said. "There's that next."

"Seems," said the superintendent, with a note of rebuke in his voice—"seems to show they've been working together all the tune. That's a new angle. Cuts out your notion that Vea might have it in for Bella now she knows it was her did in Mark Monk."

"Does it?" Bobby asked. "Or does it mean Vea wants to keep Bella for herself?"

CHAPTER XXXII
"WHY SHOULD OTHERS LIVE?"

NOW AT LAST, now that Bella Winlock was 'wanted' on a clear and definite charge, it was possible to take more forthright and decided measures to discover her whereabouts. Desirable, too—more than desirable, in fact—to find Vea as well, though in her case it was difficult to think of any excuse for detaining her, highly advisable as that course of action seemed to be. The liberty of the subject is above all things sacrosanct in every free community, but it has its disadvantages when the question is not so much the detection as the prevention of crime.

Not that there was very much that could be done for the moment, now that night was drawing in, beyond making preparations for the morrow. Plans were laid. Instructions were sent out. It was agreed that every possible means of publicity should be employed, including such things as the publication of photographs in the Press. All this completed, and nothing more to be done till morning, Bobby began to think of dinner—a subject which had been a kind of yearning background to his thoughts for some time. It was afterwards, he was in the lounge, smoking a good-night cigarette over a cup of coffee, complacently contemplating bed, that Vea Burden came quietly into the room. She stood in the doorway, looking at him, a faint smile on her thin, ravaged face where the scarlet of her painted lips showed in startling contrast to the deathly pallor of her other features. Bobby rose to his feet.

"Oh, good evening," he said. "Awfully good of you. I've been hoping for a chance of a chat. Waiter, another cup of coffee. A liqueur?"

"Thank you so much," she said, and there was a touch of mockery in her voice as she added: "Awfully good of you." To the waiter she said: "Make it double—the liqueur, not the coffee." To Bobby she said: "I've got a room here for to-night. Do you mind?"

She sat down, and they looked at each other across the small lounge table, nor did either speak. Vea's thoughts were her own, her eyes, beneath swollen, half-closed lids, were inflamed and dark. Bobby was wondering uneasily what lay behind this unexpected visit. Vea began to cough. There were still a few of the other visitors to the hotel scattered about the lounge, chatting or reading, or playing cards. All of them looked, for it was a harsh and dreadful cough, and shook her so it was a wonder that thin and emaciated form could endure it. She had her handkerchief to her mouth. When she took it away there was blood on it. She showed the stain to Bobby:

"That's why," she said. "My lip-stick, I mean. Why it's the brightest crimson I could find. Then it doesn't show. The blood, I mean."

"I see you've taken off your earrings," Bobby remarked.

"I miss them, feel undressed somehow," she told him. "I got used to them. A sort of signature tune. Only now I thought they might be getting to be too much of one. That plainclothes cop outside here, I was afraid he had noticed. Not too bright, was he?"

"Or shall we say," Bobby suggested, "not so experienced, not so well up in the tricks of the trade—of the crook?"

She began to cough again. This time the spasm was less severe, less prolonged. She said:

"I got soaked to the skin that wet day. So did you. Hasn't hurt you, though."

"I had a hot bath as soon as I could," Bobby explained.

"And I," she said, "I had no change so I lay in my wet things all night. There was a fever in my blood that I thought would dry them. It doesn't matter much. Did you see those fools all staring just now? Have they never heard any one cough before?"

"Not like that I think," Bobby answered. "You should be in hospital."

"Hospital?" she repeated. "Cemetery you mean. You think I'm going to die, don't you? Break a blood-vessel or something. So did they." With a sudden blazing fire of passion that seemed to eat her up into one fierce incarnation of angry will she said: "Why should they live—why should any one—if I've to die?"

"Would you like another cup of coffee?" Bobby asked.

She stared and laughed—no pleasant laugh, low and harsh.

"Damn you!" she said at last. "I think I hate you more than all the rest."

"Well, that doesn't do either of us much good, does it?" Bobby asked. "And it doesn't do your cough much good either to get wet through and lie in damp things all night. Tell me, what have you been trying to do all this time?"

"If you weren't a fool," she told him angrily, "you could see for yourself I had to know."

"To know?"

"To know," she repeated, "—to know what had happened, to know—to know, if it was like that, which had killed the other." She laid a hot and stinging hand on his. Her eyes were fire, her voice hardly more than a whisper as she repeated: "It was the not knowing was more than I could bear."

"Mark Monk or Bella?" Bobby said. "Victim or murderer? Which was which? or something else altogether? Well, that's what we were trying to find out."

"If it was Bella had had it, I had to help Mark," Vea went on. "That's at first how I thought it was. He was my man. I wanted him back. I think I might have got him back—I think I might have gone on living. I think I might, if it had been that way and I had helped. He might have wanted me again, have needed me. That's what I wanted. For him to need me."

"He might have for a time, needed you as long as he needed your help. Afterwards?"

"I know what you mean," she said defiantly. "You mean he killed his first wife. They couldn't prove it. She should have left him if she couldn't keep him. It was up to her. A woman ought to know her man. Well, suppose he did?" She was staring at Bobby, intently, fiercely. She drew a long, deep breath. "What about it?" she asked. "Life wouldn't be dull, anyhow. Have love from him—or death. To know every time he kissed you, what might be next."

"A fascination of horror," Bobby said with a mixture of repugnance, fear, and pity.

She nodded and was silent. Then she spoke again.

"You don't understand," she said. "I suppose you can't. Could you love a woman you knew was giving you poison in your food every day? I wonder. We could, we others. It wasn't only me. Others, too. I've seen the whisper go round the room that there was a man had stood his trial for murdering his wife, and some would shiver, turn pale, shiver away, and some, and more, would turn pale and shiver—but not away. Ever looked over a steep cliff and felt it draw?"

"The pull of the abyss," Bobby said.

"Well, then," she said.

"Does all that explain why you came here this evening to warn Bella?"

"I only wanted to know if she were here," Vea answered. "Been here all the time, hasn't she? safe and snug, in the same place as you, helping cook your dinner, while all the time you were searching for her high and low."

"One up to her," Bobby agreed. "Definitely one up to her. A young woman of imagination and resource. Still, but for you, I think we should have found her this evening. Where is she now?"

"How should I know?"

"You came to warn her, didn't you? I should have to lower my opinion of your intelligence if you tried to deny that. She went away with you, I think?"

"She didn't. She may have slipped out after me. I don't know and I don't care. Nothing to do with me."

But now she was not looking at him. Her eyes were turned away. She put one hand up to shade her face as if she feared that he might understand what he saw if he saw too clearly. Her small, feverish, restless movements that had been noticeable before, though she herself had been unconscious of them, now ceased entirely. She sat rigid and motionless.

"You told me," Bobby said, "how you felt you had to know what took place at Bexley House. You thought it must be either that Mark Monk had killed Bella or that it had been the other way. Well, we thought that, too, though we had to take into account the possibility of some one else having intervened, and of Bella having been rushed away to prevent her telling. Or even of her having gone off voluntarily with the idea of helping Mark's escape, if he had done anything. Many possibilities. But I think you only considered the first—that one of the two had killed the other. If it had been that Mark Monk were the killer, you meant to help him. But supposing the killer turned out to be Bella, what had you in your mind then?"

"I never thought it could be her," she answered, but still without looking at him. "You did, you say. Always in your mind, wasn't it?"

"As one of various different possibilities," Bobby agreed, "and I think not long before it was in your mind, too." She did not speak. "When it did come into your mind," he asked, "what then?"

"Well, there was nothing I could do, was there?" she said.

He did not repeat the question, for he saw she did not mean to answer it. Nor did he think there was much need, for he felt he knew. There was a short silence. Then he went on:

"Well, tell me—what made her kill him? She had not meant to. What was it at Bexley House that made such a deadly quarrel between them? Was it something you said?"

"Trying to pin it on me, are you?" she retorted, and then with one of those bursts of anger of hers, she answered: "Yes. Yes. I did. I told her how she had been fooled."

"You mean you told her who you were, that you were his wife?"

"That's right. I knew what it meant when they turned up that night at Bexley House. Like him to fix up for her to meet him where I was, like him to plan to go off with her under my nose. Well, I told her. She didn't like it."

"Liked it the less for the way you told it?" Bobby suggested.

"Know it all, don't you?" she sneered. "Good at guessing, you are."

"Not guessing," Bobby protested mildly. "Just getting to know you."

"All very well for you to talk," she protested in her turn, and it was odd that in this remark of Bobby's she seemed to feel an implied rebuke that somehow stung more than anything else he had said. "You've not seen your wife planning to run away with another man under your nose and just amused to think you know. I told her—oh, yes, I told her. I didn't wrap it up. I knew what her temper was under those pretty, girlish, kittenish ways of hers—kitten, tiger cat, that's her all right. Oh, yes, I meant to set that temper of hers going. I didn't mean—expect—"

"No," Bobby agreed when she stopped abruptly, "I don't suppose you did—we so seldom do. Then it happens."

"Well," she said moodily. "Well."

"You had quarrelled with Grace that evening, too, hadn't you?" Bobby asked.

"Oh, that," Vea said. "That was nothing. Grace knew I knew Alf Harper had cut her out, and she tried to be funny about Isobel cutting me out with Mark. I wasn't feeling that way, and I shut her up. Quick."

"I suppose it was you who did in my motor-cycle at the Round Table Mine and took pot shots at me as well."

"I didn't mean to hurt you," Vea explained. "Not that I cared," she added, "all I wanted was to make you think there might be something there. I wasn't sure, but I thought. . . ." She paused and added wearily: "I thought so much, so many things."

"When you saw Miss Winlock to-night, did she tell you anything?"

"She told it all," Vea answered. "That's why I came. To get her to talk. I told her I had come to help her, but what I wanted was to be sure. I said I was on her side because Mark had lied to us both. But I wasn't. She said when she asked him if it was true I was his wife and she wasn't, he just laughed. She said he seemed awfully amused at me telling her. He had wondered if I would, he said. She told him she was through with him and she was going home. He said, no, she wasn't, it was too late, and then there was the money he had let her win gambling. That upset her a lot as well. She thought she had been so clever with her winnings, and he told her it had been fixed to keep her sweet. Now he wanted it back, and any more she had with her. Pay for his trouble, he called it, still laughing at her. When she wouldn't, he tried to take it by force; and it was then she snatched up the knife from the supper-table and jabbed it at him, and it went right in at his neck and he fell down. She said she never knew before it was so easy to kill a man. Is it?"

"Very easy," Bobby agreed gravely, and there came into his mind a line he remembered from an old play he had once acted in, years before, at the University: 'Death hath so many doors whereby to let out life.'

"When she saw him fall down," Vea continued, "she said she was so surprised she screamed, and Harper came. He had found out somehow she meant to go off with Mark, and I think he meant to stop her if he could. Good thing for him he didn't try, or he might have been the deader, and not Mark. So when he saw what it was, he helped her put Mark in the car."

"That would be when he got blood on his clothes and hands," Bobby remarked, "and that's why he cut his hand to explain it. Puzzled me at the time, that bit. Surprising she didn't get him to drive the car or go with her."

"Not her; she wouldn't trust him or any one," Vea said. "Had to do it all herself. She meant to drive the car over the cliffs into the sea. Get rid of the body that way. It's a way," she said moodily. "It's one way," she repeated. "I don't know why she changed her mind."

"Thought it would be safer not to give the sea a chance to give up its dead," Bobby answered.

"I suppose what she did," Vea asked, "they could call it manslaughter?"

"If she had had the sense and the courage to tell the truth," Bobby said, "she might even have got off altogether with a good counsel and a soft-hearted jury. But now there's the hiding of the body and all that grisly drive in the car. Doesn't sound much like the innocent, frightened, bewildered little girl, who had just simply lost her head. Clearly manslaughter, though, not murder. But now there's what happened to Harper, and she won't be allowed to get away with that. A long term in prison is the best she can look forward to now."

"That's what I wanted to know," Vea said. She got to her feet. "No death sentence?" she asked.

"No. Manslaughter in the first case, and Harper still alive—though not well. Very definitely not well."

"He'll live," Vea said, "and so'll she," and her voice was low and still and dreadful. "But I'll not, for I've got to die. Why should she live, or any one, and not me? It is not just," she said.

CHAPTER XXXIII
"WE'LL BLOCK ALL ROADS"

It was at this moment, before Bobby could even try to answer—though, indeed, to such a question no answer was possible—that there appeared a waiter to say that Bobby was wanted on the 'phone by Mr Henry Smith.

This was the code name used by the police when calling Bobby, so as to avoid attracting unnecessary attention. Though a little worried by so inopportune an interruption, Bobby went to answer it, taking, however, the precaution to instruct the porter to let him know if the lady in the lounge showed any sign of leaving.

The 'phone message was to the effect that Jerry George had been stopped and the lorry he was driving found to be loaded with cases of cigarettes, a few bales of lace, and other goods plainly intended for the black market. Both Jerry and the lorry were in safe custody, and the former might confidently look forward to a probable and prolonged respite from his public—and private—activities. Bobby expressed much satisfaction at this, and asked that the senior officer in charge should be at once informed of Vea's presence in the hotel. Gould, Bobby asked, no matter how hard it might be to spare the men, a watch be placed on the hotel, in case Vea chose to disappear again? He himself, he said, would of course take part.

The senior officer who came then to the 'phone seemed more than a little worried. After all, Vea had done nothing, she had uttered no threats, there was nothing overt. One had to be so careful, with the Press always on the pounce to make some silly fuss or another. The Chief Constable would have to be consulted.

Bobby hung up the receiver. He told himself moodily that what he most unfairly called 'red tape' was probably going to cost a life or two, as it has done in the past, and probably will again. He went back into the entrance hall, where he found Vea on the point of going out.

"It's beginning to rain," she told him, and he noticed with surprise that she had again put on those long, swinging earrings of hers. "I've a letter to post I want to go as soon as possible."

"Let me post it, may I?" Bobby asked.

"I wouldn't trouble you for the world," she answered and was gone.

He did not much suppose she would return. Nothing he could do, though. He had no authority to detain her or to interfere with her movements in any way. Somehow he felt that her resumption of her earrings was vaguely ominous. It was as though she were proclaiming an approaching end, a decision taken and final. But his fear that she would not return proved unfounded, for presently he heard her harsh and dreadful cough in the hall. When he went there, he found her sitting on a chair, once again shaken, as though that frail form of hers must fall apart in such a paroxysm. One or two of the hotel staff were hovering around her, anxious to help where no help was possible. As soon as she was able she got to her feet and went up the stairs to her room.

"Going out in the rain with that cough of hers," one of the hotel people remarked. "She'll get her death of it."

Bobby was of much the same opinion, though he did not think death threatened in the way suggested. He returned to the lounge, deeply worried, oppressed by an unfamiliar sense of futility, feeling as though events had taken charge and he was but a helpless spectator—a role to which he was not accustomed, and which he did not like. The porter came presently into the room.

"That lady's gone off, sir," he said. "I thought you might like to know. She came down again and said as she had changed her mind and was going to spend the night with a friend—a doctor. She had paid her bill, so there was nothing I could do, and the manager glad enough she's gone. That cough of hers—sort of upsetting. The guests didn't like it. T.B., if you ask me, and bad at that."

Bobby thanked the man for letting him know, handed over the appropriate tip, and remarked that he thought he would go out and tell Mr Henry Smith.

"Maybe that's where's she gone," the porter suggested.

Bobby said he hoped so, and did not add that he thought it little likely. The rain was heavier now, but he went as far as the police station, where he asked that every effort should be made to obtain information concerning Vea's movements. This was, of course, promised at once. But it was added that it was late, that it was a dark and very wet night, and that the lady could not have gone far in such weather. Effective measures would probably have to wait till morning, when everything possible would be done without delay.

Bobby did not feel so sure that Vea would not have gone very far. He thought her in no mood to take much notice of rain and wind, and indeed it seemed as if the rain were already clearing. He went back to the hotel, heavy with apprehension, there to resume his interrupted progress to bed.

In the morning he was up early. It was a Sunday, and he was down long before there was any sign of breakfast. He went again to pay a visit to the police station, where he was assured by a brisk young sergeant just come on duty that all the necessary steps had been, were, and would be taken.

"We'll soon be on her tracks," said the young sergeant confidently, and in private he wondered what on earth Mr Owen was worrying over.

When he was as senior as Mr Owen, he told himself, you wouldn't catch him turning out at that hour on a Sunday morning—and a wet, cold, dark morning at that.

Bobby went back to the hotel, sat about there, was regarded with much disfavour by the staff, who found him greatly in the way of their cleaning and dusting activities. Then breakfast arrived, and at the very moment he was sitting down to it he was called away to the 'phone. This time it was not Mr Henry Smith, as he had expected, but David Pope. Pope sounded disturbed.

"I've just been rung up by Maggie," he said. "You know— Miss Kerr. It's about Vea Burden."

"Oh, yes, yes," Bobby said, disturbed, too, but not greatly surprised, for he had expected some development, though not that the attack would be delivered through Maggie Kerr. "What's happened?"

"I don't like it," Pope's voice came over the instrument. "She's asked Maggie to meet her. She asked her to hire a car—a big one. It's to help Bella. I couldn't make out exactly, I don't think she—Maggie, I mean—knew herself. It was something about Bella having been bullied into going into hiding at a cottage right away from everywhere, and Maggie was to go there with Vea to get her away and to have a car because it was so lonely. Maggie said she would, only wouldn't it be better to have a man with them, and she's asked me to go. I'm meeting them in a few minutes."

"Where?" Bobby asked quickly, but there was no answer, and he thought he heard the click of the receiver being hung up.

He knew the hotels where respectively Maggie and David Pope had been staying. He rang them up in succession. At Maggie's hotel the reply was that Miss Kerr had gone out some time previously in a car she had secured from a neighbouring garage. At Pope's hotel the answer was that he also had gone out some time previously. Nothing more was known. Next Bobby rang up the garage from which Maggie had hired her car, and got its registered number and description. It was a Bayard Twenty, capable, as Bobby knew, of doing easily a hundred miles an hour. Then he asked the Exchange to trace the recent call made by Pope. As he had expected, it came from a call-box on the main road not far from Pope's hotel. Armed with all this information, he hurried round to the police station.

No difficulty now. All the usual steps were taken at once, since Bella was 'wanted' on a definite and serious charge. The location of the call-box from which Pope had 'phoned provided a starting point wherefrom the search could radiate in all directions. Swiftly as Bobby had acted, some time had already elapsed. If, as Bobby suspected, Pope had hung up because of seeing or hearing Maggie's car arriving, then that car might already be twenty miles away in any direction.

"Making for London most likely," said the inspector in charge. "We'll block all roads out of the peninsula first."

He called up the focal points already arranged for, from Boscastle to Tavistock, and then others, till there was no police force from Bude to Plymouth but was on the look-out for a Bayard Twenty containing probably three women and a man.

"It's only putting the net into action," the inspector explained to Bobby, not sorry for a chance to show this Scotland Yard man what efficiency really meant. All ready and prepared. "A complete net from sea to sea," he said. "They'll never get through. Of course," he admitted, "geography helps us. They must try to get out of the peninsula, and if we're warned in time, then they're caught like rats in a trap."

"Suppose they go the other way—Land's End way?" Bobby asked.

"Well, that's what I'm saying," the inspector explained once more. "Caught like rats in a trap," he repeated, "if they go that way. I'm dealing with that now," and soon all the police from Land's End to Lizard Point and on to Plymouth were similarly warned to be on the alert.

Nothing now to be done but wait for news. Presently it came. The 'phone rang. A car answering the description given, driven at a high rate of speed, had been seen travelling Redruth way.

"Straight into our loving arms waiting to receive them," chuckled the inspector. "One thing about us in Redruth, we've a nice long main street it's easy to close at both ends. We mayn't be the tourist's delight, but we are practical. Lucky it's a Sunday, and not much other traffic on the road to get in the way."

CHAPTER XXXIV
"ONE WAS SCREAMING"

THEY WAITED silently. The inspector began to look uneasy. He started to 'phone again, here and there. There was no news.

"Travelling at a high rate of speed!" grumbled the inspector. "Why, they must be going dead slow. Tyre trouble, perhaps."

Bobby said nothing. He felt that Vea would not be so easily cornered. No likelihood of her driving straight into 'loving arms waiting to receive her', as the inspector had put it. She, too, he felt, was of an infinite resource, and he was uneasily aware of strange possibilities that might have been born in her tormented, distracted, disease-ridden mind.

Why was she driving so fast, he wondered? and why had she wished—as apparently she had—to be accompanied by Maggie and David, as well as by Bella Winlock? Questions to which he could not but feel there was only one likely answer, and that an ill one.

Hard to have to sit there and wait, helpless to do anything to change the flow of circumstance. At last—the interval had not really been so long, though to Bobby it had seemed interminable—the 'phone rang again. The inspector grabbed the receiver. A car answering the description given had dashed through Camborne. The summons to stop had been ignored. A constable making the stop signal had only saved his life by jumping aside at very much the last minute, and of traffic lights no notice whatever had been taken.

The inspector grunted indignantly. Ignoring traffic lights, indeed. What next? he wanted to know. Bobby made no attempt to answer, but he got up and began to study a map of Cornwall hanging on the wall of the inspector's office. The inspector was busy 'phoning. Once more the car had disappeared.

"Beats me," said the inspector crossly, "what they think they are doing. They can't get out, the net's there from sea to sea," he repeated.

Bobby, his finger on the map, said over his shoulder:

"There's one way out."

"Plymouth, you mean?" asked the inspector. "Oh, I don't know. They aren't so slow there. And a big town's easier in a way to make a stop in than these country roads, where there's always some lane or another you can dodge round by. They'll never get out of the peninsula," he insisted.

Bobby had been thinking of a way quite other than that leading through Plymouth. But he said nothing, and, turning away from the map, he sat down again. The 'phone rang. Now the car had been seen flying past Crowan Beacon.

"Round and round like a squirrel in a cage," complained the inspector. "Silly, I call it. Most likely it's Falmouth now."

But the next report came from Townshend. Here again a summons to stop had been ignored, and here again the officer making the stop signal had been driven straight at, and had only saved his life by a last-minute leap aside.

Quickly came the next report, this time from St Erth. On the bridge there a man had been seriously hurt. Trying to avoid the car's reckless rush, he had received a glancing, fortunately not a direct, blow, that had knocked him down. He had broken ribs, a broken leg and other injuries, and had been taken to hospital, lucky to be still alive.

"Must be clean off their heads," said the inspector. "Do they want to kill people?" he asked.

"It may be that," Bobby said.

"Looks like it," agreed the inspector, though he did not understand a certain gravity he thought he heard in Bobby's voice. "Going the right way to do it, anyhow. Why are they driving like that?" he demanded. "No one's chasing 'em."

The 'phone rang. This time it was to say that a motorcyclist from Hale was in pursuit.

"Some one chasing 'em now," said the inspector. "High time, too."

They waited. The 'phone rang. It was a direct report from the motor-cyclist. He said he was still alive, but he didn't know why. The car he was following had, by a tricky manœuvre at cross roads and a complete disregard of all traffic rules, been turned and driven straight at him. He and his cycle alike had been thrown into the air. The cycle had been smashed, but he himself, by good luck or an act of Providence, whichever you liked, had come down on a haystack and had suffered only bruises. But he was out of the chase.

"No one chasing 'em now," said the inspector. "We're bound to get 'em in the end. They don't think they can go on like this for ever, do they?"

Once more there they waited, silent and apprehensive. Once more the 'phone rang. The car had been seen. The speed was terrific. The driving reckless in the extreme. One of the occupants was standing up and shouting.

"Got something to shout about," said the inspector. "Bound to crash sooner or later, and that ought to mean a broken neck or two. What do you think, sir?" he asked Bobby. "Can't go on like this for long. Bound to crash."

"Unless they get first to where they may be going," Bobby said.

"Where's that?" the inspector asked. "Any idea, sir?"

"I think perhaps it may be Gurnards Head," Bobby said.

"Gurnards Head," the inspector repeated, not sure he had heard correctly. "There's nothing there. Only cliff and sea, that's all."

"Yes, I know," Bobby said.

"Well, then," said the inspector.

The 'phone rang. This time the report was from near Towed-much. There a hasty barricade had been erected. The car had charged it and smashed through. The speed was again described as terrific. It had been observed that the man passenger was not now standing up, but had apparently collapsed on the back seat. A woman was bending over him. She was wiping his face, as far as could be seen. The woman in the driving-seat and another woman by her side were taking no notice.

"Warn Zennor," Bobby said. "Say that car must be stopped at all costs."

The message went through. Zennor reported that a barricade was being placed across the road.

"It'll stop 'em or kill 'em," said Zennor, with cheerful confidence.

Zennor rang up again. The fugitive car had simply crashed through the barricade, scattering it in splinters all over the roadway. As additional precaution, a chain had been stretched across the road a little farther on. The car had simply leaped it, rising high in the air, and somehow or another preserving its equilibrium and coming down uninjured on its own four wheels. By special grace of the devil, in Zennor's considered opinion.

"Getting near Gurnards Head, only two or three miles now," the inspector said. "What made you think that's what they were aiming for? Why?"

"Recovery work still going on there, isn't it?" Bobby asked. "Aren't they still trying to get up that crashed car?"

"That's right," said the inspector.

"Can't get in touch with them, then," Bobby said. "No 'phone. Most likely they know already."

Some time before this he had asked that a police car should be in readiness. He went out to where it was waiting. To the chauffeur-constable, he said:

"Gurnards Head. About twenty miles, isn't it? Get there just as quickly as you know how."

The inspector had come out with him, and would have liked to accompany him in the car, had duty permitted. Bobby said to him:

"Could you ring them up all along the way to Gurnards Head? Tell them you are sending a car, tell them it's urgent, ask them to try to keep the road clear." To the chauffeur, Bobby said again:

"Gurnards Head. Full speed."

"Gurnards Head?" repeated the chauffeur. "Very good, sir. Fine view there, sir."

"Is there?" Bobby said. "Well, get me there to admire it as soon as you can. Go all out."

The chauffeur thought to himself that the view would not run away. He wondered if the Chief Constable would approve the use of a police car to take this Londoner to admire even one of the grandest views in Cornwall, or in the British Isles, for that matter. But the driver has not yet been born whose soul does not leap to the injunction: "Full speed. Go all out."

Nor was this driver any exception. True, he did not crash traffic lights or charge barricades; but, then, there were no barricades, and only a few traffic lights. On the long, straight, empty stretches of road both sides of St. Ives he did his best to match the speed at which Vea Burden had driven. Indeed, the memory of that Sunday morning's drive still brings a happy smile to his lips.

Even his driving, however, hardly matched Bobby's impatience, and the car had not stopped before Bobby had leaped out and was running up the steep and rough incline to the cliff's edge where men stood in groups, pale, silent, or talking to each other in low tones, still shaken and awestruck by the sudden, dreadful thing that they had seen. One man said to him as he ran up:

"Straight it went, straight and fast, straight over and down into the sea, and one of them was screaming. God Almighty! I never saw the like."

Another man said:

"There was two as jumped first."

The first man said:

"Her that was screaming wanted to, but she wasn't let."

At a little distance, Bobby saw Maggie half sitting, half reclining, on the ground. She had apparently been trying to get to her feet, but hadn't quite been able to manage it. David Pope was lying near by. One leg was crumpled under him, and his face was bleeding. Maggie got her handkerchief and began to dab at it in a feeble, bewildered way, as if not altogether certain what she was doing or why. Neither of them spoke. Not far off another man lay at full length, complaining and groaning loudly. The little scattered group of bystanders seemed all too aghast, too bewildered by the suddenness and the terror of what they had seen, to be capable for the moment of either speech or movement. It was as if they all were held in a common paralysis of overwhelming horror. Bobby ran across to Maggie. He said:

"Are you hurt?"

"I'm all right," she answered, though she did not look it. "It's David." Then, as if abruptly realizing the need for action, she called out loudly: "Oh, please, won't some one get some water?"

One of the men near, apparently galvanized into action by her cry, called: "Right-o, miss," and set off running towards some vehicles stationed near. To Bobby, Maggie said: "I saw them go. I shall dream of it ever more. He won't die, will he?"

"Who? Pope? Bless you, no," Bobby answered. "Bad shake up and a broken leg. Bad enough, but might be worse. What about you?"

"I'm all right," she repeated. "It was Vea. She wanted us to go, too, she wanted us as well. Oh, why should she? David tried to stop her, but she wouldn't, and she threw pepper in his face—at least, I think it was pepper, or something."

The man who had gone hurrying to the parked vehicles came running back. He had a first-aid box with him. He said:

"There's a chap gone off to ring up for an ambulance. It won't be long."

He and Bobby did what was possible to make Pope comfortable and warm. When they had done what they could, Bobby went across to the other man who was lying on the grass near, still groaning and complaining loudly. Bobby did not think he was much hurt—to judge, at least, by the volume and energy of his groans. A man standing by said:

"It's poor old Billy Tompkins; he copped it fair and square when them two jumped. Broke their fall when Billy caught them, though not wanting to or meaning same."

Bobby left the suffering Billy in the care of his companions and went back to Maggie, who was giving Pope some hot tea one of the men had managed to produce. She looked up as Bobby approached and said:

"Vea took Bella. Did you know? Why did she? Vea, I mean. She wanted to take us, too. What for? And her own self? All of us, all. Why? And Bella. She said it was Bella killed him. Did she? Oh, why are people so wicked? What makes them do such things—Bella and Vea, too?"

"Not so much wicked, perhaps," Bobby said thoughtfully, "as driven by forces they did not understand. Vea could not bear to think of life and love for others when she had lost the man she loved and knew she had to die so soon. She grudged you what she knew was not for her. She told me once it was not just. Bella played with love as a child plays with fire, knowing nothing of the power she was letting loose till it destroyed her."

He turned away. He had seen many strange and dreadful things, but somehow this had shaken him more than he quite realized. He went to the cliff edge and stood there, looking out and down into that awful void into which Vea Burden and Bella Winlock had vanished only a few minutes before. He thought of the vivid and strong personality of Vea, so full of a force she had known so little how to direct. He thought of Bella Winlock, who had used her charm and powers of fascination to such ill ends, and he had grief for them both. The foreman of the gang joined him. The foreman, too, was pale and shaken. He said, as he, like Bobby, gazed down into that tremendous emptiness where nothing showed but rock and sea:

"I saw it all. I think no man has ever seen the like. Lickety lick it come down the road, and we all stared. So then it swung round, and before we knew, aiming straight it was for the cliff edge. Slowed a bit—it had to, along of the ground getting steep and rough-like near the edge—so those other two had their chance to jump; but straight on the car went, bumping a bit, but fast as could be, and over, deliberate. Deliberate," he repeated, "and one of them screamed as they went, but the other held her fast, and then they were gone, and may God have mercy on their souls."

THE END

E.R. PUNSHON
CRIME FICTION REVIEWER

E.R. Punshon was for many years a reviewer of crime fiction for the Guardian *newspaper in the U.K. The following nine reviews by Punshon were published in* The Guardian *between 1935 and 1936.*

Gaudy Night, Dorothy L. Sayers (1935)

The Garden Murder Case, S.S. Van Dine (1935)

The Wheel Spins, Ethel Lina White (1936)

Trent's Own Case, E.C. Bentley and H. Warner Allen (1936)

The Penrose Mystery, R. Austin Freeman (1936)

The Man Who Murdered Himself, Geoffrey Homes (1936)

The Talkative Policeman, Rupert Penny (1936)

Fair Warning, Mignon Eberhart (1936)

Death at the President's Lodging, Michael Innes (1936)

Gaudy Night
by Dorothy L. Sayers
(13 November 1935)

"Gaudy Night," Miss Dorothy L. Sayers's new story, has the advantage of a novel and interesting environment, that of a woman's college at Oxford, with which she herself is intimately acquainted but that will be new ground for most of us. In the college there has broken out a plague of anonymous letters, threatening to drive nervous students to suicide, to bring disgrace upon the whole community, even upon scholarship itself, if scholarship shall prove a soil from which such ill can spring. That the guilt must rest upon some inmate of the college is clear, and excitement steadily grows as suspicion flickers to and fro from don to student, to staff, then back to student and don again. Miss Harriet Vane, a writer of mystery stories, and then our old friend Lord Peter Wimsey are called in to solve the mystery, and neat and clear and logical is the solution at which Lord Peter arrives after the lady has failed, though it is doubtful whether Miss Sayers intends this as an allegorical demonstration of the innate superiority of the masculine mind. But this detective work, however much the author's admirers may demand it, is so little the real theme of the book that it seems inadequate indeed to class the story under the heading of the detective novel—it is larger and escapes from any neat classification. There is in it a three-fold cord the author has woven to hold fast reader's interest: the strange events that throw the college into a turmoil; the psychology of the teaching staff under the stress of a loathsome suspicion creeping closer to them every day; the slow breaking down of the barrier Harriet Vane has erected between Peter Wimsey and herself; and of this triple cord one may say that study of the inmates of the senior common room, more especially Miss Lydgate, the English tutor, is the most successful strand and the love scenes the least so. For this is not only a detective story, not only a psychological study of a learned community under the strain of sensational events, it is also a love tale, and since it is laid in academic surroundings one may borrow from the schools a metaphor and award Miss Sayers a double first, honours in the detective tale class, honours in the orthodox-novel class as well. Incidentally, Miss Sayers has, in her stride as it were, slain half a dozen superstitions connected with the detective novel, as, item, that a detective story must have a murder in it; item, that it must have no love interest; item, that there is something immoral about writing it in good and scholarly English; item, that the characters must be puppets; item, that it of necessity must be a kind of "Who's Who," to be read only to discover Who Did It. But the worst of superstitions is that the more often they are slain, the more immortal they prove themselves; the more deeply they are buried, the more swiftly they run about the world.

The Garden Murder Case
by S.S. Van Dine
(18 September 1935)

In "The Garden Murder Case" Mr. Van Dine is neither classical nor romantic, but purely "Philovantic," to use a word current, one understands, in the United States, where Mr. Philo Vance holds much the same position as that achieved here by Lord Peter Wimsey, though with this difference, that we all love our Wimsey, whereas about Philo Vance ribald songs have been made advocating for him that extreme form of sanctions known as a kick in the pants [i.e., "Philo Vance/needs a kick in the pance"—Ogden Nash]. Certainly Mr. Vance's way of imparting information does strongly resemble forcible feeding, and, as the knowledge pumped this time into the more or less patient reader is chiefly concerned with American [horse] racing, its appeal to English readers may be limited. But Mr. Vance's intellectual powers are as remarkable as ever. He is even able to explain the hidden significance (page 21) of certain words in a message he received, though in that message (page 16), no such words occur. Proudly indeed may the United States cry, "Where's your Wimsey now?" After such a feat of intuition it is no wonder that he solves with accustomed neatness, accuracy, and dispatch a somewhat conventional mystery beginning on the roof garden of a New York apartment house. The scheme of the story brings its author face to face with the detective novelist's peculiar difficulty and paradox—that of presenting vividly to the reader the personality of the guilty individual and yet letting the identity come as a surprise. But Mr. Van Dine does not make much effort to deal with it.

The Wheel Spins
by Ethel Lina White
(12 May 1936)

More than all other practitioners of the protean art of fiction is the writer of tales of sensation and of crime bound to observe to laws of probability. The necessity is imposed upon him by the very fact that he deals with happenings outside the range of ordinary life, since how can he hope to make his tale significant unless he can succeed in relating it to actuality? Even in such fantasies as "Frankenstein" or "Dr. Jekyll and Mr. Hyde," it is their underlying and eternal truth that has made them live.

Neglect of this law explains the failure to attain the first rank of Miss Ethel Lina White's excellent new story "The Wheel Spins," a tale of strange happenings on a transcontinental train running from some vague East European country to Trieste. On the train a little English governess, Miss Froy, mysteriously disappears. She was and she is not. A fellow-passenger, Iris Carr, wonders what has become of her, inquires, and is met on every side by blank denial that any such person as Miss Froy has been on the train at all or even has any real existence. Iris is almost driven to believe she has suffered some strange hallucination, but she persists to the exciting and well-planned climax of the story. It is clear, however, that in fact nothing more would have been necessary than to appeal to the conductor, on these long-distance international trains an important and responsible official, and so at least to have ensured sufficient publicity to prevent even the most reckless conspirators from proceeding with their plans. Few intending murderers care to put their names and addresses on official record before committing their crimes. And for that matter if the conspirators had chosen to tell Iris, an entirely casual train acquaintance, that the missing woman had met a friend and changed her seat to the other end of the crowded train, Iris would never have given her disappearance a second thought. Considering how slight the story is, little more than an anecdote, Miss White succeeds in extracting from it a most creditable amount of excitement and suspense, qualities on which the book depends, since its scope allows no problem to be posed to baffle the reader or challenge him to find it for his own solution.

Trent's Own Case
by E.C. Bentley and H. Warner Allen
(22 May 1936)

That in recent years the claim of the detective novel to take its place in the great tradition of English literature has been more generally allowed is due largely to the impetus and example given by Mr. Bentley's "Trent's Last Case," published more than twenty years ago. Before then, in the early days of this century, the detective novel, declining from the heights of Wilkie Collins and of Doyle, had fallen to a level little above that of the common "shocker." During all that somewhat dreary period between Doyle and Bentley the work of only one or two writers seems to have been worth the regard of an intelligent reader.

Now, after the lapse of so many years, Mr. Bentley, not unjustified perhaps in thinking that all can grow the flower now that he has sown the seed, gives us, with the aid of a collaborator, a new "Trent." Truth to say, there is not much more than ordinary merit in the plot, with its blackmailing millionaire, its fake confession nobly made to Save Another, its climax of truth secured by means of which any defending counsel would make cheerful hay. The construction indeed is good, the clue of the champagne cork is one of the most brilliant detective fiction has to show, and that of the razor blade is almost as good, even though it brings the joint authors for some time under the dire but happily unfounded suspicion of "concealing a vital clue from the reader." Possibly some heretics will prefer Chief Inspector Bligh, so well-drawn a character one feels he must be sketched from life, even to Trent himself, who does indeed play the quotation game just a little too freely, though it may be doubted whether there are many in the C.I.D. capable of delivering themselves of so fine a piece of literary criticism as that on the work of Mr. G.B. Shaw recorded on page 64 as uttered by Bligh. The high merit of the book does not depend either upon the characterisation, excellent as that is throughout, or even from such delightful interludes as the account of Trent's visit to Dieppe, so told that henceforth no visitor to that town will be content till he, too, has striven to find his way to the Inn of the Little Universe, but rather upon the manner in which the bare bones of another no-better-than-another plot has been clothed in the magnificent raiment of true literature. Superfluous, no doubt, to praise Mr. Bentley's style were no more meant that that upon nearly every page is to be found some pungent or picturesque phrase. There is more than that, there is that this book offers to the reader the rarest and the chiefest pleasure literature can give—a sense of close communion for an hour or two with a rich and cultivated mind.

The Penrose Mystery
by R. Austin Freeman
(23 June 1936)

That in a detective novel the detective should be superb in skill, in knowledge, in observation is as excusable a convention—though one of the great detectives of fiction, Dickens's Inspector Bucket, is not so depicted—as that in a love tale the heroine should be lovely as the dawn or that in an adventure story the hero should be a judicious compound of Hercules and

Adonis. But this omniscience of the detective should always be germane to the tale, its displays springing naturally from the story's complications. It should not, as in some American books, be flung at random at the reader, after the manner of the amateur who tunes in to every broadcast station available merely to display the efficiency of his act.

In the books of Mr. Austin Freeman his Dr. Thorndyke is shown possessing a range of knowledge as large as that of any encyclopedia. But the knowledge he displays is always necessary to the development of the story. True, Mr. Freeman's austere and scientific soul is not much concerned with the literary graces, but how admirable in construction are his stories, how careful in workmanship, how ingenious in conception! His own Mr. Polton, that perfect pattern of all good craftsmanship, must surely bestow upon such fine work a nod of grave and affectionate approval. In his new book, "The Penrose Mystery," Mr. Freeman tells of the disappearance of an oddity, a Mr. Penrose, who has chosen to go through life like an incarnate crossword puzzle. When he inexplicably vanishes Dr. Thorndyke undertakes the task of discovering what has become of him, and accomplishes it by process of reasoning so simple that every reader will feel that he could have thought it out for himself, and yet so subtle that it is fairly certain that the reader would fail in that attempt. Then comes the further puzzle that the evidence points with equal clearness to the guilt of this man and of that. How ingeniously this difficulty is resolved must be learnt from the book itself, and at the same time there will be learnt a good deal about archaeological research.

The Man Who Murdered Himself
by Geoffrey Homes
The Talkative Policeman
by Rupert Penny
(14 August 1936)

That a good style is as necessary in the detective novel as in any other of the main forms of fiction is a platitude; but it may be admitted that the "purple patch" is even less desirable in crime stories than elsewhere. From America—and out of America always something new, as the old Roman tag probably meant, only it got the continents confused—has come recently a number of such tales written in a brief staccato style of which it is scarcely an exaggeration to say that the guiding principle seems to be words of one syllable and paragraphs of one sentence. Deriving from hurried and brief newspaper reports in which only the facts are set down and all comment is avoided, the method does succeed admirably in giving of the sequence of events an impression swift, clear and bright, and, by its very nature, entirely superficial, since it tells so little of causes and of backgrounds.

A good example of this style is "The Man Who Murdered Himself," by Geoffrey Homes, which has also the further merit of good characterisation, presenting to us, among others, one of those fat, sympathetic rogues for whom, since the days of Falstaff, popularity has been assured. The story itself is less satisfactory. It begins with the discovery of a dead body in the reservoir of an American city, and goes on to tell of other crimes of no subtlety and little interest as regards either method or motive. As seems usual in American books, the police are shown as incredibly incompetent and brutal, newspaper reporters as incredibly drunken and efficient. Among the characters is an Englishman of whom it is recorded that his accent grew broader in moments of emotion.

*　*　*

Mr. Penny is a new writer, and in an interesting if provocative introduction to his "The Talkative Policeman" claims the high authority of Father Ronald Knox for this thesis that the true aim of the detective novel should be to make the reader at a certain point lay it down and go perambulating the garden with corrugated brow, trying to think the problem out for himself. To which the simpler answer is that the detective novel should, at every point, hold its reader in its grip, impervious to the claims alike of duty and of dinner. Perhaps it is unkind to add that the problem Mr. Penny sets is unlikely to send many readers perambulating the garden with corrugated brows. The criminal is all too evident, even from the moment of first appearance in the story. The tale begins with the apparently motiveless murder of a country clergyman, and the best thing in the book is the slow emergence of the reason for what at first seems an aimless crime. Mr. Penny has taken pains with his story, and, demanding that the industrious reader shall do the same, offers to him a plethora of tabular statements. On the whole the story suggests that the author is more highly gifted with the critical and the analytical then with the creative faculties. Had the late Mr. Bradshaw devoted himself to detective stories instead of railway time-tables, this is the kind of detective story he would have written.

Fair Warning
by Mignon Eberhart
(18 September 1936)

The tone of Miss Eberhart's "Fair Warning" is not so much background as emotion. Every sentence throbs, every paragraph are a heartbeat, now and then a line of italics is thrown in to heighten the general effect. Marcia is one of those unfortunate wives whose spirit a cruel husband is busily engaged in crushing to the dust, and only a harsh, unsympathetic reader will wonder why she does not walk out of her torture-chamber and get work as a housemaid or a teashop waitress—commonplace job, perhaps, but surely better than suffering slow agony day and night. However, she does not walk out; when the crawl husband is found murdered she is suspected, and so is the young man who has been writing her indiscreet but welcome letters, and so are others as well. A second murder takes place, and in the end the real culprit receives "Fair Warning" that guilt is known, any little difficulty about evidence being overcome by the author's assurance that presently the police will discover lots of it. The book is more than anything else a study of the sufferings of the suspected wife under the harsh questioning of the police, and it is certain that many readers will be moved by the sustained emotional appeal of the story.

Death at the President's Lodging
by Michael Innes
(9 October 1936)

Too many writers of mystery fiction, too many publishers as well, seem inclined to think that all that is required for a detective novel is a corpse and half a dozen characters with bad records, bad tempers or bad luck to being them under suspicion. All the more grateful then should readers be when an author introduces a breath of novelty into what is too apt to degenerate into almost a mechanistic formula.

It is this welcome touch of novelty in outlook and in treatment that given by Mr. Michael Innes in "Death at the President's Lodging." There are, it seems, in England three ancient universities—Oxford, Cambridge and, situated somewhere in between them, bearing to them a strong resemblance in atmosphere and tradition, yet another, whereof St. Anthony's is a famous college. Dr. Umpleby, President of St. Anthony's, is found dead in circumstances that prove that one of the senior members of the college must be the murderer, and the interest of Mr. Innes's remarkable book lies in the subtle reactions of these acute and highly trained minds to the mystery and brutality of the crime, to the suspicions resting on them all and entertained by them all of each other. By good fortune the detective called in has a mind as subtle as any of theirs, and can bandy Kant, Montaigne, and De Quincey with the best; and if in fact, in spite of the special pleading on page 291, it is impossible to believe that any responsible body of men would engage so whole-heartedly in what in less lofty and academic circles would be known as "passing the buck," yet it may be agreed that if, supposing the impossible, they did so behave, then this is exactly how they would behave. And if that sounds just a little over-subtle, then Mr. Innes must bear the blame, for subtlety like his is an infectious thing. One thing is certain, this book will be the "chosen" detective story of the season in every common room of every school and college throughout the land.

www.ingramcontent.com/pod-product-compliance
Lightning Source LLC
Chambersburg PA
CBHW070927190726
48292CB00004B/1130